# Revolt in Berlin

## Part One

*A Spy Story*

By
**Noel Hynd**

*REVOLT IN BERLIN* – Part One           NOEL HYND

A tremendous **Dankeschön** to my friend, Mary Jean Jones, for help and guidance throughout this manuscript.

*

Published by
Red Cat Tales Publishing, LLC
PO Box 34312
Los Angeles, CA 90034

For comments and corrections, including typos and printing glitches, please contact: Red.cat.tales.publishing@gmail.com

*

© 2024 Noel Hynd
{240105-k/p}

Second printing. January 2024

# Author's Note

This is a continuation of the *Flowers from Berlin* saga which began more than three decades ago. The series will run for ten volumes, following American intelligence agent William Cochrane and his various tours and assignments in Berlin for a quarter of a century, from 1938 to 1963, a fairly substantial chunk of history. It's my contention that Berlin was the most important city in the world in the twentieth century. So what better place could there have been for a complex and enduring career in espionage?

There are stories within stories. This, the fifth book in that series, is the first part of a two-part tale that encompasses 1952 and 1953, years that took the United States from Truman to Eisenhower and the Soviet Union from Stalin to Khrushchev. The same years also took East Germany, as it was then known, from a complacent, repressed, satellite country to a nation in armed angry revolt. The Soviet Union had to send tank divisions into East Germany in 1953 to put down the suppressed rage of the populace.

*Revolt in Berlin: Part One* is a story about 1952.

*Revolt in Berlin: Part Two* will be a story about 1953. The book will arrive in late 2024. It should be listed on Amazon by January 2025.

I should mention also that this book is illustrated by a few of the propaganda posters that were ubiquitous on the streets of Berlin in 1952, little daily messages extolling the supposed wonders of communism to a populace that by and large didn't believe it for a moment. The artwork, striking in its cheerful deceitfulness, set the mood of East Berlin, even if thousands of people tried to ignore it.

I've used the poster artwork to establish part of the atmosphere of this book. I've also done my best to track down the creative rights to these images created by unknown artists seventy years ago. For lack of any evidence to the contrary, they appear to be in the public domain.

Readers can contact me at Nh1212f@yahoo.com. I like to hear from you, even if you're correcting me about a tiny detail that I got wrong. I try to respond to everything.

Well, everything within reason. ☺
Thanks for reading.

Noel Hynd
Los Angeles, CA
December 2023

# Previous Novels in this Series

***Flowers from Berlin***
***Return to Berlin***
***Judgment in Berlin***
***Betrayal in Berlin***

*Coming in Winter 2024/25*

## *Revolt In Berlin – Part Two*

*REVOLT IN BERLIN* – Part One      NOEL HYND

**Dr. Walter Linse
West Berlin – June 1952**

*REVOLT IN BERLIN* – **Part One**          **NOEL HYND**

*"The assistant director of the Stasi, the East German police, is a vicious pint-sized little Red named Erich Mielke. Usually, he's highly visible. But sometimes he disappears. He goes underground. He's invisible for days at a time. No one knows where. Maybe he's in Moscow with Stalin. Even East Germany's communist boss Walter Ulbricht doesn't know. On these days trouble is brewing, and Erich Mielke is more dangerous than ever."*

**Article in *Time* magazine, 1952**

# Chapter 1
## Eberswalde, East Germany – Late Spring 1952

Wolfgang Reymann was a quiet, engaging, German war veteran with wise gray eyes and an easy smile. He was a distant nephew of a Nazi general named Helmuth Reymann who had the unenviable task in 1945 of being the last general to defend Berlin as the Red Army rolled inexorably westward from the east and crushed everything in its way.

Wolfgang never talked about his uncle, who had been captured by the Russians, much the way he never talked a lot about himself. Wolfgang never talked about the war, either, even though some kids in the town of Eberswalde, where he now lived, one day said that he had a box that was full of medals. It was obvious that he had been a soldier. Usually, he kept the box hidden in the single room he had in the main farmhouse that stood on the collective farm where he worked. What he couldn't hide were the dark scars along the left side of his head and the small section of an ear that was missing. But everyone had war wounds. That or they were already dead.

The kids in the village liked him and addressed him as Onkel Wolfgang, a title that brought a smile to his face and which he met with a shrug. That was Wolfgang's usual way of greeting developments these days: a smile and a shrug. Life, he knew, could end abruptly. No use fretting about what a man couldn't control.

Wolfgang had first arrived in Eberswalde in the summer of 1948, carrying a small cloth bag that had once been a potato sack. The sack contained everything he owned: a coat, a change of clothing, and the box of medals. Shortly thereafter, Gustav Zeitler, the thin, dour, bespectacled, local commissar of agriculture, received Wolfgang's work papers. They were unusual in that they had originated in Moscow.

*REVOLT IN BERLIN* – **Part One**     NOEL HYND

Zeitler knew not to ask questions, however. Zeitler's orders were to put Wolfgang to work on the state collective farm. So that was exactly what Zeitler did when the ex-soldier arrived.

Eberswalde had a heavy recent history. In 1938, local Nazis had joyously burned the town's only synagogue. During the war, several factories of military equipment employed inmates of the Ravensbrück concentration camp. Toward the end of the war, the German Luftwaffe attacked the town center in an unsuccessful attempt to slow the Soviet advance. The attack didn't work. The remaining people of Eberswalde surrendered to the Red Army without a shot being fired. When Adolf Hitler learned of this in his underground bunker, he concluded that suicide was the next best career move.

Wolfgang was a popular name in Germany, very traditional and Teutonic. It meant "traveling wolf" or "the way of the wolf." It suggested a certain power and majesty, as well as traveling. There was something about Herr Wolfgang Reymann that suggested such things. After all, it seemed he traveled a considerable amount. There weren't many men left in the town. Eighty percent of the male population had died during the war. To the other remaining men – many of them blind or missing limbs – who became his friends now in Eberswalde, he admitted that he had been among the brown bears, lynxes, and wolves in the Carpathian Mountains, as well as Poland, Hungary, and Slovakia. Wartime stuff, it was obvious to his new friends. They knew not to ask more than an ex-soldier was willing to tell.

These days, Wolfgang lived less stressfully. Lots of smiles, lots of shrugs.

He trucked the farm produce off to work the markets at the end of the S-Bahn in East Berlin. Turnips, cabbages, and onions, which were suited to the flat terrain and poor soil. He always returned with money for the farmers and Comrade Zeitler, the commissar. Somehow the adults knew they could trust him. He had a sense of honor and justice. Zeitler was deferential to him if one watched carefully. Zeitler was a devout communist who had studied in Moscow during the war. He spoke German, Polish, and Russian and had a worldview beyond the village, though not one that most Germans in the village cared for.

Gradually a story got around, mostly in whispers: Wolfgang had been in a certain Soviet prison camp near the Polish eastern border for three years. The camp was known for "reeducation and rehabilitation," meaning it either worked male and female prisoners to death or it addressed the issue of turning around men who had been useful for the Reich into good comrades of the new People's Republic. The Soviets had the evidence – so they said – to prosecute him for the war crime of being a sniper. But they had more creative ideas for his future.

When the alternative is either a firing squad or working eighteen hours a day in a steel mill or a coal mine, reeducation can be a wondrous option.

So, Wolfgang worked as a field hand and delivery driver on a collective farm ten kilometers east of the end of the S-Bahn line in East Berlin. Those who knew him knew that he had been in the Wehrmacht during the war. His hands were shaky. Now he lived in a single room in one of the old farmhouses near the apple orchard on the farm. He had discharge papers from the Wehrmacht that stated that had had been born in Anzing, Bavaria on December 22, 1921, meaning he was an even thirty years old in the spring and summer of 1952.

Anzing was about twenty miles from Munich. Around it lay the Ebersberger Forest, which had been severely damaged during the war but was now growing back. When Wolfgang was a kid, he had gone hunting in the forest. It was filled with deer and game birds. He learned to be a good shot and an expert marksman. Now the kids asked him if he had carried a rifle and used his shooting abilities in the war.

After much thought, he answered. "Yes," he said.
"Did you kill people?" they asked.
"Yes."
"Russians?"

*REVOLT IN BERLIN* – **Part One**     NOEL HYND

"The enemy," he said.

"How did you shoot a weapon with shaky hands?" a boy of ten once asked.

"Very carefully," Wolfgang answered. "And my hands were not shaky when I was young. Plus, they are still very strong hands: the hands of a laborer." He made a gesture of throwing a mock punch at the boy. The boy ducked, laughed, and knew not to ask more.

"Are you old now, Onkel Wolfgang?" another boy asked.

Wolfgang laughed and winked. "Yes," he said. He had a rural Bavarian accent that amused the kids and the adults in his new town. "Very. I'm thirty and I fought a war. Wars make you old fast. See?" He motioned to his dark hair streaked with white, souvenirs of horrors too great to discuss. Whenever such questions came up from the young people, he would deflect the inquiries and then he would change the subject. Yet sometimes the boys or some of the men would watch him when he didn't know he was being watched. There would be this contemplative, empty look on his face, which the men understood, and the boys did not.

Wartime stuff, once again.

One thing he did talk about was his baptism. He was descended from several generations of pig farmers. He was baptized as a Catholic when he was two days old, on Christmas Eve in the Pfarrkirche Saint Sebastian church, a simple white building that dated back hundreds of years and had once been a monastery. He was raised with his two sisters and two brothers on the farm where he refined his skills as a marksman. Around his neck, Wolfgang still wore a small plain silver cross on a silver chain that his father had given him "to protect him" when he joined the Wehrmacht. He credited it with guiding him though the war. He wore it inconspicuously inside his shirt and occasionally engaged in a subconscious habit of rubbing it between his forefinger and thumb.

Now, in 1952, he was the sole survivor in the family. The two brothers had died fighting for the Third Reich. His parents and two sisters had disappeared. He was still a Christian, though, as were many other people in the village. Religion was officially discouraged in the nonsecular Marxist state of East Germany. But a small contingent of two dozen people still met secretly in a barn at the end of town and celebrated the Christian sabbath. They would have been afraid of Commissar Zeitler ratting them out to higher authorities, except Zeitler had been a practicing Lutheran before the war. He was now one of the communicants.

The presence of Onkel Wolfgang was a gain for the town. Many of the boys between eight and twelve were fatherless from the war. They followed around Onkel Wolfgang and even formed a little squad that helped him gather produce. A blond boy named Hector was their leader. He was the son of the town's only remaining jeweler. Recently a girl named Gerda had joined them, as had her younger sister, Inge. The crew of kids numbered eight to ten on any given day. They picked bugs off the potatoes and onions that grew in the field and killed the insects with their fingers. They also had contests throwing stones. They removed many from the fields to improve the production of vegetables. At the end of each day, the boys would have contests to see who could throw the most over the treetops. Hector, the biggest and strongest, usually won. The boy had an arm.

The *Kinder* helped Wolfgang load the truck that went to market. Sometimes Wolfgang allowed one or two of them to come into East Berlin with him to unload. He would cadge a few extra pfennigs out of the receipts and buy pastries for himself and his young assistants.

*Onkel Wolfgangs kleine Helfer,* the people Eberswalde called the gang of boys and girls. Uncle Wolfgang's little helpers. They followed him everywhere. They teased him about what they felt was his funny way of talking – a Bavarian accent that embraced vowels, didn't care much for consonants, and rolled in the manner of Romance languages.

Wolfgang accepted this with a shrug and a smile. The kids were the family he hadn't had since the war. Increasingly, the shadow of the war and its horrors began to recede. As a man, he grew more tranquil. He enjoyed solitary walks in the woods, which reminded him of his innocence as a kid before the brutalities of the war had just about ruined and killed him. He enjoyed working in his newly assigned and now adopted village. He was at his core a simple man. He enjoyed the idea of raising food and successfully working on a farm. He found the work relaxing and the woods rejuvenating. At times when he was free, and when daylight and seasonal temperatures permitted, he was not above napping under a tall old tree, his cap pushed down over his face and his back against a sturdy trunk.

As the weeks passed, Wolfgang's steadiness increased. He gained a few pounds, and the contemplative, empty look became less frequent. To Zeitler, Wolfgang looked like a man who had finally gained some peace in life, if only for the time being and while it lasted.

# Chapter 2
## West Berlin, West Germany – 1952

The Berlin that William Cochrane returned to in the early summer of 1952 had three million people, four zones, two governments, two police forces, two police chiefs, two sets of laws, and several hundred codes and regulations – some written, some unwritten, some frivolous, some serious, and some nonsensical. It was a rough and tumble place, scarred by war, divided by politics, ugly, sensitive, brash, and beautiful all at the same time. The city had a horrible recent past and was struggling to find its rightful future. Berlin was, as usual, Berlin – a world capital in turmoil.

The area under Soviet control, the Soviet zone or sector, was often called the *Opera Magistrat*. It governed one million people, a third of the city's population. Or at least it tried to.

The one million people had no choice in the matter. In the first citywide postwar elections in 1948, East Berliners were not allowed to vote. The Soviet overlords – the Red Army and the Moscow-trained politicos – chose the Magistrat's members, a harbinger of things to come.

The nominal head of this entity was the *Opera Burgermeister*, Mayor Friedrich Ebert. Ebert was the son of the first president of the Weimar Republic, a man of the same name who died of septic shock after a failed appendectomy in 1925. He might have lived longer but his Nazi political opponents kept him too busy to seek medical attention until his illness grew worse. When he finally saw a team of doctors, it was too late.

The younger Ebert in 1952 was barely more visible day to day than his deceased father. The Soviets often held him at an undisclosed location in the Eastern zone and relayed what they said were his edicts for the city. The Soviets had installed him in office for the propaganda impact of his socialist surname. They relayed his wishes for Berlin and Berliners in the Soviet-controlled East German press. Since the Soviets would have refused to accept the results of the 1948 election because their side would certainly have resoundingly lost, Ebert remained their mayor in East Berlin.

In West Berlin, there was a government elected by the people in those same 1948 elections. The people had chosen a man named Ernst Reuter as mayor. Reuter was a courageous, pugnacious Social Democrat, a former communist who had denounced Marxist ideology in midlife. He had spent several years in Nazi concentration camps before he escaped to Turkey in 1943. He eventually returned to a battered Germany after World War II.

Reuter worked with a city council and a West Berlin city parliament. The authority above them, however, was the Allied Kommandatura, which once had been the four-power governing board of Berlin, but which now continued as a three-head hydra that was more formally known as the three Western military governments: the French, the English, and the Americans. On paper, they were three equal partners. But the Americans were enjoying their finest hours of the twentieth century: They had the military might and the money. They had the right personnel and the willpower. They were the strongest, so they did the bulk of the political and diplomatic heavy lifting.

Ernst Reuter, the West Berlin mayor – a pleasant, intelligent, thoughtful, and occasionally outspoken man on behalf of a city he loved – tried to maintain law and order with a police force headed by a quiet, scholarly, chief named Johannes Stumm. But because there were two mayors, there were also two police chiefs. The police chief of the Soviet sector, East Berlin, was the often-clownish, occasionally pompous Paul Markgraf, the son of a bread baker. Chief Markgraf was a onetime professional Wehrmacht soldier and officer. He had converted to Leninism after his capture at Stalingrad, conversion being preferable to life in a labor camp.

So both mayors had their own office and their own police chief, along with their own police force. Markgraf had until recently been the chief citywide, but Reuter had fired him for failing to enforce the law in West Berlin. Markgraf said he refused to be fired. Reuter responded that he was fired anyway and installed Stumm in a new office in West Berlin. Markgraf remained in the old office in the Soviet zone.

Stumm had radio cars and the support of American, British, and French military police to assist him. Markgraf employed thick-browed communist thugs – mostly Germans, but with some Poles and Russians tossed in – and the sinister Soviet secret police, whose tactics had already begun to terrorize all quarters of Berlin.

Both governments and both police forces claimed sole jurisdiction over the city. Both of them exercised their authority in their respective territories. Both encroached into the other's territory when it was considered important, but the Eastern police did it more consistently and brutishly. More recently, though, the East Berlin police were acting under orders to arrest any policeman working for Johannes Stumm who came into their half of the city – a tit-for-tat move in reaction to Reuter's dismissal of Markgraf. Similarly, while citizens were free to move around from the Western zone to the East – there was no wall yet – cars with license plates from the American, French, and British zones were prone to arbitrary seizure while in the East. Starting in early 1952, no resident of the American, British, or French sector ever went into the Soviet one without the fear of being arbitrarily arrested by the Eastern "people's police" and never again seen.

Postwar crime had never been uncommon in Berlin. Back in 1949, two young German women in their late teens were riding bicycles one day in front of the headquarters of General Lucius Clay, the civilian high commissioner for Germany, in what was considered a "secure" area of West Berlin. The area was also where the American PX was located as well as the American mess halls.

## *REVOLT IN BERLIN* – Part One            NOEL HYND

It was the noon hour, a warm, balmy day in Berlin. Two Russians in a Soviet Jeep stopped the young women by swerving in front of them. The Russians drew pistols, shot them on the spot, and stole their purses and wristwatches in full horrified view of hundreds of American employees who were going to lunch.

General Clay was outraged by the event when he heard of it. He took the matter to Marshall Sokolovsky, the Soviet governor. Sokolovsky insisted that this was not the work of Soviet soldiers but "capitalist bandits" in Soviet uniform. Clay then took the matter to Chief Markgraf, who laughed at him.

Up until this time, General Clay shared the attitudes of his colleagues in Washington. He was determined that the Americans would have a good relationship with the Russians, that they would be able to find a way to work together to de-Nazify Germany and recreate the German state. The Americans and Russians had worked together during the war, after all. That must have meant something, the reasoning went.

Now Clay changed his mind. He suddenly understood the Soviets' true ambitions: to eventually absorb all of Germany, recreate the state in a communist image, and send the Americans home. He now saw the Russians as a major threat to American policies in Europe. Then it didn't matter what he thought. Clay's tour ended. He was replaced and returned to the United States.

By 1951 and 1952 crime worsened, particularly in the Western zone. West Berliners complained that they were incessantly the victim of thugs and criminals from the Soviet zone, often armed East German police who were off duty, out of uniform, and not using their vehicles and weapons. Chief Markgraf refused to investigate. Then there were several horrendous, high-profile, violent incidents.

Almost immediately, day-to-day life in the city got worse. More ominous. More dangerous. More combative. Not too long after the slaying of the two girls on bicycles, a similar incident occurred on the banks of the Spree with a woman in her twenties left dead. Two weeks later two young German women were murdered by a Soviet guard near the final station in East Berlin on the S-Bahn. Two male students from the Free University disappeared from the S-Bahn on a produce-shopping trip and were never seen again. The East Berlin police investigated none of this.

What they did, however, was to ramp up enforcement of an arrest-on-sight policy against their counterparts in the three Western sectors. There hadn't been any incidents with American MPs, but the city had been on edge for months. Several days earlier, four Western sector policemen were seized over the weekend when they entered the Eastern sector. They remained in custody.

These were things over which the Allies had very little control and were an enormous problem for the new German police forces. The new West Berlin Chief of Police, Johannes Stumm, had been head of the KRIPO, the Criminal Police. He had been one of Europe's finest operational policemen. But now he was overwhelmed. He was confronted constantly with calls for help from people who were being threatened or had been actually kidnapped by Soviet intelligence personnel, police personnel, or just thugs.

There was no end to it.

There were smash-and-grab incidents every day at the railroad stations. A famous one at the Anhalter Banhoff resulted in three Soviet soldiers being shot by an American captain who was a former police captain from Detroit, Michigan.

The incidents were not just constant, they were epidemic. Markgraf shrugged off allegations against the Russian or East German agents and tried to serve arrest warrants in the West.

By June of 1952, things became even more brazen as bands of "off-duty" East Berlin police – which their Western counterparts called *Schägertrupps* – or thug squads – roamed working-class West Berlin neighborhoods and terrorized residents, particularly those who earned hard currency by working for American and British reconstruction projects.

East German detectives and patrol officers barged into homes in the middle of the night, accusing the residents of dealing drugs. They handcuffed them or held them at gunpoint, beating and torturing them into confessing or providing information on which of their neighbors were doing anything illegal, or working for Western powers. All this according to dozens of people who said they witnessed the assaults or were victims of it.

The West German residents described the violence that sometimes went on for hours and seemed intended to strike terror into targeted Germans. One night a thug squad of four men in a dilapidated Jeep ambushed and shocked an airport baggage worker when he was walking home at six AM. They beat him and choked him, and as he lay submerged in a flooded ditch, rammed a stick down his throat until he vomited blood.

A week later, what may have been the same squad ambushed and choked a bakery worker with an industrial cord when the man was walking to work in the early morning. In the same neighborhood on the same night, an owner who flew an American flag was beaten in his supply room until the walls were spattered with his blood. His store was attached to his home. Members of the raiding party searched the home, dragged his terrified wife half-naked from her bed, tore off the rest of her clothes, jabbed flashlights threateningly at her body, and demanded her jewelry.

The assault might have continued unchecked if a neighbor had not heard the commotion and come out to the street and fired a contraband American shotgun in the air, alerting West Berlin police and American military police from the airport. The assailants fled through an eastern access road. The residents then formed their own evening militia.

By early summer the streets were tense and alive with danger. There should have been little surprise then, about the atrocity that took place in the American zone on July 8, 1952

# Chapter 3
## West Berlin, American Occupation Zone
## July 8, 1952 – 7:30 AM

At seven-thirty on a warm summer morning Dr. Walter Linse, age fifty-two, unlocked the iron gate that protected his home and several others on cobblestoned Gerichtsstrasse in the American zone of Berlin. Linse, a prominent economist, attorney, and journalist in the postwar German Republic was also a crusading anti-communist.

Since the war ended, Walter Linse – a Wehrmacht veteran – had completed his doctorate in law and worked as an economic law expert for the Investigative Committee of Free Lawyers in West Berlin. During the first week of July 1952, he had been preparing a detailed report for an upcoming international law congress in Berlin. The report focused on the unending and brutal violations of law in East Berlin and the German Democratic Republic, colloquially known as East Germany.

Dr. Linse had lived under two dictatorships in Germany, first the Nazis and now the Stalinist regime that had installed itself since the end of World War II. His ideals, which he termed "Justice and the Rule of Law" put him on a collision course with both of them. He was not a man easily frightened or intimidated. He was well respected and prominent in the "new" Germany that was recovering from the war. But he was used to having his head on a swivel.

Linse stepped out onto the sidewalk with a black attaché case that carried the results of this inquiry to date. The results were explosive. They were within hours of being dropped off to a top Western intelligence agent and days of being publicized around the world, perhaps the worst publicity for the East German regime of Walter Ulbricht since the ill-advised blockade and airlift of a few years earlier.

## *REVOLT IN BERLIN* – Part One                 NOEL HYND

East Germany had the fastest-growing economy of any of the Soviet satellite nations in Europe. But compared with West Germany, the development was poor. Citizens of East Germany all had jobs, but the pay was terrible, the currency was weak, and there was little to do with the money other than trying to buy food or coal, and both of these commodities were scarce. Worse yet, the contrast with West Germany was extreme. East Germans who went to the West to visit relatives often chose not to return. Stores were full of consumer goods and grocery shelves were filled. A heavy population of Westerners – including American and British troops – kept the economic cauldrons bubbling. Life in the East was as drab as the rubble-strewn landscape. The fighting had stopped, but the deprivations of the war continued. Worse, East Germany was a police state, one of the most repressive places on the planet. Linse wanted the world to know it.

Swivel time: Linse glanced both ways to assess whether it was safe to leave his home. He had the keen sense that he had been under surveillance recently. How could he not be? He had no idea whether the watchers were Russians or East Germans, but to him, there wasn't much difference. The enemy, he had long since concluded, was whoever was trying to stop him from doing his work or trying to get him killed. The enemy was whoever denied individuals their freedom.

He had, in other words, more enemies than he cared to count.

And the enemy didn't need a name. The enemy was simply the enemy.

Linse was at the time deeply involved with publicizing specific human rights violations, labor camps, and secret trials in the Soviet occupation zones of Berlin and East Germany. He was the acting president of the Association of Free German Jurists. The results of his investigations were prominently displayed in the Western press, much to the embarrassment of the pro-Moscow regime of communists who controlled East Germany.

As soon as Linse was too far from his front door to turn back, a large, rough-hewn man approached him, stepping out of a narrow alleyway a dozen meters from his home.

"Dr. Linse?" he asked.

The man startled Linse. The lawyer's heart began to race.

The man mumbled a string of incomprehensible words in low German and made a motion of asking for a light on a bent, unlit cigarette. The man was half Linse's age, forty pounds heavier, had a misshapen nose, and missing teeth. He came across as one of those violence-prone, deranged thugs that littered Berlin's postwar streets, more common in the Eastern sector than the Western. Linse didn't like the looks of him. He accelerated his walk, stepping around him when the man abruptly blocked his path, then broke into a slow run.

There was a single car parked near the corner where Gerichtsstrasse intersected with Drakestrasse. Linse noticed as he passed that two men were in the car, their eyes turned toward Linse. The first man, the one who had initially accosted Linze, fell into stride with the West German lawyer and continued to pester him for a match. He was so close that Linse recoiled from the man's foul breath and body odor.

Linse shook his head and kept moving, particularly when the man made an ominous grasping gesture with his arm. But Linse was sufficiently distracted to take his eyes off the two other men.

They jumped out of the parked car. Linse heard the sound of the car doors opening and then the hurried footsteps behind him. Next, in the fraction of a second that passed before anything actually happened, Linse guessed he was probably going to die.

The two men from the parked car grabbed Linse from behind. They quickly overpowered him. Linse screamed for help. He dropped his attaché case. He fought furiously, flailing with his arms and elbows, kicking with his feet, jabbing at his assailants with his knees.

The men behind him pinned Linse's arms to his sides. The first man walloped him across the face with a sand-filled blackjack, a homemade street weapon common to the Berlin streets, bloodying the attorney's face and mouth. The blow stunned Linse. It broke several of his teeth on the left side of his face. Linse had a fencing scar that he had carried since the time between the two great wars. Blood gushed from the old fencing wound.

Linse's glasses shattered and flew to the sidewalk. One of the men from the car stomped on the glasses, crushing the frame. The first assailant then drove a powerful fist into his gut, doubling him over and quickly taking the fight out of him. Then the same man threw a second blow into his gut, this one more powerful than the first.

One of the assailants kneed Linse in the kidneys. When Linse continued to scream, the assailants pulled a leather gag around his mouth. Then another pair of strong hands quickly dropped a hood over the lawyer's head. The abduction team dragged him toward the car, which sat idling with all four doors open and waiting.

Linse dragged his feet to slow the abduction. The move didn't work.

Linse could hear the voices of other members of the kidnapping team. Their German was guttural and crude: peasant voices from the rural eastern regions, perhaps near Saxony where Linse had spent the war. Within seconds his hands were bound behind him, and his abductors were pushing him into the car. He resisted and flailed again but he was no match for three men, all of whom were bigger and stronger than he.

For one glorious moment, he broke free. He staggered awkwardly, then six powerful hands were on him again. The sound of horrified protesting voices swirled around him in the street.

Neighbors' voices. Men. Women. Children. An entire choir of enraged onlookers.

*REVOLT IN BERLIN* – **Part One**     NOEL HYND

A woman screamed to call the West Berlin police or any available American soldiers. Linse stumbled and fell as his assailants pushed him again toward the waiting car. His forehead hit the stones of the uneven sidewalk. Then the strong hands of his abductors hauled him up, slammed him against the door of the car, and threw him into the rear seat. He landed roughly, and other members of the kidnapping team held him.

The car rumbled to life. It began to move.

Linse could still hear agitated voices. German was the only language, though he wouldn't have been surprised had he heard Russian. Russians were the real enemy, after all, something he knew well. Linse had always been a devout anti-communist, which was how he ended up being a victim on this day.

Linse's head throbbed. He cursed at his abductors and received a chop to the back of the neck. He could feel the jerky motion of the vehicle as it began to move even before the rear doors were closed. The vehicle accelerated and careened through the quiet Tuesday morning streets of the residential neighborhood. It picked up more speed as it crossed Karwendelstrasse. The adductors now pulled Dr. Linse's legs into the car. As they struggled to close the door, one of Linse's shoes tumbled out onto the street.

Outside the car, as it moved, a shocked West German truck driver shouted at the kidnappers to stop. Another woman who watching the event cried out for help. Unbeknown to Linse, the truck driver tried to follow. Linse, terrified, knew that his assailants were not about to surrender him. One of Linse's abductors pulled a pistol. Gunfire from the car followed. From the sound of the bullets, Linse – even blindfolded – knew the assailants were firing.

As the car moved down Drakestrasse, the abduction team dropped caltrops – small tire-puncturing spikes resembling jacks from a child's game – to deter anyone from following. The pursuing truck hit the spikes, skidded noisily, spun, and hit a lamppost, abruptly falling out of the chase as the kidnap car hit sixty miles an hour. The shooter in the abduction car laughed and fired a few extra bullets his way. Meanwhile, one of the other abductors used leather bands to strengthen the ties on Linse's hands.

The fleeing car crossed the bridge above the Teltow Canal and made a sharp skidding turn down Deisendorferstrasse and Berlinerstrasse. The truck sped eastward through several additional streets. There was little vehicular traffic in East Berlin. That was normal: there were few vehicles other than police, military, and Communist Party bigwigs.

The vehicle took a few sharp turns and came within sight of a vehicle barrier – one that resembled a bar that could be raised or lowered for trains – that marked the division of American and Soviet zones.

There were military guard booths on both sides of the barrier. Two East German soldiers in uniforms manned the sentry booths. They recognized the van and hoisted the barrier when they saw the abduction car approach. The other two guards wore Soviet army uniforms. They performed their duties and watched impassively.

The car rumbled forward at top speed, its top gear grinding. It hit a pair of speed bumps, one after the other, and awkwardly left the ground as it careened through. Now the German and Soviet guards grinned to each other as the van fishtailed, then continued onward after crossing from one half of the divided city to the other. The car disappeared into the Soviet occupation zone of Berlin with the vehicle barrier dropping quickly to help seal the abduction.

The car continued on Friedrichstrasse. There was an array of modest stores and huge bold posters proclaiming the glory of socialism and the beneficence of East Germany's Soviet friends. The propaganda posters were ubiquitous in the Soviet zone, stunning for their bald-faced lies about the great life in the Workers' Paradise. Not that Linse could see any of it from where he was pinned by two heavy bodies in the back of the van, but the surroundings grew increasingly gray and grim.

Two minutes from the center of East Berlin, as the van bounced along cratered, pot-holed streets, entire blocks still lay in ruins, seven years after the end of the war. Not much had changed since the last bombs of 1945 had fallen. People in bedraggled clothes populated the streets, moving as if in a collective trance, wary of strangers who could be informants. They shuffled and kept their eyes ahead of them. In the Soviet zone, it was wiser to shuffle quietly and avert one's eyes than to move quickly and notice the unusual.

The car took a prearranged course toward a section of Berlin called Karlshorst. The driver already knew that no one from the West had followed. In the distance now behind them, a new Soviet Zil automobile which belonged to the Stasi – the East German secret police – kept pace and kept watch. The lower carriage of the car was low to the ground from four immense security men within. In the center in the back, however, sat a small trim man in a gray suit. The man said nothing but watched the operation with approval. He had not ventured into the American zone. He never did, as he might have been arrested for crimes dating back to the 1930s. But today in the Eastern zone he was in command and liked what he was seeing.

The car carrying Linse proceeded two more minutes and entered the heavily guarded "restricted area" in Karlshorst. It took a few final turns and approached a barricade with four soldiers in a pair of sentry booths, one booth on each side, the same setup as the zonal crossing. There was barbed wire on top of the brick and stone walls and a long, gray macadam road on the other side of the sentry area.

The car with Linse arrived at the gate. Two soldiers emerged from the sentry booths and watched the street. Another soldier who seemed to be in charge eyed the car's cargo – the captive Linse. The soldier smirked, nodded, made some sort of cruel joke, and signaled that the gate should rise.

Noisily, the gate cranked and rose upwards. The follow-up Zil peeled away and returned toward the administrative enclave at Ruschestrasse in Friedrichshain.

The car passed into the foreboding compound, which was something straight out of *1984* or *Darkness at Noon*. The vehicle continued down the cracked macadam roadway toward a sturdy gray building with narrow windows on the upper floors and bars on the lower portals. It came to a halt in front of an ominous gray cement building with guards and iron bars on all the windows. The kidnappers roughly pulled their captive from the rear of the car. They pushed and shoved him toward the main entrance and its massive wooden gate.

The gate opened. Within ten minutes of the time he had left his home, he had been forcibly abducted across the border from Lichterfelde in West Berlin to neighboring Teltow in East Germany. The physical difference was four kilometers. But in July of 1952, it was a world away. Walter Linse, who had been a free man when the day began, was now a prisoner.

For Dr. Linse, a hell on earth was just beginning.

*REVOLT IN BERLIN* – Part One     NOEL HYND

**DDR Propaganda poster 1950s: Learning from the Soviets is learning how to win!**

# Chapter 4
## East and West Berlin
## Early Summer 1952

Postwar Berlin in 1952 remained the spy capital of the planet.

West met East in Berlin, for better or worse, which meant that Western ideas and liberties, plus unbridled capitalism, ran straight up cheek to jowl with the snarly Russian bear, samovar, vodka, Bolshevik ideas, and a victorious Red Army. The stakes were high. The fate of Berlin would signal the fate of Europe and neither the Soviets nor the Western Allies were willing to retreat, led by President Truman's vow to "stay in Berlin" in the late forties and Dwight Eisenhower's deep distrust of the Soviets when he was wartime commander.

At the top of the political pecking order in Berlin were figures who were familiar – or all *too* familiar – from before the war.

By 1952, the Federal Republic of Germany, the FRG, or *Bundesrepublik Deutschland*, had risen miraculously from the ashes and rubble of World War II following its creation in May 1949. Known to most people in English as "West Germany," it had been cobbled together as a political entity during the Allied occupation of Germany after World War II, established from the dozen states formed in the three Allied zones of occupation held by the United States, France, and the United Kingdom.

The FRG's initial capital was Bonn, the proverbial "small town in Germany," though Bonn had had its outsized, strategic importance during the war. These twelve states were re-organized into ten, with Berlin, or the Western occupied portions of it, considered an unofficial eleventh state. While legally part of West Germany, the city was under the control of the Allied Control Council (ACC). A U.S. High Commissioner governed the city though Ernst Reuter was the mayor.

Reuter was best known in the West for an impassioned speech before a hundred thousand Berliners in 1948 when he begged the Western powers to not abandon the city. Reuter also came to be nicknamed *Herr Berlin* after a laudatory cover story in *Time* magazine for the way he had stood up to communism. Barely a day went by, rain, snow, or blazing sunshine, when he wasn't seen around the city's trouble spots with his trademark black beret pulled down to the facial latitude of his bushy gray-black eyebrows.

Colloquially the new nation was also occasionally referred to as the *Bonner Republik*, or the Bonn Republic. Heading this reestablished nation, whatever one wished to call it, was a statesman, Konrad Adenauer, the first German to bear the official title of chancellor since Hitler. Adenauer, the mayor of Cologne in the 1930s, was known for his intense work habits and his brilliant political instincts. As a Catholic and fervent anti-communist, Adenauer was deeply committed to a pro-West foreign policy, an alliance with America and Britain, and the restoration of a noncriminal Germany on the world stage. West Germany saw itself as the direct descendant of the German Reich which had existed from 1871, the era of Bismarck, to 1945, when a certain megalomaniac from Austria brought ruin upon the nation.

On the opposite side of the Elbe presided an old-line communist named Walter Ulbricht who, as the first secretary of the Socialist Unity Party, was the chief decision-maker in East Germany. He was also the East German head of state, as the party controlled the state. His power derived from his relationship with Stalin, a powerful standing army backed by the Soviet Union, and a brutal reliance on the Stasi, the secret police agency of the German Democratic Republic, or colloquially, East Germany.

The Stasi was the most hated and feared institution of the East German communist government. They had earned the distinction, and no one was in second place. The word was a

*REVOLT IN BERLIN* – **Part One**     NOEL HYND

conversational term for state security and referred to the East German Ministry for State Security, abbreviated as MfS . The Stasi was both intelligence service and secret police.

The first head of the Stasi was a German communist named Wilhelm Zaisser, a politician and sometimes foreign diplomat. Born in 1893 in Germany's turbulent Ruhr, Wilhelm Zaisser developed a taste for blood-fighting in Germany's World War I army, in which he rose to the rank of lieutenant. When the bloody "workers' rebellion" broke out in the Ruhr in 1923, Zaisser organized workers' brigades. He was already known as the "Red General of the Ruhr." Taken prisoner by loyal German security forces, he escaped to Russia. There he became a Soviet citizen and a colonel in the Red Army. During the Nazi regime, he returned to Germany, a leader and organizer of the communist underground.

Stalin eventually launched him on a world tour. He worked as a spy for the Russians and from 1925 to 1926 as a military advisor to Syria. He excelled at what he did. He went on to work as a military advisor to China from 1927 to 1930 and the Czechoslovak Army from 1930 to 1932, an assignment upon which he first met and worked directly for Laurenti Beria, creator and head of the Soviet MGB, Josef Stalin's intelligence agency and secret police force since 1946.

His covert life was eventually rewarded by full membership in the Communist Party of the Soviet Union in 1932. In 1936, Zaisser traveled to the Second Spanish Republic under the covert identity of "Gomez" and had a successful time rooting out anti-Stalinists in the Republican army and arranging for them to be shot. For all this and more, he was rewarded with full Soviet citizenship in 1940, just in time for the biggest war yet.

The resourceful Stalin remembered him when Germany attacked Russia in 1941 and gave him a position indoctrinating German officers taken prisoner. Zaisser helped build a renegade German army inside Russia. But it was four years before Stalin let him go back to Germany. In 1945 he turned up in Saxony-Anhalt in East Germany as the pro-Stalin chief of police. His real job was building up the 130,000-man Volkspolizei, the paramilitary communist police army in East Germany. He was made state security minister in the East German government. In 1950, Zaisser gained membership in East Germany's Politburo and the Central Committee of the SED, thus becoming one of the most powerful men in the country. In the same year, Zaisser was appointed director of the Ministry of State Security. Using his vast knowledge of intelligence work, Zaisser built the Stasi into a powerful organization.

These days, though, Zaiser was more of a desk general. A technocrat. He had also mellowed into a porky middle age, gaining several dozen pounds since the 1920s. Even more lethal now in 1952, however, was Zaisser's deputy, Erich Mielke, who was more involved with street operations against Western targets. Mielke also had strong connections to Ulbricht. Both had been active as triggermen in political assassinations in Berlin in the 1920s and 1930s, the most significant of which had been the notorious Bülowplatz assassination of Paul Anlauf, the forty-two-year-old captain of the Berlin Police's Seventh Precinct. Captain Anlauf, a widower with three daughters, had been nicknamed *Schweinebacke*, or "Pig Face" by the KPD. During the last days of the Weimar Republic, the KPD had a policy of assassinating two Berlin police officers in retaliation for every KPD member killed by the police. Mielke and Walter Ulbricht had been complicit in the murder of Captain Anlauf. Both had then fled to Moscow, working with communist troops during the war, only to return to Germany on a Russian aircraft in 1945 to take prominent positions in the new government of East Germany.

They were still accused murderers, but the new pro-Soviet regime didn't care. Or, worse, they favored that detail. Ulbricht had a beard, after all, one that resembled that of Lenin. To old-line Reds, how bad could the man be?

By 1952, the Stasi had plenty to do. Berlin to them was a lawless place, crawling with spooks, would-be spooks, retired spooks, street thugs, and criminals. There were hustlers, grifters, con artists, war profiteers, political hucksters, soldiers, wounded veterans, disabled civilians, plus several hundred thousand normal citizens just trying to survive and get by day to day. They were just trying to keep order among the various social vermin and counterrevolutionaries.

The four occupying powers – the Americans, the French, the British, and the Soviets – all had at least two official intelligence services at work, and each believed each of the others had several more. The Czechs maintained a service based on the Russian MGB and so did the Poles. The West German police had an intelligence unit and so did the East Germans. The East German government of Walter Ulbricht claimed that the Western powers had "almost a hundred" intelligence services, but American authorities sniffed that there were probably no more than two dozen, officially anyway.

A cottage industry had even grown up among hundreds of people who had survived the war but had no livelihood other than to sell espionage secrets to either the West or the East, depending on who bid the highest. Some of the info was pure gold, some of it was completely made up. Golden fleece, as one American spy put it, more aptly than he might have intended. Then there was a significant cadre of professional ladies who jumped from bed to bed to bed and reported for a fee what they had seen and heard.

The American OSS contingent remained quartered at Föhrenweg 21 in an angular red brick house behind a high iron fence. The house had been the headquarters of Field Marshall Wilhelm Keitel during the war. The house, with three layers of bunkers underneath as protection against air raids, had been designed by Albert Speer. Keitel had been chief of Hitler's high command.

Keitel had been the Oberkommando der Wehrmacht (OKW), the high command of Nazi Germany's armed forces, during World War II. He was loathed by his Wehrmacht peers as Hitler's "yes-man". Field Marshal Ewald von Kleist labeled

Keitel nothing more than a "stupid follower of Hitler" because of his servile "yes-man" attitude toward Hitler. His sycophancy was well known in the army, and he acquired the nickname "Lakeitel," a pun derived from *Lakai,* the German word for *lackey,* and his surname, Keitel.

Hermann Göring's description of Keitel as having "a sergeant's mind inside a field marshal's body" was a feeling often expressed by his peers. He had been promoted because of his willingness to function as Hitler's mouthpiece. He was also known by his peers as *Nickgeselle* after a popular metal toy of a nodding donkey, the *Nickesel.*

Keitel no longer enjoyed the red brick mansion that had once been his. After the war, Keitel was arrested and indicted by the International Military Tribunal in Nuremberg as a major war criminal. He was found guilty and swung from a rope in Nuremberg in October 1946.

While the OSS enjoyed Speer's architecture and Keitel's old digs with an assignment of fewer than a hundred operatives, Soviet intelligence was headquartered in the Karlshorst district of East Berlin in the building that had once been the Saint Antonious Hospital. The new compound that housed Soviet intelligence was now close to two hundred acres, including hundreds of operatives, footmen, snoops, agents, and tech assistants. Close by within the same compound, not by coincidence, was the Red Army's Berlin Garrison, which was five thousand soldiers strong, complete with housing for soldiers and embassy personnel. A high fence surrounded all of this, with barbed wire across every inch of it, surrounded by elite Stasi guards. It was impossible to get in or out without several layers of official permission.

There was one significant flaw, however, in the no-nonsense, utopian, socialist system: human nature. Within the vast and various GDR government compounds – from the administrative areas to the military barracks to the prisons – corruption was both rampant and a way of life.

Payoffs could be petty or grand. The unseen warp in the system took many forms.

On a higher administrative and governmental level, corruption often involved higher-level prison and security officials. Some prison officials had been implicated in the late 1940s in accepting payoffs. Those caught were shot. But it didn't end corruption because the odds of getting caught were low. In other cases, prison and military supervisors had been accused of covering up violations by correction officers or others within the prison by shielding human rights abuses. Rumor had it that Dr. Walter Linse had worked these angles and paid for tips and stories from anonymous sources within the system. The larger rumor was that he had used CIA money to bribe people.

But on the most basic level, security officers accepted cash bribes, tobacco, liquor, or sexual favors to smuggle weapons, drugs, or messages to inmates in prison or workers who were not allowed off base, or to provide inmates with other benefits, such as "looking the other way" if those assigned to state housing wanted to slip away for an evening of fun. Political or criminal prisoners were not allowed off base but almost everyone else could find a way not so much to beat the system but to sidestep it here or there.

It was a way of life. And in the cold, gray world of Eastern Europe after the war, it was sometimes a breath of fresh air, no matter how polluted the air was.

There was one other consideration, an unseen principle that lurked beneath everything. The Western Allies of World War II did not formally acknowledge the East German state, nor did they recognize the GDR's right to remain in its self-proclaimed capital of East Berlin. Instead, Allied forces recognized the authority of only the Soviet Union over East Berlin. According to Western intelligence leaders and agents, anything that East Germany, the GDR, did could be traced back to Moscow.

Sometimes everything was just that simple; and sometimes it wasn't.

# Chapter 5
## East Berlin – July 8, 1952

In the late 1940s, the central Soviet administration for detention and transit camps in East Germany had moved their administrative offices into a building in Berlin at Ruschestrasse in Friedrichshain and their prison at Hohenschönhausen on the Genslerstraße, deep in the Eastern or "Soviet" zone about eight miles northeast of the Brandenburg Gate.

The stone and concrete building that formed the prison had been a nineteenth-century fortress. It had been partially destroyed by Allied airstrikes during the recent war. Previously, it had been a Nazi prison since the 1930s. But now it had new uses for a brutal new regime.

The Soviet Secret Service, then known as the NKVD, initially established it as a "restricted area" in 1945. It appropriated a large part of the surrounding industrial zone, including the long-standing site of a foul and filthy slaughterhouse and meat-processing plant, which was brought down by explosives.

Soviet soldiers and forced laborers then contained the area with sturdy fences with barbed wire or broken bottles at the top, creating one of the largest Soviet-restricted zones in the former German capital.

Before 1946, the sectioned-off area in Berlin-Hohenschönhausen contained "Special Camp No. 3," a Soviet detainment and transit camp, which was converted into a Soviet prison and labor camp in use up until the blockade and airlift of 1948 and 1949. The Soviet Ministry of Internal Affairs Special Camp Department was located in the restricted area. In addition, the Soviet State Security Central Investigation Department was housed here from 1947 to 1951, using the cellar of this former canteen and food store as its main remand prison.

The GDR State Security Services assumed control over the restricted area in 1951. Apart from the main remand prison, labor camp "X," and the two departments responsible for instituting criminal proceedings, the area was also used by a number of departments under the control of the Ministry of State Security, known in the English-speaking world as the MfS, an arrangement of letters which could be as intimidating as NKVD or MGB or eventually KGB.

By 1951, Hohenschönhausen Prison was extended and partially converted into a prison hospital. In the new area, in addition to medical and psychiatric units, three enclosed exercise cells were added to the hospital's eastern wing. The exercise cells were left open to the sky but covered with barbed wire nets, leading the prisoners to call them the *Tigerkäfige*, the tiger cages.

The prison hospital was positioned under the Ministry of State Security's Central Medical Service, highly convenient for the East German regime that operated it. The hospital had two dozen beds, with leather restraining straps that remained in locked cells. The other facilities included an X-ray ward and a so-called "treatment ward." Then there was a collection of small "operating rooms" and – most ominously of all – "laboratories" that were nothing short of hell on earth. Few survivors ever emerged. No man ever emerged unbroken or undamaged.

To make security all the more rigid, the Hohenschönhausen Prison in Berlin was located in a large, restricted military area, accessible only to authorized personnel. For those outside, all that was visible of the restricted area were the tall, grey buildings with every window shaded, the closed metal gates, the dark, terrifying watchtowers, the hundreds of surveillance cameras, and the formidable, armed security personnel.

The latter all belonged to the East German Ministry of State Security (MfS) guard regiment that monitored the entire area, including parts of the Genslerstrasse, Freienwalder, and Lichtenauerstrasse stations. To make things complete in this new world of intimidation and terror, none of this officially existed. The restricted area never appeared on GDR street maps. It was simply left blank.

It was to this facility that Walter Linse, who had peaceably started his day with his wife and family and was walking to the bus stop to travel to work, was taken. He had landed here – this bleak, crushing, unreal world that offered no hope of escape – within an hour of having finished his last sip of coffee at breakfast.

# Chapter 6
## West Berlin, American Occupation Zone
## July 8, 1952 – 10:00 AM

In contrast to Dr. Walter Linse, William Cochrane was enjoying a much more pleasant time in Berlin, at least to the extent that no one was currently trying to abduct or kill him. In fact, no one was paying Bill much unfavorable notice at all – not yet, anyway – since his return to Berlin in late May of 1952 and his informal meeting with a group of young people who would be his students on Thursday, July 3, the week before his class would begin.

All of that suited him simply fine, assuming that appearances could be believed.

Bill knew well that appearances could not be believed. The truth, if any such thing as absolute truth existed at all, was like those bloody Russian Matryoshka stacking dolls that were in all the tourist shops in East Berlin: the wooden nesting dolls, little figures of decreasing size placed one inside another. Truths within truths, they might be considered, or, more likely with Bill's increasingly cynical view of the world, lies within lies within lies, then followed by more lies.

Notwithstanding all of that, Bill was generally in good spirits and a good place in life. At age forty-six – "closer to ninety than to zero," as his dear wife, Laura, liked to gently tease him – Bill Cochrane gave all the appearances of having settled into a comfortable middle-life as a quirky but engaging university lecturer. He now filled an attractive adjunct position that had been specially created for him at the Free University in West Berlin. After several years away in New York and Washington, he had returned to a city that was very much in his blood by now. He was back in Berlin with his wife, Laura, and their daughter, Caroline, who was now seven years old. To

*REVOLT IN BERLIN* – Part One  NOEL HYND

Bill's great relief, both of the ladies of his family had also taken well to the city, war scars and all. It must, he mused to himself, have been somewhere in the Cochrane genes as well as Laura's. If so, it was a happy coincidence. So far at least.

The home life of the Cochrane family was comfortable. The university assignment was accompanied by a generous living space, a secure eight-room brick house that had somehow survived – more or less – the British, American, and Russian bombs that had fallen on Berlin. The home had once belonged to an anti-Nazi German professional couple who had disappeared during the war. It was in a secure and quiet stretch of the city in the American zone. It had been requisitioned after the war and repairs were done in 1947. Security had been retrofitted, including a giant iron fence around the building where the Cochranes lived and four other such homes in the small complex. In 1948, a distinguished American general named Max Albertson, his wife, and two daughters had moved in. The commander, an intelligence officer who had frequently been involved in set-tos with Soviet counterparts, had remained there with his family until the general's retirement in late 1951, upon which he announced in a profanity-laced diatribe that the city would be better off if the Russians all drowned in the Spree. *Stars and Stripes*, the daily American military newspaper, printed the quote, much to the amusement of all whom Albertson had served with in Berlin.

On the two mornings that Bill gave classes at the university, which had begun in the first days of July 1952, he was close enough to walk or take the S-Bahn, the tram. Bill served as a guest lecturer on the subject of American literature of the Jazz Age, the 1920s.

*The twenties*. Bill remembered the decade very well and with a certain affection. Having been born in 1906 and having celebrated his twentieth birthday in November 1926, the twenties had always been the decade that most fascinated him. Part of the attraction had to do with the stretch of buoyant years being intertwined with his youth. But he recalled the decade as a progression of ten years – more or less – with unbounded optimism in America even though it followed the first great modern horror: World War I.

The twenties was a formative decade for him as he lived through it, one of great intellectual and creative ferment, much of it evolving from those who had survived the carnage of the war. That was the bright side. The dark side was that it was a decade of disabled veterans in all countries, many of them in poverty and feeling betrayed by their governments. The social inequalities gave rise to Bolshevism in the Soviet Union and fascism in Spain, Italy, and Germany, as well as England and the United States where it did not take hold as readily.

Stalin, for example, had succeeded Lenin in 1922 and now thirty years later remained the head of state as well as of the Communist Party in the Soviet Union. The rise of Hitler and Mussolini had begun in the twenties, also. While both men were now safely dead, the legacy of their horrors continued to live after them.

*The twenties.* The mention of the decade generally speaking meant from the end of the first great war until the collapse of Wall Street in 1929. Now here Bill Cochrane was at age forty-six in 1952, smack dab in a vibrant middle-age, explaining the writers and writings of an optimistic America of two and a half decades ago to a select group of German university students.

Privately, Bill Cochrane might have conceded that it was questionable whether this academic post had sought him, or he had sought it. Nonetheless, he filled it. He had been in Berlin for many years from the late 1930s till the 1950s. Berlin, warts and all, was one of his two favorite cities, New York being the other. As a student of history and a witness to a good recent part of it, Cochrane considered Berlin the most important city of the twentieth century. He knew the city, its mood, its history, its subcultures, its currents, and its darker corners. He knew America with equal fluency. So, fine and dandy, he said to himself, he was the perfect man to explain

America to young Berliners while keeping the keen professional eye of a working intelligence gatherer on the city from close range.

Greater truths often lurk beneath comforting surfaces, of course. And this was the deeper reality of Bill Cochrane being in an academic post at Freie Universität Berlin. A post in academia was not a bad place to keep an eye on things, an innocent "cover" occupation that allowed him ample free time to circulate and take the measure of what was going on in the ongoing back-alley conflict of East and West. Looked at one way, there was never a dull moment as the great powers wrestled over the fate of the city as well as the future of Europe. On the other hand, there were plenty of dull moments between the various punches, bombs, abductions, and shots from an ambush that each of the great powers threw at each other.

Then again, Americans had a certain swagger and self-confidence these days in Germany. American interests may have been self-serving at times, but nonetheless, most Germans welcomed the protection. With their British allies, they had kept Berlin open and part of the free world during the blockade and airlift of 1948-49.

Bill Cochrane had more eyes and ears working in West Berlin than he would ever care to admit. From his involvement in the airlift, Cochrane kept a local "network" at Tempelhof, good solid men – German and American – who were both trustworthy and dependable. Noteworthy among them was Master Sergeant Jimmy Pearson, now in motor and transportation. There was also Otto Kern, Cochrane's master electrician, and former Wehrmacht soldier, who often enforced Bill Cochrane's own foreign policy positions with both muscle and firearms. Through Otto, Bill also made use of a couple of men named Cyril and Max. Cyril and Max liked girls, fast vehicles, guns, and fights. Cochrane couldn't have asked for a better-extended family. And this was just part of the "home team," as he thought of them, in West Berlin. He also had a few hearty souls stashed away among the fens and punts of

Cambridge, "the road team," for rainy days that he knew would eventually arrive. And then there were his Corsicans, about whom the less said the better. Bill assumed they were still in the occasional employ of the unsuspecting American taxpayers and was under the impression that he could work them into an operation as needed. They were, however, once removed from his own authority.

All of them received money every month to keep their households afloat during the tough postwar days. Rampant unemployment remained everywhere across the continent. Bill rarely put his hands on the monthly baksheesh. In Berlin, it came out of an agency black fund that arrived by courier at Tempelhof and found its way into Sgt. Pearson's locker on the eighth day of every month. Pearson, honest as a choir boy, took his share and acted as paymaster, distributing the rest. In England, a woman named Frau Swensen performed a similar task.

As a de facto office for tasks Bill did not wish to do at home or at the university, Cochrane still kept a small ten-by-ten-foot office at Tempelhof. It was secure on the ground level where the pilots' lounge was and with a sign on the door that read, "Janitorial – *Reinigungdienstungen.*" Cochrane had plenty of eyes and ears working the place.

Today Tempelhof, reconstructed in 1946, belonged to the Americans – one hundred percent. The airport could just as easily have been America's forty-ninth state. In an earlier time, Hitler had built sprawling, intimidating, troop quarters and air-operations buildings at the field. Workers who now lived in the apartment buildings on Tempelhof's fringes were as anxious about the low-flying incoming and outgoing aircraft as the pilots were about the five- and six-story buildings around the landing fields. Yet at this location, the Kaiser's special troops had once paraded. Many of these same imperial soldiers had attended regular Christian services in the adjacent German military chapel or been interred in the attached burial grounds. Both the church and cemetery had been obliterated

*REVOLT IN BERLIN* – Part One     NOEL HYND

by wartime bombing, as had the aggressive dreams of first the Kaiser and then the Führer.

Tempelhof in 1952 remained the most significant airport in Berlin. But there were now two others. The British maintained a sputtering but functional airfield at Gatow, known formally as RAF Gatow, except to the French who pronounced it as "gateau." Pilots frequently joked that landing there was a "piece of cake," which it actually wasn't, particularly in the fog and in thunderstorms. Nor was it centrally located, perched as it was on the distant west bank of the Havel River, not far from Spandau Prison. The British field lay in the flat, open countryside. It provided fewer mental hazards to the fliers but more difficulties to the truckers that had to haul tons of bulky, incoming freight into Berlin proper.

RAF Gatow was also primarily a military base. As a military base, however, it was quirky. It was the home for the only known operational use of flying boats in central Europe – the Havel River serving as a landing strip for these airborne curiosities – as well as a spanking new squad of de Havilland Canada DHC-1s, known as the Chipmunks. The Chipmunk was a tandem, two-seat, single-engine primary trainer aircraft. It was increasingly recognized for its excellent flying characteristics and its capability for aerobatic maneuvers. Much to the annoyance of the East Germans, the RAF soon began to use Chipmunks for photographic reconnaissance missions over East Germany.

Even the French got into the airport business. The new French airport at Tegel in the French zone, still not entirely complete, had risen – sort of – from an expanse of choppy, sandy, wasteland next to a stagnant canal. The field still looked like a barracks camp, lit for night work, rather than a finished modern airport. One would have thought that a French place would have had more style and joie de vivre, Bill Cochrane frequently thought. But it didn't. None.

The French had not actively participated in the airlift of 1948-49, but they did make some contributions. And they had a knack for getting under the skin of the Soviets.

## *REVOLT IN BERLIN* – Part One          NOEL HYND

By 1948, they had built a new airport complete with a new runway – built from crushed bricks and rubble from bombed-out buildings – that was more than a mile long. The opening of Tegel enabled more landing opportunities in Berlin, to the dismay of the Russian commander.

There was also the infuriating issue of an antiquated, nonworking, Soviet radio tower that stood in the French sector and was blocking part of the British-American flight path into Berlin. French general Jean Ganeval, commander of French troops in Berlin, whom Bill Cochrane knew personally from the months of the airlift, asked for weeks if the Soviets would dismantle the transmitter.

As was their usual approach to such matters, they ignored the request. Finally, General Ganeval ordered the tower blown up. Soviet Military Commandant of the Soviet Sector of Berlin, Aleksandr Kotikov, expressed outrage face to face over the destruction of the irksome transmitter. He demanded to know how Ganeval could do such a thing.

The French commander replied with classic Gallic insouciance "Easily, Comrade," he said. "With French engineers and dynamite." The story of Ganeval's remark appeared in no newspaper or periodical. But it gradually made the rounds.

Even General de Gaulle, out of power now but maneuvering behind the scenes, had been amused. De Gaulle and his shadow government in exile had returned from Algiers to Paris postwar. There he headed two successive provisional governments, until in 1946, he brusquely resigned, having had enough of the bickering political parties that had formed his coalition government.

In November 1946 the Fourth French Republic was declared, and de Gaulle eloquently fulminated against its weak-kneed constitution, which, he raged, was likely to reproduce the political and governmental instabilities of the Third Republic.

In 1947 de Gaulle had formed the Rally of the French People, *La Rassemblement du Peuple Français*, known also as the RPF. It was a mass movement that was not a political party but gathered such momentum and grew so rapidly in strength that suddenly, overnight, it turned into a political party during the elections of 1951. It won 120 seats in the National Assembly.

The movement expressed de Gaulle's hostility to the constitution, to the party system, and, in particular, to the French Communists, whom he despised because of their unswerving loyalty to directives from Stalin, whom he despised even more. The French military establishment – like de Gaulle – was heavily Roman Catholic and instinctively anti-communist. The French – the army at least – were frequently seen as the little brothers of the Americans and the British, but quietly would facilitate whatever Americans like Bill Cochrane wished to accomplish, as long as it was done quietly. The radio tower reduced to rubble was a fine example.

Few working people of the Western powers that had defeated Hitler were fully aware of how anti-Nazi the city of Berlin had been. The city had always displayed its characteristic independent, irreverent, in-your-face flavor, much like Paris, which had in many ways been Berlin's sister city in the 1920s.

Now in 1952, this attitude had morphed into a deep loathing in West Berlin for those who governed and oppressed the East. Those in West Berlin were willing to hang tough, to support the Americans, French, and British as they battled the Soviets. It was no secret that if the Allies were forced out, or gave up, Soviet tanks would roll westward the next day and the great German capital would be swallowed up by Ulbricht, Zaisser, Mielke, and Stalin and that one little glimmer of light shining through Europe's Iron Curtain would fade out for generations if not longer.

It was a time when the villains of the postwar world were ascendant, and many of those allied against them were war-weary and turning inward. But it was also a time when men and women like Bill Cochrane instinctively dug in, toed the line, and waited for the next atrocity the other side could throw at them.

"French engineers and dynamite," Bill laughed to Helmut late one evening at the Bar Ritter. "Damned good one, eh?"

"The best I've heard since the last time you were in Berlin," Helmut agreed.

They clinked their glasses together and drank to the health of General Ganeval who not only knew his military tactics but his psychological ones as well.

*Sir.* Helmut was in never-never land in terms of how to address Bill Cochrane. Helmut knew he went by the name of Lewis, but his name was actually something else. Nor did Helmut know how his mentor wanted to be known at any particular moment. It was all part of who he was, and if asked, Helmut knew that Bill worked for his country and his country's interests. As those interests had frequently been on the side of Helmut and Bill had helped him get a toehold into a solid, postwar business, Helmut was fine with all of that.

Yet how to address Bill was perplexing. They had never discussed it. But "sir" fit perfectly.

There was a flip side to all of this, however.

Berlin could be more than treacherous during the stiflingly hot summer of 1952.

There was even a somber echo of Berlin in the twenties: a prosperity – in West Berlin at least – that had excluded many, including a population of wounded and disabled veterans and legions of militant poor littering the streets. If Bill Cochrane looked beneath the surface in most places, he could easily find suggestions of danger or menace. He kept Laura far from it and Caroline even farther. Yet at the same time, the city had been rebuilt. Blocks in the French, British, and American zones that he remembered as piles of rubble in 1948 and 1949 had miraculously come alive again with shops, beer gardens, restaurants, movie houses, and clothiers. An even stranger phenomenon could be seen after dark with new "clubs" popping up with names reminiscent of the seedy days of the Weimar Era.

There was, among others, the Weisse Maus, which was wicked and raucous. Heaven and Hell, it promised both, and elegantly delivered such across the street from the ruins of a church.

The Blue Stocking was favored by mulatto prostitutes in skimpy dresses, cocaine sniffers, pickpockets, "Alphonses" and transvestites. Even the Red Mill Cabaret, the lowest of the low, relocated from its former location in what was now the Eastern sector and merrily reopened on a cul-de-sac street in the American sector. The Red Mill was a rough-and-tumble joint, a place with a floor show of barely glad girls, appreciated by pimps, crooks, cheap hookers, and usually a tableful of American MPs having a look-see taking in the foreign culture, a can't-miss place for conscripted sons of farmers from the Midwestern dairy states to gawk at stuff they never could have imagined back home.

The doors to these places were closed to the street, usually with heavy, sober-visaged guards in front of them. But beyond the doors, Berlin nightlife had returned in all its gloriously seedy, pervy, off-kilter, pre-Nazi glory, permeated with a blue haze of powerful cigarette smoke. It was wise to wear sturdy shoes because it was common for one's foot to brush against a syringe that had been dropped on the floor.

The moralistic stick-up-the-backside socialist leaders of the East, from Ulbricht on down, frequently railed and inveighed against the moral decay and degeneracy of West Germany in general and West Berlin specifically, but there was rarely a night in any of the racier clubs when one didn't hear loud Russian spoken above the din or a live band or sound system playing American music. It was common to see a bare-breasted waitress or two bouncing on the lap of a drunken, high-ranking Soviet army officer in a boxy civilian suit or even a Czech, Hungarian, or Polish diplomat breaking free of Marxist ideology for an evening just to experience first-hand how deplorable life could be in the West.

If life wasn't deplorable enough in the main seating areas of the storefront clubs, there were usually backrooms or cellar chambers for further degradation for those who dealt in Western currencies. Berliners who liked to go slumming were welcome, as were tourists, mostly English and American, many of whom departed without their passports, rings, watches, wallets, or unattended coats.

Bill Cochrane visited a few of these hellholes in the line of duty, not to socialize but to watch what was going on. From a table in a corner where he sat and nursed a whiskey, he could see the talent spotters from Washington, London, Ottawa, and Paris as they trawled for middle-range defectors and snitches from the Soviet zone.

Business, Bill observed on those times when he was present, was brisk.

Bill made no secret to Laura about where he had been or what he had been observing. She took it all in stride, as worldly English ladies of her generation had learned to do. She entertained only one lingering question.

"What in heaven's name is an 'Alphonse'?" she asked Bill one evening as they settled into bed to sleep one evening.

"A pimp. A procurer," he said.

"Of women?"

"Well, not to put too fine an edge on it," he answered, "but a procurer of whatever the paying customer so desires, I would think."

"Oh." A thoughtful pause, then. "Innocent me. I see."

"It's the term the Berliners use."

"Where, if I may ask, did they get that name? 'Alphonse'."

"I wondered, myself," Bill said. "I asked at the university, where they would know such things. Turns out that the term evolved from a remote play by Alexander Dumas *fils*, who wrote *Monsieur Alphonse*. Haven't seen it or read it but I can guess the subject matter."

"And how do *you* know something like this while *I* do not?" she laughed.

"It's obvious. You obviously spend your time with a better class of people," he answered.

"Indeed," Laura answered with mock propriety, smiling and shaking her head. "Well, we both knew that already, didn't we?"

"We did, Laura."

After a moment's thought, "I guess I've led a sheltered life," she added with an edge.

"We all have to some degree. I'm certain Berlin will cure us all of that, sooner or later," Bill said.

He turned off the bedroom lights. But it didn't clear his ever-teeming mind.

Surely, he told himself with an amused grimace, thinking back to those risqué clubs that had sunk new roots into old Berlin – Alphonses, blue clouds of tobacco smoke, lovely ladies *en deshabille* and all – what other consenting adults do with each other on their own time was their own business. But surely a world war hadn't been fought solely to resurrect the depravity of the Weimar years in West Berlin.

Had it?

He turned the question over and over in his now misty consciousness, found no conclusive answer, and moved along to other more important things. The latter quickly bored him. He spent enough time on such things in his waking hours.

The thought line dissolved. He slept peacefully with his wife breathing steadily and equally in peace beside him and his daughter safe and secure in the adjoining bedroom.

He settled in to sleep, Laura next to him. In a tough, uncompromising, and intimidating way, Berlin amused and entertained him. He reassured himself that he and his family were safe in the retired general's former digs.

He slept soundly.

# Chapter 7
## Moscow and Korea – 1952

On March 10, 1952, Soviet Foreign Minister Andrei Gromyko gave a formal diplomatic "note" about the solution of the "German problem" to representatives of the three Western "occupiers" and proposed a four-power conference. The note came from the Soviet general secretary and premier, Joseph Stalin, and was later to be known as the Stalin Note. It caught the Western powers by surprise.

The note offered Soviet recognition of a reunified Germany if the Western powers agreed to not join any military alliance: NATO, for example. The proposal suggested German reunification and neutralization with no conditions on economic policies. There followed the usual Soviet hogwash about "the rights of man and basic freedoms, including freedom of speech, press, religious persuasion, political conviction, and assembly" – guarantees that they had no history of following through on in any land they had conquered.

There was also another catch. The eastern border of the proposed reunified Germany would revert to the Oder-Neisse Line and the old Prussian territories would be ceded to the Soviet Union and its Polish satellite, presumably forever.

The offer was dead on arrival. The three Western powers rejected it summarily, each with its own reason. The immediate dismissal of the note played perfectly into Walter Ulbricht's plans. Ulbricht flew to Moscow where he met with Stalin. He convinced Stalin to allow the GDR to protect itself with a firm and defensible border.

Stalin agreed. Immediately construction began on a strip of land known as the Inner German Border, the new formal frontier between the German Democratic Republic and the Federal Republic of Germany. It was three and a half miles wide and almost nine hundred miles long. It meandered through Central Europe from the Baltic Sea to Czechoslovakia. The work was done by unlucky local conscripts from villages along the border.

On its eastern side, it became one of the world's most heavily fortified frontiers, defined by a continuous line of high metal fences and walls, barbed wire, alarms, anti-vehicle ditches, watchtowers, automatic booby traps, and minefields. It was patrolled by fifty thousand armed GDR border guards who faced tens of thousands of West German, British, and U.S. guards and soldiers, frequently close enough to wave to each other. As the weeks passed in the spring and early summer of 1952, more than a million NATO and Warsaw Pact troops assembled on opposite sides of this new border. They awaited the possible outbreak of war in the hinterlands behind the border,

The border was the Iron Curtain in person as well as in concrete and wire. One had to risk one's life to attempt to cross it. Most people knew better.

There were twin rows of concrete tracks up hillsides to a watchtower. Rapid access to all parts of the border line was required to ensure a quick response to escape attempts. This was initially a problem for the East Germans: few patrol roads existed. Patrols – soldiers or Stasi with rifles – typically used a footpath that ran inside of the fence, alongside the control strip.

Strips of bare, plowed earth were flanked by a concrete road on one side and a row of barricades and fences on the other with buildings visible in the far background.

The control strips – *Kontrolstreiffen* – were lines of bare earth running parallel to the border fences. They were not an obstacle as such but provided a simple and effective way for the border guards to monitor unauthorized travel across the border. It was almost impossible to cross the strip without leaving footprints, thus enabling the border guards to identify otherwise undetectable escape attempts. They could learn how many individuals had crossed, where escape attempts were being made, and at which times of day escapees were active.

*REVOLT IN BERLIN* – Part One     NOEL HYND

From this information, the border guards were able to determine where and when surveillance needed to be improved.

There were two control strips, both located on the inward-facing sides of the border fences. The secondary strip, two meters wide, ran alongside the signal fence to the rear of the *Schutzstreifen*. The strips ran uninterrupted along the entire length of the border. In places where the border was prone to escape attempts, the control strip was illuminated at night by high-intensity floodlights installed on concrete poles, which were also used at vulnerable points such as rivers and streams crossing the border. Guards also patrolled the strips day and night, usually with three officers armed with rifles. On the western side of the border, the control strip became known as the "death strip", *die Todesstreifen*, because of the shoot-to-kill orders given to the border guards. It also picked up the underground term, *Pieck-Allee*, "Pieck Avenue," after Wilhelm Pieck, the Soviet-puppet president of East Germany who presided over it, usually by three officers armed with rifles.

Anti-vehicle barriers along the inner German border grew increasingly impenetrable throughout its existence. In the early days, the East Germans blocked border crossings by simply tearing up the road surface, digging ditches, and using the earth and rubble to build ramparts that physically blocked the carriageways. These were then enhanced with wire and wooden posts. As border fortifications developed into permanent barriers, purpose-built obstacles became standard. The most common types were "Czech hedgehogs." These were constructed from three or four pairs of five-foot-long rails welded together to form a steel obstacle weighing over a thousand pounds, heavy enough to stop a motor vehicle or a team of strong men from pushing them aside. They quickly became a common sight along the entire inner German border.

Dog runs – *Kettenlaufanlagen* – were installed along high-risk sectors of the border. The dogs were usually tethered to steel cables running up to the length of an American football field. The dogs were occasionally turned loose in temporary pens adjoining gates or damaged sections of the fence.

The border fences were constructed in a number of phases, starting with the initial fortification of the border in May 1952. The first-generation fences were crudely built barbed-wire fences – *Stacheldrahtzäune* – standing between 1.2 and 2.5 meters (3.9 and 8.2 ft) high. The fences were overlooked by watchtowers located at strategic intervals along the border.

However, as in most of East Germany, corruption and incompetence came into play. The border barrier was in certain locations so poorly constructed or maintained that chickens, pigs, and cattle were able to wander unhindered across the border. In a few places, gaps were purposefully left with lowered gate poles in front of them and anti-vehicle Czech hedgehog barricades behind.

*

On the other side of the world, not by coincidence, a similar scenario was playing out on another enforced border. The Empire of Japan had annexed Korea in 1910 and ruled Korea as a colony until World War II ended in August of 1945.

The Soviet Union and China brought their influence quickly to bear on North Korea. The United States propped up a feeble democracy in the South until it turned into an ugly dictatorship under President Sigmund Rhee. The war began on June 15, 1950, when North Korea invaded South Korea following years of animosity between the two countries. North Korea found support from China and the Soviet Union. The United States supported South Korea. United States forces fought battles against Chinese troops and were in conflict with Soviet aircraft providing support to North Korea.

After a year of fighting and tens of thousands of casualties, North and South Korea remained intent on continuing to fight, but their Cold War sponsors were growing weary of a war that seemed doomed to be an eternal stalemate. Lulls fell on some battlefields and while air strikes continued, both sides dug into defensive positions around a strategic line

– imaginary in most places – that stretched across the Korean peninsula more or less at the 38th Parallel. It ranged from forty miles above the 38th Parallel on the East Coast to twenty miles below the parallel on the West Coast.

Both sides exchanged heavy artillery fire throughout 1952, and in June, the 45th Division, in response to increased Chinese ground action, engaged in an intense period of fighting with the Chinese, successfully establishing eleven new patrol bases along its front. By the beginning of 1953, however, the larger picture was still one of continuing military stalemate, with few changes in the front lines, reflecting the deadlock in the armistice talks.

For many weeks, all was quiet on a large scale. But the war remained red hot on another level. Close to the front, a new faceoff had developed, one that played out with military sharpshooters taking frequent potshots at each other from a distance of four hundred meters or more.

The sharpshooters, of course, were called snipers. And each country's army had scrambled to assemble as many good ones as possible.

DDR Propaganda poster 1950s: Korea for The Koreans!

# Chapter 8
## West Berlin, American Occupation Zone
## New York City, Winter 1952

The Free University of Berlin was concurrently a political gambit and a noble undertaking. It was founded in West Berlin in 1948 with heavy American financial and political support. It was a Western continuation of the Friedrich Wilhelm University, or the University of Berlin, which had been Nazified in the 1930s and 1940s. It sought to reexamine the traditions that the Nazis had destroyed. There was another university in Berlin, the Friedrich Wilhelm University, which had been renamed the Humboldt University. But Friedrich Wilhelm University, being in East Berlin, faced strong communist repression; the Free University's name referred to West Berlin's status as part of the Western Free World, contrasting with communist-controlled East Berlin. The Free University of Berlin was founded by students and scholars in December 1948. The creation of the university had been strongly connected to the beginning of the Cold War period.

The Free University had staggered off to an inauspicious start after the conclusion of World War II. The University of Berlin had been situated in what became the Soviet sector of Berlin. The Soviet Military Administration in Germany granted permission to the university to continue teaching in January 1946. However, the university came under immediate communist interference and repression. It became a battlefield for the political disputes of the postwar period as well as philosophical differences between Western freedoms and a Soviet brand of socialism. When the Soviet Union tried to suppress free thought and critical thinking at the university, there were widespread protests by students critical of the East German political system.

Enter the Soviet Secret Police, or the MGB, to restore academic vigor, Bolshevik style.

A crackdown on free thought was brutal and immediate. Between 1946 and 1948, dozens of students were brutally beaten and arrested or persecuted by the MGB or their newly formed allies in the East German secret police. More than a dozen students were executed, usually by Russians.

By the end of 1947, thousands of disgruntled students were agitating for a new university free from political influence. The climax of the protests was reached in April 1948 just as the Soviets were preparing to blockade Berlin. Three students were expelled from the university without a trial, triggering a mass protest of twenty-five hundred students at the Hotel Esplanade, an iconic, old, luxury hotel that dated from 1907, which once loomed above Berlin's busy transport and nightlife hub, Potsdamer Platz. By the late 1940s, however, the Esplanade had gone from being one of Berlin's most luxurious and celebrated hotels to a bombed-out heap of rubble lost in the wastelands of the postwar era. Nonetheless, a small section of the hotel remained standing, and rebelling students made it their focus of protests until they were routed out by Russian and German security brigades.

The situation, however, was not lost on some of the wise American authorities in postwar Berlin. By the end of April 1948, the military governor of the United States Army, Lucius D. Clay, gave the order to legally examine the formation of a new university in the "free" Western sectors of Berlin. On June 19, 1948, a "preparatory committee" laid the legal groundwork for a "free university" in Berlin, the Western version of the renowned University of Berlin.

The local Berlin government in the Western zones accepted the by-laws in November 1948. The first lectures followed in the same month. By 1949, the Free University had registered nearly five thousand students. Many students came from the Soviet sector, much to the chagrin and embarrassment of the Soviet governors and their new East German socialist allies.

There was an engaging, round man with a pink face on the administrative side of the faculty at the Free University. He was Dr. Bernard Kreitler. Cochrane had met him the last time he had been in Berlin. It was a given that he supervised all hiring and was a Dulles crony going back to Geneva in the 1930s.

"If I get this straight, the Free University is ninety percent academic and the other fifty percent political," Cochrane said to his intelligence contact, Larry DeWinter, who had finalized Bill's assignment back in Washington over far too many drinks at the bar of the Madison Hotel in the waning days of 1951. "Does that add up to you?"

"Yes, it does," DeWinter said. "I've always admired your facility with numbers."

"It's a skill I've acquired," Cochrane said. "Necessity more than force of habit."

"Roamin' numerals, huh?" DeWinter said with a wise-guy grin, finishing his fourth Scotch and signaling Sid, the indulgent bartender, for a fifth. Sid had the right bottle ready. He poured for DeWinter and looked to Cochrane, who held up a palm to decline.

"Speaking of Rome," Cochrane asked, "whatever happened to those three bloodthirsty Corsicans we used two years ago? Are they still in the fold?"

DeWinter nodded, quite drunk now. It was a grand moment for Cochrane to get information out of his handler. DeWinter had the habit of being too gabby when he was drinking with friends. Cochrane was careful not to say too much in return.

"Who might that be?" DeWinter teased. "I don't recall any Corsicans."

"Vito, Sergio, and Nino," Cochrane said. "Those were the names by which I knew them."

"Oh. Them," DeWinter said as if there were other Corsicans. "Alive and well. Still on the roster for Mr. Dulles.

Along with many other teams. Some men collect cars, others collect women, and some men have a penchant for assassination teams. Don't you worry if you ever need some blood and guts."

"Why would I need that?" Cochrane asked. "I'm to be a lowly academic preaching the American literary gospel in a foreign city. Doubt if very much trouble could find me at all."

"Ha, ha!" DeWinter said. "Sure thing, Bill. I suppose you'll also tell me that you no longer have your very capable supporting cast, your sub-agents as they might be known. Scattered all over Berlin, the south of England, and who knows where else."

"I wouldn't dream of denying that," Cochrane said pleasantly. "Why would I? And by the same token, I'd never dream of revealing who and where they are. These are my people, and they will remain so. Fair enough?"

"Sure," DeWinter said. "I'll pass it along."

"Of that, I have no doubt," Bill said.

A pause, then, "Listen, buddy," DeWinter said with an air of finality for the evening, "the DCA, General Smith, is going to make some changes in the Berlin command. And if Eisenhower gets elected this fall, Dulles may be back." A pause, then, "I suppose if Stevenson gets elected, the CIA will be run by Henry Wallace, someone with a direct line to Stalin."

"You're drunk, you know, Mr. D.," Bill said. "Talking too loud and talking too much."

"Am I? Just wanted to give you a heads up."

"I assure you that you succeeded."

DeWinter finished his drink and was eyeing Sid and the bottle when Cochrane interceded. Bill paid the check and delivered DeWinter to a taxi. A few days later, Cochrane conjured up a cover story that led him to some research files in Virginia where he managed to access a file on Dr. Bernard Kreitler. DeWinter's story checked. Kreitler had first come into view by Allen Dulles in Switzerland where he was teaching classics at a private school in Geneva. He had been

*REVOLT IN BERLIN* – **Part One**     NOEL HYND

on the faculty of the University of Berlin until the Nazis had beaten him one time too many and he fled the country in 1939 for the shores of Lac Leman.

The pretext for the beatings was that his mother was Jewish, but that was more of an excuse than an established fact. What Hitler's thugs really didn't like was that Bernard Kreitler didn't like them and had said so to his students, at least one of whom ratted him out to an arm-banded goon squad. By his writings in an exile publication in Switzerland, which were in the American files and which Bill Cochrane read carefully, he didn't much like the communists, either. That left him in a lonely place in Germany. But it was a pedigree that appealed to Allen Dulles, and, happily, it also appealed to Bill Cochrane. More recently, Kreitler had studied law in Germany after the war, worked as a news correspondent in Amsterdam and London, then returned to Berlin where he wore several hats, some more surreptitious than others.

Kreitler looked great on paper. More than great. Cochrane had liked him when they first met, also, sharing pastries in a faculty lounge in the spring of 1950.

To Bill, all of these details plus gut instinct sealed the deal.

Laura had reservations, but in the end, no objections. So several months later, the Cochrane family had returned to West Berlin, flying from New York to Paris, spending some days with old friends, and then continuing on to a resurgent West Berlin by train.

Bill's classes at the university were soon to begin, plus, he knew, whatever fate threw in his direction in defense of his country.

# Chapter 9
## Eberswalde, East Germany – July 1952

Wolfgang Reymann's new life disintegrated the morning that two sour-tempered, uniformed police officers from Berlin came looking for him, arriving in what had once been an American Jeep, but which had been repainted with DDR markings.

The names of the police were Glienicke and Berg. They wore sidearms, big new Lugers. They were a Mutt and Jeff combo: Glienicke the tall thin one, Berg eight inches shorter and pudgy. No one had to announce to anyone that they were Stasi. Their uniforms announced what unit they served. The people of the town scattered and did their best to avoid them. But the visitors were persistent.

They arrived in the town square of Eberswalde shortly before noon. Berg carried a large, brown, oblong, canvas sack that looked like a weapons bag. They were in the company of a third man – ramrod straight posture, short blond hair, military swagger – who wore civilian clothing. He towered over the other two. He was at least six and a half feet tall with wide shoulders, made even wider by the heavy, military-style black coat he wore, even on a summer morning.

The man seemed to not have vocal chords because he didn't say anything for most of the visit. But it was a given that he would have plenty to say – none of it pleasant – if he got started. They asked around, the two Stasi, trying to determine where they could find a man named Wolfgang Reymann. No one in the village wanted to help. The third man tailed them, listened, and kept silent. The two Stasi showed him great deference. He neither gave a name nor used one.

They persisted. They had an address for Commissar Zeitler. They located him in the two-room cabin that he shared with his wife. The three men entered without knocking and confronted the commissar as he sat at his kitchen table. Now the Stasi men went quiet, and the third man spoke for the first time. He spoke in native Russian.

"Where will we find Comrade Reymann?" the Russian asked, formal and unsmiling. He had a face that conveyed a threat without announcing one.

Commissar Zeitler shot to his feet as soon as he heard Russian. He broke into an immediate sweat and answered in Russian.

"You will find him laboring in the fields of the collective farm above the town, Comrades," Zeitler answered. "He will be honored by your inquiry and visit. As we all are," he added quickly.

"I hope so, Commissar," the Russian said. Then he repeated, barking this time for emphasis. "I hope so!"

"That is where I assigned him, Comrade!" Zeitler insisted.

"Let's hope he is obedient," the visitor said, barking again. With a jerk of his head, the Russian indicated that the Stasi should return to their vehicle.

Zeitler's legs were reduced to rubber. He stayed standing until the visitors departed, one of the Stasi turning halfway to give him a contemptuous glare. The men went out to their vehicle. A brief conference took place. Then the Stasi men waited as the Russian returned to Zeitler's small home. He walked into it without knocking.

"Comrade Zeitler!" he bellowed.

Zeitler appeared from the kitchen. He stood quietly at attention.

"Show us!" the Russian said.

The Russian prodded Zeitler along and the four men piled into the former Jeep.

They took the only road that continued beyond the town. They drove up a dirt road that was bumpy with stones. At the top of a hill, they came to a clearing, which seemed to border on an orchard. There were several local people working in the area, tending to small patches of crops. The truck that was used to deliver produce to the farmers' market at the final terminal of the S-Bahn stood idly at the edge of an open field. Apple trees stood beyond. The trees were young, having been planted after the war.

Wolfgang Reymann was kneeling in the grainy soil of an onion patch, eyeing a potentially disappointing harvest, when one of the boys who helped him indicated the visitors. Reymann's heart jumped when he turned and saw the visitors looking in his direction. He stood. His young helpers gathered around.

"You boys, go," he said.

"We'll protect you," one of them said.

"No. You must go!" Wolfgang said. "Now!" He gestured with his hand. The boys took off. Commissar Zeitler sent the other workers home. The two Stasi and the Russian approached Wolfgang. They met twenty meters from the edge of a thick stand of apple trees.

"You are Wolfgang Reymann?" asked the Russian in heavily accented German.

"Yes."

"The Great Stalin, the Great Architect of Communism, sends you his greetings."

"All hail the great Stalin!" said Reymann with fake enthusiasm that passed for the real thing.

The Russian eyed Reymann closely, up and down, then eye to eye. Reymann did not flinch. Then, "We have something to discuss," the Russian said.

"I would be honored to hear it," Reymann said without emotion.

There was much to discuss with Comrade Reymann.

Conscripted into the army, Wolfgang Reymann and his skills as a marksman – honed as a boy shooting small game in the forests of Bavaria – trained in the Wehrmacht as a sniper from January to June 1942 at the Truppenübungsplatz Seetaler-Alpe in Steiermark. Graduating with high honors, he was then assigned as a Feldwebel, or sergeant, to the 3rd Gebirgsjäger Division. His mission was to gain a furtive advanced combat position and target Soviet officers as the

63

Wehrmacht proceeded south from Poland through Eastern Europe.

Reymann was nothing if not lethally effective. Wehrmacht records credited him with more than two hundred confirmed kills. This was an excellent total. For this, Wolfgang Reymann received the Knight's Cross of the Iron Cross on April 19, 1945, less than a month before the Reich collapsed. As a German, he was more proud of the award than of what he had done to earn it.

In the military of the Third Reich, the only "kills" which were confirmed as "effected" were those witnessed by a superior officer. Wolfgang Reymann's estimated kills were many times higher than his total of confirmed. Feldwebel Reymann engaged in battle against Soviet forces in the Carpathians, Hungary, and Slovakia. Throughout the war, he carried with him three weapons: a Walther P-38 pistol as a sidearm for when the fighting came within fifty meters, and for long-range, two long rifles, a Karabiner 98k sniper variant with six-power telescopic sight, and a Gewehr 43 with a four-power telescopic sight. The Karabiner was his weapon of choice, depending on wind and weather. It worked better than the other long rifle in the cold.

Wolfgang had another distinction in comparison to his peers in the long-rang killing profession. He rarely wasted a round. If he fired, he hit his target lethally an astonishing eighty-two percent of the time. If an enemy was in his sights, the enemy was as good as dead.

His longest confirmed kill was a shot that reportedly covered more than a thousand yards before hitting a Red Army tank commander named Sokolov in the center of the back, a perfect shot from a tree that shattered the Russian commander's backbone and ripped through his heart, bringing bone fragments with it. The kill, like most of Reymann's, was instantaneous.

On November 25, 1944, Wolfgang suffered a head injury from Soviet artillery fire and was awarded the Wound Badge, *Die Verwundetenabzeichen*, a week later. He lost part of an ear and some shrapnel remained under his scalp. But he returned to his unit on December 12 and stayed with it till the end of the war.

Wolfgang arrived at a Soviet POW camp in May of 1945, surprised to be alive. He might have been sent to a forced labor camp in Siberia or been summarily executed for all those Red Army officers he had killed. But his superiors looked at his Wehrmacht records now that the war was over. Noting his skills as a sniper, they took interest and sent him instead for reeducation, meaning indoctrination as a communist, in Ukraine where many postwar camps were located. He was given rifles from the Great Patriotic War, as the Soviets called World War II, and asked to demonstrate his proficiency. He did. He showed how he could pick apples off a tree with a bullet from four hundred meters or bring down a soaring bird in the sky from six hundred meters. His handlers were impressed.

Wolfgang had never cared much for politics. His military service was to the professional army, not the SS. He was spared the brutal forced labor that was mandatory in the postwar gulags and prison camps. He was given indoctrination in Marxist theory, Stalinism, the evils of capitalism, and Russian culture. He took to it as he understood it was keeping him alive. He knew he was being treated better than other POWs due to his sniping skills. The only question was whether he would now be impressed into the Soviet army or the East German Army. It turned out that neither would be the next path for him.

"You will go to a village called Eberswalde near Berlin," said his Soviet handler one day. You will work on a collective farm. There are many young German widows there. Select one if you wish. Do farm work and wait. You will be contacted in the near future for special assignments. Do you understand?"

No smile, no shrug this time. Just a crisp, "Yes."

Now, many months later, and several hundred miles away, the Stasi policemen Glienicke and Berg arrived to screen a selected "patriotic volunteer" for the special assignment. They made sure the field was clear of all the farm workers. They shooed the kids farther away. When the young people didn't move fast enough, the Stasi berated them in obscene, profane German. The boys and two girls started to run. Then the Russian drew a Russian pistol out from under a coat and, before Wolfgang could intervene or say anything, fired two bullets in their direction, though well over their heads.

Then, smirking, he tucked the weapon away and muttered. *"Kleine Gören,"* he said. Little brats.

"You shoot poorly," Glienicke said. "Kill one. That will get the attention of the others as well as their peasant parents."

"Yes," Berg said, escalating the challenge. The children had stopped running and were grouped fifty meters away. "Kill one of the dirty little farm girls. See if you can hit the blonde one from the group."

The Russian looked at the two Stasi as if they were joking. They kept stern faces.

"All right," the Russian said, annoyed at their audacity but provoked.

He drew his pistol again. He turned toward the group of children. He raised his pistol, brought it down to firing position, closed his eyes— and thought that his arm had been chopped off when Wolfgang brought the full force of the stock of the Karabiner down across his forearm.

The pistol discharged and a shot went into the ground. The children ran in panic and disappeared.

"The Russian, clutching his arm, turned furiously on Wolfgang. They were eye to eye. Wolfgang, an inch taller, glowered down at the Soviet.

"You don't shoot children!" Wolfgang said.

"I shoot whoever I want."

"Not here!" Wolfgang said. Then, reloading the rifle, he said, "You want bottle-shooting, I'll give you bottle-shooting."

The Stasi stepped back. Glienicke indicated that Zeitler should stand guard several meters away and prevent any townspeople from returning. The three visitors stood in a half-circle around Wolfgang.

Wolfgang and the Russian exchanged a cold stare. They knew each other. Not well, and not as friends, but they knew each other. There was much Wolfgang could have said, but none of it came forth. He wondered, however, if he was about to be killed.

"You are pleased with your life here?" the Russian asked. The two Stasi men stood behind their leader and kept quiet as large stones.

"I am pleased. My thanks to the great Stalin."

A pause, then, "Do you still shoot?"

"Only game. Deer. Pheasant. Rabbit."

"You were assigned to practice."

"Too much practice can be a bad thing. It arouses suspicion."

"So you are out of practice?"

"That is not what I said." Searching for more, Reymann added. "I have a medical difficulty with my hands," he said. "They shake."

"Show me."

Reymann held forth his hands. They quivered.

"Alas," said the Russian.

"Alas," said Reymann.

"Let's see how bad it is," the Russian said.

Berg opened the sack. From it, he withdrew two empty wine bottles. The glass was light green, suggesting that the vintage had been a light German white. The Russian jerked his head toward the far end of the open stretch of farmland.

"Don't waste time," the Russian said.

Berg handed the bottles to Glienicke. The latter hustled down the length of the field, a hundred meters or so, and set up the bottles as targets on a tree stump. As he hustled back, Berg reached into the sack and pulled out its most important item: a newly produced model of the Karabiner 98k.

"That's your preferred weapon, isn't it?" the Russian asked. "A new model of what you used to use."

"Mine had an eight-power sight," Reymann answered. "This one has an iron sight."

"Show us what you can do."

The Stasi watched as the Russian glared.

"I regret. My hands are not good today, Comrade."

"Shoot the bottles," the Russian said. He handed Reymann two live rounds.

With a hint of anger, Reymann turned toward the bottles. He held his carbine to his chest and took the measure of his targets. His breathing, which had been heavy a moment earlier, became lighter and more even. He felt six eyes on him, none of them friendly. He loaded his rifle. He glared back.

Abruptly, Wolfgang raised the rifle and aimed it down the field, the butt finding a secure spot in his shoulder. He looked at the distant bottles. He peered down the sight.

He pulled the trigger. Then he moved the rifle slightly toward the other bottle and fired again. He came to a rest position with his weapon.

"My hands shake," he said.

"That is disappointing, Comrade," the Russian said. "Perhaps you do not realize the seriousness of our purpose here. You have been living comfortably here on the state. Now the state wishes you to help. You do not seem to have any value if you cannot shoot. Perhaps your next reeducation should be in Moscow. I assure you it will be brief. During the war, you murdered hundreds of Soviet patriots. Enough men to fill two military companies. And now you display your ingratitude in front of witnesses."

The Russian turned and looked at the two East German police officers. Their eyes were fixed on Reymann like a pair of hounds.

The Russian snapped his fingers. Berg handed him two more cartridges. The Russian held out the bullets in his open palm.

"Perhaps you were nervous," said the Russian to Wolfgang Reymann. "Fortunately, a soldier's nerves often settle when his life is on the line. Is that not so?"

The Russian glanced at the standing bottles, then back to Reymann. He offered a thin grin and stepped back. "Do we have a sniper or not?" he asked. "Or does a distant labor camp have another 'volunteer'?"

Wolfgang drew a long breath and considered his options, which were few. Then, "I want four bullets, not two," he said.

Berg found them. Wolfgang loaded his Karabiner. He looked at the two Stasi and the Russian. A certain steel came to his face, the same metal that had led him to survival through Hungary, Poland, and the Carpathians.

He turned and looked at the standing wine bottles, then he shouldered his weapon. He fired once and blew the top of the left bottle off at the neck. He fired a second time and blew away the neck of the second bottle. He went back to the first bottle with his third shot and demolished it with a direct hit. A moment later, he cleared the stump with a shot that demolished the remains of the second bottle, hitting it in what remained of its label.

He lowered the weapon. A quick glance at all three men. He pushed the weapon back at Berg.

Wolfgang took a step to walk away. The Russian's hand clamped down hard on the German's shoulder. The Russian had noticed something with a silvery glimmer within Wolfgang's shirt.

"What's this?" the Russian snapped.

He reached into Wolfgang's shirt, pushed the cloth away, and spotted the small silver cross.

Wolfgang stood his ground. "A gift from my father many years ago," he said. "My father who was abducted and presumably murdered by the Red Army."

"While you were dutifully away murdering patriotic Soviets, correct?" the Russian said.

Wolfgang kept quiet, not taking the bait.

The Russian yanked the chain and broke it. It came off Wolfgang's neck. He shoved the German to the ground and broke the silver chain a second time with a sharp hank of his hands. He turned angrily and flung the chain and the cross as far as he could. It flew over a low row of shrubbery into the tangled forest beyond.

"Now get up," the Russian said. Wolfgang stood. "I should shoot you right now for disobedience and insolence. But you are needed. Do you have anything to say for yourself?"

"You know where to find me. You come back when you wish to reassign me," Wolfgang said. "I know how the system works. All hail the great leader, the General Secretary Joseph Vissarionovich Stalin."

Today, the bright sun was high in the noon sky as Wolfgang walked back to the village center by himself. As he walked, he heard the battered, refitted Jeep approach him from behind. Then it passed with its dour occupants, two Stasi, the Russian, and Zeitler, on their way back to Stasi headquarters in East Berlin.

Far behind, cowering at the orchard, was a small group of boys who were normally Onkel Wolfgang's helpers, plus Gerda. The young Germans had seen everything and had even overheard some of the conversation. They could see how well their Onkel Wolfgang could manage a rifle and they had witnessed how distressed and upset he was when dealing with his unexpected visitors. They had even seen the silver item yanked off Wolfgang's neck and hurled into the foliage of the nearby forest.

But they also were aware of the horrible words the Russian visitor had shouted at them, as well as the pistol shots above their heads. They were too scared to move. They didn't creep home until just before dark. Only Gerda was brave enough to explain to her parents what they had seen.

DDR Propaganda Poster: As American military and
bankers try to control Berlin,
"Our Answer!"

# Chapter 10
## West Berlin, July 8, 1952 – 10:00 AM

In a lecture hall recently renovated through Marshall Plan funds, Bill Cochrane moved his morning lecture and dialogue toward its conclusion. He and his class were in a small, ground-floor amphitheater that served as a lecture hall. The seating started up high in the room and descended downward to where Bill Cochrane delivered his remarks. There were nearly a hundred seats in the hall, fifteen rows running from the first and uppermost level where one entered, down to where Bill stood on a small stage behind a lectern. The room was about half-full.

On the two mornings each week – Tuesdays and Fridays – William Cochrane lectured and taught. He felt good each time he walked into the classroom. The course he presented was conducted in English and German with advanced students of English filling the seats. The readings were in English, however. That was part of the design of the course: to elevate the individual student's knowledge of English, and with it, to convey the strengths of Western democracy, American style.

Like most times of good feelings, of course, it was fragile.

The author Bill discussed today, the second day of the summer session, was Sinclair Lewis. Lewis was a personal favorite of Cochrane. Lewis was the author who, in Cochrane's opinion, started the literary movements of the 1920s with his phenomenally successful publication of *Main Street* in 1920, nominally the first year of the new decade.

"*Main Street* was not Sinclair Lewis's first book," Cochrane told his students. "It might not even be his greatest. But it was what brought him before the reading public to start this most extraordinary of decades."

The class discussion today bounced back and forth between English and German. The course was designed to introduce the Free University's top students to American culture and politics, a study that most of their parents had been prohibited from taking.

"In the late teens, Lewis had been employed by newspapers and publishing houses in America's upper Midwest," Cochrane explained. "Lewis developed a skill at quick, shallow, popular stories that were purchased by a variety of magazines. He published a series of potboilers during the First World War. Fair enough, right? An author has to support himself or herself if he or she wishes to continue to write, after all. But then Mr. Lewis turned to more serious writing as he became more prosperous. He moved to Washington, D.C., the capital, and devoted himself to creating more complex and challenging stories that changed the course of American writing."

There were thirty-one students in the class, twenty-one of them men, and – Cochrane was pleased to see – ten women. He was already getting to know them personally. Three of the men were former German war veterans, two were DPs, the children of Berlin airport workers. There was one set of twins. As a class, they looked at him with bright expectant eyes, ready to dig in and grasp whatever they could of the world on the other side of the Atlantic Ocean. Like most young people in a devastated Europe, America – whatever ills it may have had – was a beacon, a light to which they were attracted. English was the most important language in the world, and America was the most important country. What other nation in its finest hours would have stood up to the Red Army, as the United States had done during the airlift, and dropped candy to the children of their recent enemy in the process?

But about a quarter-hour into today's class, in the back of his mind, something suddenly registered upon him. While he was in the middle of his remarks, indulging for a few minutes in a riff on how Lewis's very plain-vanilla, bland appearance, rural manners, and air of self-importance had made making friends difficult during his university days at

*REVOLT IN BERLIN* – **Part One**     **NOEL HYND**

Oberlin and Yale, Bill realized that he had heard the door to the lecture hall open and gently close.

When this settled in on him, somewhere in the back of his mind a calculation went off that reminded him that all thirty-one students were already present. So as he continued to speak, he raised his eyes to glance upward to where the doors to the room were located.

For a moment, he was startled. He had a visitor. There was a man of maybe forty or more, dark suit, white shirt, deep navy tie. Glasses. A pale expression. Not quite an academic face, and not – blessedly – the face of an assassin or thug, either.

So who was he and why was he sitting in on the lecture? Why had he selected a seat a few rows down but hadn't integrated himself among the rest of the students? Why was he twice the age of anyone else in the room other than Bill?

There were, after a moment's thought, several palatable explanations. Bill tried to ignore the man. In Cochrane's life as an intelligence agent, he had ignored worse than this clumsy interloper. And, thinking it through further, the most likely explanation was that this man was a university administrator or even someone from the faculty, just sitting in to catch the flavor of the class or even – heaven forbid! – learn something about Sinclair Lewis.

Well, so be it, Bill told himself.

Cochrane continued with his class. He ignored his unexpected guest for several minutes and talked about the America of the 1920s, the years in which Lewis had been active. There had been great prosperity upon the land, for white middle-class people at least. Jazz, dance marathons, mahjong, and flagpole-sitting made headlines. Paced by Babe Ruth, baseball shrugged off a gambling scandal and became the great American pastime. Jack Dempsey, an unpopular mauler of a heavyweight boxer, accused of being a slacker during the First World War, got knocked through the ropes at the Polo Grounds in New York, got up, got pushed back into the ring, and demolished an adversary, Luis Firpo, an Argentine heavyweight, and became an American hero: the guy who got knocked down but got back up. There was a booming stock market, an economy that was white hot, and an optimism to match it. Any American who worked hard could have a new automobile, and any man with a pulse who wanted a wife could find one.

Or so it seemed.

Cochrane glanced beyond the students in the amphitheater. The mystery man was still there, watching Bill carefully. Their eyes met. The man smiled slightly.

*At what?* Bill wondered.

Cochrane circulated around the room continuing an hour-long recap of the literature of the Jazz Age in America. He had chosen his remarks today on the overall feeling in America after the great war, one of hope and one of knowledge of America having arrived as a world power. He managed to push the irritating visitor out of his mind. Then Bill's eyes rose inadvertently to where the visitor had been sitting. Bill was astonished and disappointed to still see him there. And he had moved two rows closer.

Why? To hear better? To see better? The man was even inclined a little forward. The bells of suspicion were going off through Bill's psyche. Maybe, he told himself, he had had just about enough of these spy games in Berlin if he couldn't even focus on a class. Maybe it was time for him, he mused to himself as he continued to lecture, to go back stateside and do something more mundane. He wasn't going to push Stalin's army out of Berlin by himself, so why did he seem to tell himself that he could?

Well, he told himself, he would finish his class and his remarks and then confront the gentleman afterward. Truth was just a few minutes away, he reasoned.

He turned back to what he was doing, staying on subject, teaching, educating, rambling to the anxious, accepting, young minds of a fine bunch of twenty-somethings.

But Bill still had this gut feeling. The man in the sixth row brought with him an uneasy aura. Bill had been around trouble often enough in the last twenty years to have a gut feeling for it. And his guts were on alert right here.

The man's eyes locked with Bill's. Damned if the man hadn't just given him another little flicker of a grin. Nothing more, nothing less. But it suggested that if they didn't know each other yet, they soon would.

Bill looked away. From a crate of books freshly arrived from the United States, as Cochrane circulated around the room, he passed out copies of the first book on the summer syllabus: An English language translation of Sinclair Lewis's *Main Street*.

Many of the students in the room had heard of Lewis. In 1930, Lewis had become the first American author to win the Nobel Prize for Literature. The award had not been entirely surprising, as Lewis's work drew upon the plight of the poor and the oppressed. During the Nazi Era, Lewis had been on the banned and burned list. No fascist bonfire was complete without several of Lewis's seditious works burning.

"As early as 1915 and 1916," Cochrane said as he proceeded through the room, "Mr. Lewis had started taking notes for a realistic novel about small-town American life and the clash of cultures between liberal, urban America and conservative, religious, fervently Christian, rural America. The manuscript which became *Main Street* was completed by 1920. When the author had completed *Main Street*, Lewis's literary agent had the most optimistic projection of sales at twenty-five thousand copies. In its first six months, however, *Main Street* sold almost eight times the prediction. Within a few years, sales climbed past two million, an enormous success. The book made Mr. Lewis a wealthy man," Cochrane said to much amusement among the class.

"The money permitted Mr. Lewis to write what he wanted to write for the rest of his life," Cochrane continued. "Lewis followed up this first great success with *Babbitt* (1922), a novel that satirized the American commercial culture and boosterism. The story was set in a fictional town in the American Midwestern town of Zenitha, a fictitious small town in a fictitious state, Winnemac, a locale to which Lewis returned in future novels, including *Arrowsmith, Elmer Gantry, Gideon Planish,* and *Dodsworth.*"

A hand rose from a young German male in the fourth row of seats. "If capitalist America had treated him so well, why does he then criticize it?" the young man asked in near-perfect English.

"Good question," Cochrane answered with a smile. "Maybe he felt guilty. Or maybe he just felt he was writing the truth no matter where it took him."

"Do American writers feel an obligation to do that?" asked Hana, a blond girl in the third row.

"The best ones do," Cochrane said. "Good question. Good point."

"Is Herr Lewis still alive?" a boy, Johan, asked from a side seat in the second row.

"No," Cochrane said. "Mr. Lewis unfortunately had a lifelong problem with alcohol," Cochrane said. "He died in Rome early this year."

"Pity," said a kid with some sarcasm.

"Indeed, it was," Cochrane said. "He was only sixty-five."

"That is old, Herr Cochrane," a girl said. "Sixty-five is *ancient*." The class laughed with him. Young heads nodded.

"I used to think that, too," Cochrane answered. "To me, it doesn't seem so 'ancient' anymore."

There was more laughter, as there frequently was in the classes Bill Cochrane led.

"Had he lived, say, another seven years to seventy-two and stayed active for five of those years," Cochrane suggested, "he might have produced two more books. One of them might have been his greatest work. The world is a poorer place without it," he concluded as he distributed the last copy of *Main Street*.

"So he drank himself to death?" Hana asked.

"Not exactly," Cochrane responded. "Sinclair Lewis had a heart attack a few weeks before his death. His doctors advised him to stop drinking if he wanted to live. He refused to stop drinking. Eventually, he died when his heart ceased to function."

There was morbid and nervous laughter around.

"Then why do we read a man if he couldn't even manage his own life?" a young man named Peter asked.

"Good question," Cochrane said. He returned to his lectern in the front of the room. "The other writers we will read this summer are Fitzgerald, Hemingway, Dos Passos, and Faulkner. Compared to the others, Lewis lacked style. Yet his impact on modern American life was greater than all of the other four writers together."

"How?" Hana asked.

"By writing the book that you are about to read," Cochrane said.

In the corridor a bell rang, marking the end of a class period. Cochrane raised a hand to slow the movement toward the exits. "Keep in mind this notion I have. Ask yourselves why you read at all. Why are we together in this room in a city where the cloud of the last war still hangs over us? Why do we read books?"

Bill let the question hang in the classroom air for a moment. Then he answered his own question. "Sometimes in books, the characters who involve us find their sense of honor and morality. In the best books, and that is what I'm attempting to assign here, the reader does, too. Good luck with it. You have a week to read *Main Street*. We'll discuss it next week. That's all for today."

Bill gave a smile to his class as they departed. Then, remembering what had been bothering him for forty-five minutes, he looked for the distracting man who had visited. His eyes shot around the amphitheater. For a moment, Bill expected the man to emerge from a klatch of students and approach him.

But no. The man was gone.

Bill looked in the corridors of the university hall as he exited, and he took a cautious scan of the streets and parks around the university enclave.

No man. No nothing.

*Niemand. Nichts.*

It was as if he had never been there at all. But Bill Cochrane had been involved in games like this since the 1930s. These appearances didn't happen in a vacuum. Not in a place like Berlin. A shoe had dropped, and Bill knew there would be more.

# Chapter 11
## West Berlin – July 8, 1952

After class, Bill walked directly to the office of Dr. Bernard Kreitler who had been instrumental in offering him a position at the university. Bill knocked on Kreiter's open door.

Kreitler, a pudgy man with pink cheeks, never looked up. He was immersed in some document on his desk – two or three pages that looked to be on some sort of telegraph paper – which he made no effort to hide.

"Hello, Bill," Kreitler said, still with no direct eye contact. "Nice of you to drop by. Come in and sit down. Give me a minute. Something just exploded."

Bill entered, leaving the door open. He sat and waited in a roomy leather chair to the right of Kreitler's wide desk. Cochrane noticed that Kreitler had come up in the world since their last meeting. The man had an office that commanded a view of the street and sidewalks in front of the building, but the venetian blinds were arranged in such a way that by leaning forward he could see down and out while no one on the street could see anything of interest by staring up and in.

An imposing Yale safe, American-made, stood in a corner: a concrete and steel presence, four feet high, hulking like a small version of King Kong, the famous movie monkey. The safe was bolted to the floorboards, which showed signs of having been reinforced to hold it, a suspiciously odd addition to the office of a purported academic.

Cochrane looked at it and grimaced.

The man's office, Bill began to notice, was awash in sturdy, heavy objects: a massive wooden bookcase, which looked as if it had been carved from the gates of a medieval monastery, a mahogany grandfather clock – standing, ticking, and looming, of Swiss manufacture with wild bears carved in the woodwork, and the Yale safe. There was even an oversized floor globe in one corner – complete with outdated, prewar national borders – and an equally oversized marble ashtray on Kreitler's desk. It was deep maroon, a foot wide, and oddly deep with two cigar butts perched on the edge. Kreitler himself rounded out the collection. There wasn't much space left for anything else – maybe some pens and pencils and some paper.

Finally, Kreitler grunted and folded his three-page document into an envelope. He looked up. He said nothing at first. Then politely and with the erudition one would expect from an academic, he softly let loose with a long torrent of inventive obscenities.

"Something academic or something more relevant, say, to Berlin of 1952?" Bill asked with a nod to the paper.

"What are you talking about?"

"Whatever it is you're reacting to," Bill said.

"Berlin '52. A lot of unnecessary belligerence if you ask me, which I suppose you just did," Kreitler answered with an indulgent grimace. "The crap I just read I'm talking about. Tell you about it in a minute. I got kicked upstairs here, you understand," he continued, deftly sidestepping Bill's question. "My first love was the Elizabethan poets. Not just the overrated Bard of Avon, but Spenser and Marlowe. Jonson and Donne. Now I push turgid papers and read postwar horror stories as I merrily approach my retirement and dotage, whichever comes first. Pays more but it's less than inspiring. Damn, damn, and damn again." A lengthy pause for an extended breath. "Okay. How was your first class, Bill? Break up any brawls?"

"None. Seems like a capable group of kids."

"Good. Then what's on your mind?"

With his large right hand, Kreitler reached for one of the half-smoked cigars in the ashtray. He produced a gold lighter from some obscure vest pocket in his suit, lit the smoke, and leaned back to listen.

"The lecture went well, the back and forth with the students went fine. I had an unregistered visitor, however,"

Bill said. "Didn't know whether you'd know anything about it."

"Why would I?"

"Oh, you just might."

"Details?"

Bill described it. Kreitler shrugged. It didn't register at all. Or so he said, and Bill believed him. Gut instinct again.

"So I shouldn't make anything of it?" Bill asked.

Kreitler lowered his voice. "No. Happens all the time, really. People drift in and out of classes here. A lot of administrative people drop by classes just to get an earful and size up the pretty German girls. Got a lot of single men here. Ex-military, a lot of them. Trawling for wives. Some are actual academics. Some are here with the same dubious background that you and I share. They're not out to screw you over, they just snoop by instinct. I wouldn't think much about it."

"No?" Bill asked.

"No," said Kreitler. "If it doesn't bother me, it shouldn't bother you. Does that make you a happy adjunct professor?"

"No," Bill answered.

"Why not?"

"I can think of a million reasons, but you still might not tell me. I won't even run through them here."

"Well, then, my meager explanation and opinion will have to suffice for now, won't it?"

"So be it," Bill said. He glanced at the standing safe, the gray whale from Yale. "Those papers you just read; do they go back in there?"

"Maybe," Kreitler said.

"When I worked for the FBI in Chicago and Kansas City there were a lot of companies that used that same safe. Sensitive documents and cash for the next day's payroll. The most popular ways for thieves to access what was inside was to either simply blast them open with a stick of gelignite or cut them open with acetylene torches."

Kreitler gave Bill a cold but appreciative look.

"I wouldn't want you to have a false sense of security," Bill said.

A long look followed from Dr. Bernard Kreitler.

"You're a bit of a mongrelized Renaissance man, aren't you?" Kreitler intoned amiably after a further moment of consideration. "Down and dirty with the crooks and the proles, then up high and ethereal with Dulles's coterie of homicidal eggheads and Princeton graduates. Frankly, I like that. I can see why you landed back in Berlin. Sophistication, articulation, and a gentle touch blended with a possibility of inspired violence. You'll do well here."

"Thanks, I think. And I believe I already have."

"I believe you have, too. Thanks for the tip on the safe. What makes you reckon that I'd be dumb enough to put anything in it other than, say, a sandwich? I didn't plant that monster in this room. How the hell do I know who else has the combination?"

"You don't," Cochrane said.

"I keep all the important stuff in my suit pockets," Kreitler said. "So? Got anything else for me? Tips? Advice? Additional reports of suspicious visitors?"

"No, I don't," Cochrane said, getting to his feet.

"Well, I have something for you," Kreitler said, his tone changing. "I was just about to send a girl from the steno pool to go fetch you. So shut the damned door and please be reseated."

Cochrane kept his eyes on Kreitler as he gripped the doorknob and pushed the door shut. The latch caught gently. Bill sat.

"Have you had a radio on this morning?" Kreiter asked.

"No. Why?"

Kreitler picked up the papers he had been reading. Cochrane could now see that they were telex communications. The paper looked fresh, as if it had just been spat out of a machine somewhere in the building.

*REVOLT IN BERLIN* – **Part One**　　　　　　NOEL HYND

*Somewhere* probably meant the southern side of the third floor where there was a row of busy unmarked offices. Cochrane had taken more than one exploratory stroll of the premises and heard a telex machine rattling away behind a locked – he tried the knob – door. On the same stroll, he had loitered in the hall. He lit a cigarette but didn't smoke it. He caught glimpses of the adjacent two offices when the doors speedily opened and shut and female employees scurried in and out, carrying closed manila files. He took the offices for code rooms and radio rooms having nothing to do with the university. The disproportion of female employees sold him on the idea: they were intuitively better at those tasks and more dependable than men.

Kreitler crumpled the pages into a tight ball, stuffed it into the ashtray, used the gold lighter again, and set fire to it.

"Do you happen to know a lawyer and journalist named Walter Linse?" Kreitler asked.

Bill sat rock-still at the invocation of Linse's name. Approximately two years had passed since Cochrane had seen Linse. Linse had been in the habit of frequenting the Bar Ritter, just to chat and listen. Nothing unusual there: a lot of Western journalists dropped in regularly. Linse also used to appear at some of the embassy events that Bill had also attended. Bill couldn't remember who had introduced him, but he thought it had been one of the intelligence officers at Tempelhof.

"I *do* know him, actually," Bill said.

"You know him well?"

"We met a few times. In the line of work, follow?"

"Oh, I follow. Maybe too well."

"Why do you ask?" Cochrane inquired.

"Walter was abducted this morning from the doorstep in front of his house. East Berlin kidnapping team."

*"What?"* Bill asked, jolted. In the ashtray, the flame burning the telex danced and then diminished. Smoke filled the room. Kreitler reached behind him and opened a window a few inches.

"I don't really need to repeat, do I?" Kreitler asked.

"No. And as I recall, Walter lives in the American sector."

"He *lived* in the American sector until this morning. Past tense. Snatched off the street. Assaulted. Bound and gagged. Kidnapped. Shanghaied. Whatever the goddamned hell you want to call it! Chances are he's in an East German jail right now," Kreitler said, practically barking, his face reddening. He was suddenly furious. "Hohenschönhausen, I'd guess, knowing too much about how they work. Do you know about that wretched place, Bill? Hohenschönhausen?"

"I know of it," Cochrane said with a shudder.

"They've got another place, too. Another circle of hell that Dante didn't even dream of. It's a halfway house for the prisoners on their way to Moscow. It's called Lichterfelde Kaserne."

"I remember it. It was a Nazi training barracks in the thirties."

"That's the one," Kreitler said. "The poor bastard, Linse. He'll end up in Moscow, mark my goddamned words. Be lucky if we ever see him alive again."

"Who are we talking about as abductors?" Bill asked. "Stasi? Street thugs? Gangs? Military? Russians?"

"All of the above," Kreitler said. "When did you leave Berlin last?"

"Spring of 1950," Bill said. Then thinking, "April first I arrived in New York actually. I recall because it was a date I promised my daughter."

"Lucky you," Kreitler said with a harrumphing sound. "Then in case no one has shared this with you, there have been scores of kidnappings since then. Most of the victims are high-profile critics of the Soviet Union or the Ulbricht regime. They just grab people off the street. Even in West Berlin. None of the zones are safe. Is this news to you?"

"Somewhat. And who is 'they'?"

"Don't be obtuse, Bill," Kreitler said, his eyes still betraying his intense anger and resentment. His thick fingers set down the cigar in the ashtray. "Surely you know."

"No, sorry. I don't We're in a university building, Bernard. Educate me."

"'They' are the East German government. 'They' are also the Russians. 'They' are Stalin and Beria. It all leads back to Moscow. But there are no fingerprints, you see. They use pimps. Thieves. Murderers. Dope addicts and pushers. Highly trained burglars and black-market operators. Throw in some dumb muscle and getaway drivers and you've got a team. One of several."

Bill was still processing this when Kreitler, backtracking, threw in more.

"The East German security apparatus has only been in existence for a brief time. But they've adopted a system that is effective. The Stasi leaders visit professional criminals in their prison cells and create arrangements with them. Here's how it works, friend."

Kreitler crushed out the cigar, obliterating it with a strong hand.

"An inmate might be serving a sentence for child rape or murder, something with a long sentence and a strong possibility of dying in prison," he began, leaning back again. "He'll be moved from a cell for eight to a single with a real bed, a shower, and a toilet. He'll wonder what's going on. Then he'll be approached by a Stasi case officer after a day or two. Maybe a team of two or three since they all spy on each other. The Stasi bring liquor, cigarettes, and a whore to the cell on the visit. The inmate gets to keep the contraband and enjoy the woman. A special guard lets her out. Then another team of recruiters comes in a few days later. Usually two. Sometimes one is female. The inmate gets another whore. The team starts talking to their prospect, floating sweet ideas. Maybe, like about how a twenty-year sentence can be reduced to time served. Immediate freedom. How? The Stasi team puts the knife in fast. The subject has to join the kidnappers' club. He's going to be part of a professional snatch team and life will be great again. The inmate can answer yes and join the squad. Or he can say *Nein* and be sent back to Special Unit Thirteen at Berlin-Hohenschönhausen. Thirteen is in the Soviet section and in the cellar. Heard of it?

"I've heard of Hohenschönhausen but not that unit," Cochrane answered.

"Unit Thirteen is for the prisoners who are to be sent to Soviet labor camps in Siberia or to the Butyrka prison in Moscow for execution. The prisoners selected for the squad are usually mulish, Bill. Dumb as doorknobs. Stubborn as mules. Limited intelligence. IQs like low prime numbers. But they're smart enough to accept the deal and go to work. Like what you're hearing?"

"Jesus," Bill muttered.

"Right," said Kreitler. "I don't, either. Illuminating, huh?"

"Who runs the squads? Germans? Russians?"

"Erich Mielke's bloody fingerprints are all over it. That's Stasi. He's the operational bastard. But let's not be dumb."

"This wouldn't be going on unless it was covered by Mielke's boss in the Stasi, as well as Ulbricht," Bill offered in agreement.

"Sure. And try to prove it. That's why the Stasi and the MGB let the criminals run it. The big guys claim they have no control over criminal activity. Sometimes when they're feeling particularly belligerent, they blame American or Italian crime groups." Kreitler paused, then,
"And for that matter, come on! Stalin's up to his Bolshevik ass in it, also. Hell, Mielke's a constant visitor to Moscow. Stalin gives him special presents: antiques from the dead tsar's palace. Beria provides little girls for him didn't you hear? Chances are Mielke ran this one past Uncle Joe and Uncle Joe nodded. They're pals from the war."

"I knew that part," Cochrane said.

"And now you know the other. We're dealing with some of the most vicious and venal people on the face of this planet, Bill. Do yourself a favor today. Get yourself a secure taxi or a military car and driver and go home. There could be some big-time trouble and fallout from this. Stay off the streets till this cools down. Give your wife and daughter an extra hug when you get home and stay safe. Okay?"

"Sounds like good advice."

"I dispense nothing but. Want me to call you an MP with a Jeep?"

"No. I still know some folks at Tempelhof. A lot of them in fact. I'll call one of them. Might have a good conversation, too."

"Got it. You have a private network of several people, I'm told. Yes?"

"Depends who told you," Bill answered.

"Available?"

"Depends who's asking," Bill said.

"Put on your thinking cap. Chances are that we'll need some work done on the side to discourage this sort of thing. You know, officially there's not a lot we can do about kidnapping teams. But unofficially…well?"

Kreitler shrugged.

"Giving me ideas, huh?" Bill asked.

"If you leave the university today inspired, Bill, then I've achieved my goal as an educator. How's that?"

"That's fine," Bill said, standing.

"Larry DeWinter's flying into town to talk with some people. I'm sure you'll be one of them."

"And my class?" Bill asked.

"What class?" Kreitler answered.

"The one you hired me to teach here."

"Oh, *that* one!" Kreitler said as if there were another one. Feel free to continue to teach. The immersion in literature always refreshes the soul, doesn't it?"

"Sure," Bill said. "A lot of surprising things, do."

Cochrane sighed. Kreitler opened the office door, gave him a nod of thanks, and sent him on his way. Bill had not traveled ten feet along the hall corridor when he was jolted again, this time by a tremendous crash that came out of Kreitler's office.

Instinctively, Bill whirled and came back. He pushed open the door, not knowing what he expected to see or find. Kreitler was standing in the center of the cramped room, swaying very slightly, his face crimson, steaming with anger.

"Sorry, Bill," Kreitler said. "Walter Linse and I were law students together in Frankfurt in 1947. I'm afraid my attention lapsed here. I dropped the ashtray."

Bill surveyed the damage. The pieces of the maroon ashtray were all over the floor. It had been shattered by a tremendous impact, not a clumsy, inadvertent drop. Bill's eyes found a spot on the Yale safe where the ashtray had hit, hurled from short range by a tremendous force.

When Bill's eyes returned to Dr. Kreitler, the man had pulled a handkerchief from his pocket. He was mopping his forehead and left cheek where shards of marble had flown back at him and cut him, drawing small rivulets of blood. His chest was heaving. His doughy chin was folded over his collar and necktie.

"I'm okay, Bill," he said.

Cochrane nodded. "Sure," he said.

"No. Really. I am."

Bill started to withdraw again. Then, "Hey," Kreitler said. He motioned with his head that Bill should draw closer. When Bill was within punching distance, Kreitler bent his own neck lower to have Bill's ear.

"Something else in the telex," Kreitler said, his voice barely above a whisper. Might as well give you a head's up. Orders from Washington and Langley. There are going to be some big changes in Berlin. Significant ones at the top of the food chain. Berlin's the ball game right now, you know. Or that's what they've concluded back in the States. And now that China's been lost to the Reds, I suppose it is.

Bill stepped back.

"Should I be worried?" Cochrane asked.

"About what?"

"Anything. My services no longer needed?"

"Ha!" said Kreitler, still fussing with a red and white handkerchief. "You should be worried that your services will be too much in demand. I never warned you, okay? Just roll with it."

"Okay," Bill said. Cochrane eyed the blood. The flow from the scrapes, cuts, and scratches had ebbed.

"I'll be fine, Bill. Honest. Be on your way. Scram, okay?"

Bill nodded and stepped from the doorway and out into the deserted hallway.

The unusual meeting was over. Dr. Kreitler's door closed gently from within.

# Chapter 12
## West Berlin – July 8, 1952

Bill stopped in the lobby and phoned Sgt. Pearson at Tempelhof. Pearson said he would round up a Jeep and a driving partner and would be there as soon as possible. He also mentioned that the military was on alert following the abduction that morning. Soldiers were to travel in pairs at a minimum. Pearson would be bringing a trusted friend.

"Not a problem, Jimmy," Cochrane said.

As he waited, Cochrane prowled through some of the debris in his memory. He tried to recall when he had last seen or spoken to Walter Linse in person.

After half a minute, he thought he had it.

He and Linse had run into each other at a place called Das Neue Café Größenwahn, on Kurfürstendamm in West Berlin. The café was a street-level operation with a billiards room in the front of the first floor and a large busy café and pastry shop in the rear. There were embassies and consulates nearby, jammed into the same new buildings as several Western publications and the office of a Ukrainian "agricultural commission." So the back room of the Café Größenwahn was often littered with diplomats, embassy staff, and newspapermen. Often one went there, Bill recalled, sat and waited.

The place was renowned and drew customers because it stocked daily newspapers from around the world. There were racks and racks of them, available upon request to any customer in good standing with the owner, a large blond Alsatian named Franz.

There was a hunchbacked waiter there, an old man known as Richard. He had red hair and had been the "newspaper waiter" at the artsy Bohemian Romanisches Café in the 1920s. As the Romanisches Café had been an epicenter for the freest of free thinkers in Weimar Berlin, it had been a frequent target of Nazi goon squads. Richard had received his share of black eyes and broken bones in that era. As a *Bucklige,* a hunchback, he considered himself lucky to have not been sent to a death camp in the '40s.

Delivering the newspapers to a table was the job of a specific waiter, here as in many similar cafés in the big German cities. In this venue, Richard was the newspaper waiter. He was also a conduit for unofficial meetings. If a journalist, or a covert representative of a foreign government or a political movement, wanted to speak to someone he saw in the Größenwahn, he would whisper such to Red while he requested a newspaper.

Red would set things up and both snitch and contact would soon be at the same table. A few new Deutschmarks or American one-dollar bills would change hands.

Linse, the last time he saw Bill Cochrane, had instigated such an encounter. They spoke German. Linse was just back from Prague where he had the scoop on two hellhole "psychiatric wards" that Beria's MGB maintained for troublesome dissenters. The wards were on the top floor of a ten-story building in Prague. Recently two "ailing" dissenters, a man and a woman, had gone out a top-floor window within a few minutes of each other.

"With strong encouragement from Moscow," Linse had said to Bill. "Plus a little nudge from some soldiers just before the plunge." Linse paused. "Nothing new or unusual in Czechoslovakia, is it?" he said. "A plunge from a window is almost a normal death."

"Reprehensible, all this," Bill said. "But why are you telling me this?" Cochrane had asked.

"I'm told you will be repatriating to America soon," Linse said.

"Temporarily, most likely," Cochrane had answered. "And very few people know that. Maybe five. Six. How do *you* know that?"

"We obviously have a few friends in common. Maybe Five. Six."

"I guess we must," Bill said.

"When you see your friends in Washington, tell them what will happen here. Budapest. Warsaw. Prague. Berlin will fall like a domino if America loses heart and commitment."

"To quote President Truman," Bill said, "America 'will stay in Berlin.'"

"Your government may turn to the isolationists," Linse said. "It happened in 1920. It can happen again. But oh!" Linse had laughed. "There's good news from Prague also."

"What might that be?"

"Klement Gottwald, the Stalinist president, is very ill. He is a lifelong alcoholic and now has heart illness brought on by untreated syphilis. His coronary arteries are fragile. He will soon be dead."

"I'll tell Allen Dulles myself," Cochrane said. "He'll be thrilled."

"Yes. You do that," said Linse. "In person, I hope. It's all in here. A report from Prague," Linse said quietly, though the din in the café would have covered everything short of a car crash. The German leaned under the table and handed Bill a business-sized envelope. Bill accepted it and quickly pocketed it. It felt as if it contained three to five pages, typewritten.

"Should I read it?" Cochrane asked.

"You should, maybe, yes," Linse said. "Open, read, seal. That way you can report even if the papers get destroyed."

Bill read it and passed it along to Larry DeWinter who forwarded it by hand to General Walter Bedell Smith, who had become the director of the CIA in October of 1950. Smith had previously been chief of staff to General Dwight D. Eisenhower until Eisenhower's departure from Europe after the war. Smith had negotiated and accepted for the Allies the surrender of Italy in 1943 and of the Third Reich in 1945. He later became ambassador to the Soviet Union.

In the Größenwahn, as Bill now clearly recalled it, Linse had seemed jittery. Moments after handing over the envelope and getting it off his person, he cited another appointment to keep. He came to his feet quickly and exited. Bill watched him go.

Inside the front entrance rotunda on the first floor of the university building, Cochrane alternately glanced at his watch and checked the street through the glass panels by the front door. Then as Linse no sooner faded out of Cochrane's mind, Sgt. Pearson's Jeep arrived in front of the building. Seven minutes had passed since Cochrane had phoned. Jimmy knew how to move in and out of Berlin traffic.

Bill quickly stepped from the building and moved briskly to the Jeep. The vehicle was a four-seater, enclosed on the sides by heavy canvas.

Pearson was in uniform, wearing a forty-five-caliber sidearm. He brought with him a marine corporal whose nameplate said LAZZIA, also in uniform, also with a pistol, and with an M-1 lying casually at his feet. Both soldiers knew better than to salute Bill in public.

As Bill squeezed into the back of the Jeep, he noticed through the canvas window at his side that there was a team of two men across the street. They were taking pictures with cameras that had the markings of cigarette packs. They each wore a felt *Seppelhut* as headgear and a tan raincoat on a sunny day. One carried a bag, the other a cane. Bill guessed that the cane was more than just a cane.

Why were they there, Cochrane wondered. Yes, the Free University had been partially funded by the CIA. Almost everyone knew that. But why was there an opposition snapshot squad? General principles or something more specific? Were they after East Berlin students taking courses at the American place? There were plenty of those. Or bigger game? Bill adjusted his hat to kill their view of him.

Sgt. Pearson spotted them, too.

"Ever seen those creeps before, Jimmy?" Cochrane asked as his eyes met Pearson's via the rearview mirror. "The ones not doing such a good job concealing their cameras?"

"No, Sir. Plenty of others. But not those two."

"Pretty crude stuff. Stasi? Russians?" Bill asked. "Got a guess?"

Pearson looked back at the two watchers, who saw that the U.S. soldier had spotted them. For whatever reason, the plainclothes opposition gave the uniformed American military a wide berth. Quickly, the cameramen looked away and started walking in different directions. One dropped his camera in a coat pocket, the other ditched his into his bag. The man with the cane carried it but didn't use it.

Jimmy Pearson's Jeep started to move.

"Not very subtle, are they, Sergeant?" Bill asked, leaning back.

"No, Sir. Could be either, Sir. Russian or German," said young Pearson, who was developing a good eye and a solid gut for such things. "I'd guess German. Never seen a Russian in a German hat. Probably against their religion."

"Good thinking, Jimmy," Bill said. "I agree with you."

The Marine kept his eyes on the road ahead, which was an excellent idea.

No one followed the Jeep. All three occupants kept an eye out for a tail. Pearson took a cagey, indirect route anyway. He gave the steering wheel a violent twist on Friedrichstrasse, did a three-sixty turn, meandered through some back streets, and delivered Bill at the front of his home twenty-two minutes after leaving the university.

When Bill entered, he found Laura listening to Radio Berlin on the console radio. She looked up at him with apprehension in her eyes.

"Yes," he said. "I heard."

*

Later that evening, in the more countrified home that he kept in a quiet, wooded neighborhood, just beyond Berlin's city limits, Erich Mielke set down by the phone on his desk. He leaned back in his luxurious chair and grinned. He was pleased with himself and Beria, and the other powers in the MGB were pleased with him. They had wanted Walter Linse and Mielke had snatched Linse for them. It was only a matter of time before the meddlesome journalist landed in Moscow. What the Soviets did to him there was their own business and none of Mielke's. Mielke's job was to run the Stasi with an iron fist and keep order in Berlin. And he was doing just that. But the task was increasingly difficult. The students at Humbolt University, which was controlled by the government, were increasingly hostile and impatient. And the workers didn't want to work anymore. Wages were low and the economy was stagnant. If things got out of control, the Soviets would send tanks in. But for now, no....

There was a magnificent Fabergé oil lamp on the desk, ornate, deep blue with gold. A prized possession, he was told. The tsar had once owned it and Stalin had given it to Comrade Mielke. Now, as he often did at the end of the evening, he admired the pleasant soft light that the beautiful lamp cast across his desk and his study.

Behind him, there was a large window that was open. The lamp had burned whale oil, which gave off an odd scent even now with this special oil that Mielke used, a commodity that a contact at the Soviet embassy slipped to him just for "Stalin's lamp." The fuel had been mixed with traces of lavender oil to make it more palatable. But the window sash was up, allowing ventilation into the room. The scent of the oil he hated, he mused to himself, the lamp itself he loved.

He leaned forward and admired the flawless craftsmanship on the stained glass and the buff on the bronze base. Then he sighed. It was almost midnight. Time to retire. He was normally at his office at six AM and would be again the following day.

Well, he told himself, he had struck a firm blow for world socialism by putting Linse out of business and into prison. Miele would have been happy to do that for any number of those irritating Americans, also.

Why didn't they just go home, the whole irritating, uncivilized pack of them? They had no legitimate business in Germany. The Soviets had won the war, not the bloody Yanks.

He closed the window and carefully shut down the oil flame on his precious lamp. He smiled. If Nicholas II knew where his one-of-kind table piece had ended up, the old tyrant would be turning in his grave.

Mielke liked that idea and left the room pleased with his day's accomplishment.

# Chapter 13
## East Germany and the Soviet Union – 1951-1952

Since the 1930s the use of military sharpshooters, or snipers, had been an important part of Soviet foreign policy. There was even a bloodthirsty philosophy behind the development of Soviet snipers.

In the Red Army of the 1930s, a training program began to train individual long-range shooters and marksmen. The field weaponry of the day had changed. Long-range rifle ability had been lost to ordinary troops when submachine guns, which were developed for close-range, rapid-fire combat, were implemented by European and Asian militaries.

Starting with warfare against Japan in 1938, Soviet military doctrine quickly initiated the successful use of snipers for providing long-distance, suppressive fire. Additionally, Soviet military leaders began to strike "targets of opportunity," especially leaders and officers. During the wars of the late 1930s in Manchuria and the initial warfare of the 1940s, Soviet commanders in the field discovered that enemy military organizations encountered difficulty replacing experienced, non-commissioned, and field officers during battles. They also found that more expensive and less rugged sniper rifles could match the cost-effectiveness of the enemy's cheaper assault rifle if put into the hands of the right shooters, given solid personnel selection, training, and discipline.

Soviet snipers were estimated to have a 50-50 result of taking out a standing, man-sized target at nine hundred yards and a four-out-of-five score of killing or hitting a standing enemy soldier at 600 yards. For distances of two hundred yards or less, the probability was measured to be close to ninety-five percent, almost an automatic. To hit these plateaus of accuracy, a marksman was not to target more than two such targets per minute.

Well-trained snipers had played a crucial role in many Soviet battlefield victories during the Great Patriotic War. Lurking in the shadows, stalking by night, dug in and concealed in frozen foxholes, a sniper poised in one spot for hours or even days, Soviet snipers waited out their prey and struck with deadly accuracy. The Red Army trained new snipers in the art of camouflage and meticulous firing. At the height of the war, the Red Army produced more than three hundred snipers a year.

Teaching new snipers varied by location. At a bombed-out chemical plant in Stalingrad, instructors stood over their students, instructing them as they fired at straw dummies, captured German helmets, rectangles the size and shape of observation slits, or silhouettes of human torsos crudely painted on a far cement wall. In the open countryside or on the steppes, sniping specialists were trained in open areas where they could learn to dig in and blend with the environment.

Soviet sniping specialists, many of whom were female, rose in stature and importance during the early years of the war when the Soviet Union was on the defensive side, the final act of which was the Battle of Stalingrad. After that, the momentum changed as the Red Army destroyed the German Sixth Army at Stalingrad and began to roll east.

At this point, the balance shifted to Wehrmacht snipers such as Wolfgang Reymann, who lurked in the rubble-strewn streets of destroyed cities or half-buried himself in the snow of the barren plains of Poland. Reymann and men from other sniping teams he served with actually stole a tactic from the Soviet system, working in six-man crews – three pairs of two-man teams – with high positions encircling battlefields. Thereafter, the momentum jumped to German snipers, men like Wolfgang, as the Red Army rumbled westward across the remains of Poland and toward Berlin.

But Wehrmacht snipers could only slow the Nazi advance. They could not stop it. The reason was that in the rubble-filled streets of Stalingrad, or on the steppes, the Red

*REVOLT IN BERLIN* – **Part One**  NOEL HYND

Army weapons specialists trained new snipers in the art of concealment and precision firing.

Snipers would conceal themselves in high ground, in buildings that had been reduced to rubble, in drainage or irrigation pipes, in charred cars, and under water pipes. High ground, under rubble, under water pipes.

At the height of World War II, the Red Army produced between two hundred fifty and three hundred snipers. The most famous Soviet sniper was Captain Vasily Zaitsev, who had killed an estimated four hundred Germans by the summer of 1943. But other snipers had also written impressive numbers in blood. Red Army Sergeant Nikolai Turtsev killed 135 Germans. Sergeant Mikhail Markovichenko had killed two hundred twenty Germans and demolished damaged three tanks, plus their occupants. Sergeant Fedor Pekov picked off close to three hundred fifty Germans. They would all take time off from the front lines to teach the tactics and mechanics of sniping to aspiring students. The students included women snipers. Major Lyudmila Pavlichenko, considered to be the most successful female sniper with 309 kills, became a sniper instructor after she was wounded by mortar fire. The instruction paid off on the battlefront, as unsuspecting enemy soldiers dropped abruptly by the hundreds, victims of precision shooting.

Zaitsev's students alone killed more than six thousand Germans. The Russian snipers' efficiency with rifles also had an effect on enemy soldiers not killed: the Germans became afraid to lift their heads in daylight hours.

Very often snipers worked in teams and fought bloody wars within wars.

Zaitsev had been a shepherd before the war, a peasant kid growing up in the Ural Mountains. He honed his prowess with a rifle by hunting deer and wolves with his grandfather and older brother, who also became a soldier. The legends of snipers, sometimes embellished, sometimes not, spread among the troops they served with, then spread to the enemy when some soldiers were taken as prisoners. The snipers from one side knew all about the snipers from the other, their background, and their traits. Wolfgang Reymann learned that Vasily Zaitsev was a onetime shepherd who had perfected his marksmanship hunting deer in the Ural foothills. In odd moments, since Zaitsev's background was similar to his own, Reymann began to think about the psychology of the Russian assassin and understand how the man thought. He reasoned that Zaitsev was comfortable in reasonably open spaces. He would never conceal himself in an abandoned tank or bunker or a bombed-out pillbox: there was no unseen escape route. Reymann reasoned they might someday meet and engage in a dance till the death. It never happened, fortunately for both men. Both men survived the war.

But when Red Army intelligence officers realized that they had captured one of the most efficient killers from their vanquished enemy, they saw him as something potentially useful for the future.

On a trip to Moscow in March 1952, Erich Mielke heard the boastful Beria saying they had "this Nazi sniper Reymann, reeducated, ready, and waiting on the outskirts of Berlin." Mielke did not command an army. He commanded a secret police force. He knew that the day would come when crude abductions and executions would no longer have a place and something quicker and more lethally efficient would take their place. He knew he could someday have use for such a man.

Mielke dispatched two of his top lieutenants, Glienicke and Berg, with a Moscow-trained supervisory security agent from the MVD, the Ministry for State Security, to visit Eberswalde. The MVD was the Soviet state security apparatus now dealing with internal and external security issues, secret police surveillance, arrests, and foreign and domestic intelligence and counterintelligence. It was the successor to the MGB; not by coincidence, the agent, Mikhail Vishinski, had been a principal in Wolfgang's "reeducation."

Comrade Reymann did not have to like his visitors or his new obligatory service to the state. But he knew too well the potential price of disobedience.

**DDR Propaganda poster 1950s: Socialist Construction is the only way out of need and misery.**

# Chapter 14
## West Berlin – July 1952

The next day, after dealing with some administrative formalities at the university, Bill Cochrane took himself to lunch at one of his favorite places in Berlin, the Bar Ritter, the bar and informal dining spot run by his old friend, Helmut. The bar, which had grown into a small café and restaurant now, sat across a wide vehicular and pedestrian thoroughfare from Tempelhof Airfield.

Bill planned on a quiet lunch and some small talk with Helmut, but one never knew what lay ahead in Berlin. Today lunch was anything but quiet and the talk was far from small. The abduction of Dr. Linse was on everyone's mind. Dr. Linse had worked out of a legal office in the neighborhood and wrote for two periodicals, which were also not far away. He had been a patron of the Bar Ritter, not every day, but often enough to have known Helmut and many of the regulars. Like Bill Cochrane, he considered it a good place to chat and listen, to pick up rumors and stories he wanted to follow.

Reaction to the abduction ranged from seething resentment to wide-open, unabashed fury. Linse's friends and acquaintances were apoplectic. The brazenness of the abduction represented so much of a Berlin that threatened to go in the wrong direction. Someone, people muttered aloud, needed to stop the game and smash the Soviets back good and hard.

Cochrane had only met Linse on a few occasions, such as the time at the Café Größenwahn. But he knew well who he was, which side he was on, and for what he stood. Everyone did, it seemed, in the American zone. The man was prominent. Rumors had been circulating for months about one or more special teams operated by either the Stasi or the Russian police, who shamelessly swiped bothersome West Germans right off the street.

"Who did this? East Germans or Russians? What do you hear on the street?" Cochrane asked Helmut in German when he could get the man alone at the end of his bar.

*"Was denken Sie?"* Helmut growled in German, low and angry. "What do *you* think?"

Helmut was nearly fluent in English by now, using his second language almost interchangeably with German with his patrons, though it still had its hitches. Conversations with Bill tended to bounce back and forth between the two languages. Helmut had spent some time learning the language of the Brits and Yanks who patronized his place. It made for a cozy time, but it also made Helmut a better eavesdropper. In a few limited instances, Bill also noticed that Elfriede, his daughter, had also developed a good working knowledge of English. The girl had a great mind. She soaked up books and music.

"I think that the East Germans don't do a damned thing without running it past their big brothers in Moscow," Bill answered. "Come on. It's Walter Ulbricht who's Stalin's proxy boy, not the other way around."

"Too true, friend," Helmut said, switching to English, confirming what Dr. Kreitler had also reasoned.

Helmut now smoked brown cigarettes that smelled like old-fashioned American five-cent cigars, the type of thing that old men in gas stations and general stores puffed during Bill's boyhood in Virginia. Like the stogies of Bill's youth, these were stinkers. Charitably, Bill decided that Helmet deserved his petty vices like any other good man.

Helmut's establishment was doing well these days. He was even able to hire two new servers, German women named Petra and Liesel, war widows whom Sgt. Pearson had first noticed when they worked the food carts that serviced the aviators who flew during the airlift. Petra and Liesel easily met Helmut's hiring requirements. They were attractive, charmingly efficient, spoke English and German, and did not go unnoticed by the mostly male clientele.

Helmut lit up one of the smokes, took a long drag, and set the remainder of the cigarette down in an ashtray that bore the trademark of a vintage scotch of high quality. Macallan, fifteen years old. The brand was the same that Cochrane used to pass along from the officers' club at Tempelhof during the airlift – a half-dozen bottles at a time. Selling pops of scotch had kept Helmut in business in the lean days after he had just opened. Bill retained a sharp memory for minute details but couldn't remember whether he had filched the ashtray across the street and passed it along. It annoyed him that he couldn't quite remember. The recall of minutia could save a man's life.

Cochrane watched Helmut's gaze as it drifted not to his customers but to the spinet piano that stood against a side wall, the one played by his daughter Elfriede many evenings to entertain customers. "Hell of a thing," Helmut muttered, staying with the abduction.

Helmut's gaze came back to Bill.

"How's your young lady?" Bill asked, changing the subject.

"She's good. Thanks. Taking some summer music courses at the American School."

"That's good to hear," Bill said.

"Thanks for setting her up over there."

"It was nothing," Bill said. "Glad to do it."

"How's your girl? Caroline? How old is she now?"

"Seven," Cochrane answered.

Cochrane expected a smile from Helmut but didn't get one. He received a vague frown, instead. The Linse abduction and the chaos that had tumbled into his café had thrown him into a dark mood.

"Hell of a city to raise a daughter," Helmut said.

Bill murmured respectfully that it was. He was trying to think of something more cheerful to add, but Helmut was called away to manage some small kerfuffle in the kitchen. Bill retreated to a table by himself with a beer and two bratwursts and measured the anger in the café. Helmut took care of a few customers at the bar, then circled back and sat down next to Bill.

Helmut scanned the room to look for unfriendly faces. Apparently seeing none, he made a motion to Bill to slide down a few seats farther from anyone who could overhear.

"I knew Walter Linse during the war and before," Helmut said. "He was a member of the Nazi party in the late thirties and during the war."

"SS?" asked Bill, curious.

"No. He served at a desk. Administrator. No combat. He was assigned to an agency that stripped Jewish families of their possessions. He had done this in Germany. Then in Poland. Then Austria. I don't think that many of his new friends, you know, since 1945, knew this part of Walter's past. He never talked of it. During the Nazi period, Linse handled the Aryanization of Jewish property down near the Czech border."

"Dresden? Leipzig? That area?"

"Chemnitz. 1943-44. But it's complicated, man." He smoked for a moment. Then, "I knew a family. A Jewish doctor, Federman his name was, who lost everything," Helmut said. "Art. Silver. Their home. Then finally his family. Wife and sons deported to one of the filthy death camps. I heard that Linse often slowed down the process when he could. But the Nazi machine. You know how it was. The Reich would always grind forward until the Red Army overran it."

"True enough," Bill said.

There was a longer pause than usual in the conversation between the two men. Helmut smoked and Bill sipped at his drink. "Linse was a complicated man," he said, a thin film of sweat accompanying the worry across his brow. "And we live in complicated times. Linse lived a life affected by two dictatorships, first Hitler now Stalin. As a German, I believe he was a good man, a man who did what he could for those around him. But he also needed to survive. Don't judge him quickly. You are at risk to judge him wrong."

"I understand," Bill said.

"I may ask you something, can I?" Helmut asked in not-quite-perfect English.

"Of course," Bill said.

"You wearing a gun these days?"

"No."

"Why not?"

Bill looked him in the eye. "I'd prefer not to," Bill said.

"For real?"

"For real," Bill said.

"Do you have one?"

"I have one," Bill said. "I have more than one if I look around. Know what I mean?"

Helmut patted the right side of his bulky apron, a spot just above his hip. There was a bulge from a piece of hand artillery.

"But like right now?" Helmut pressed. "Nothing?"

"No."

"Pity," said Helmut. "That's how Walter Linse felt also."

Bill felt himself stiffen slightly. He gave Helmut a friendly glare – if there was such a thing.

"I love you like a brother, Bill. But sometimes you're too much of a gentleman. The American idealist."

Cochrane laughed. "Oh, I assure you that I can be as venal as any man, given the provocation and the proper circumstances."

"Really?" Helmut asked.

"Really. Why do you doubt that?"

"I have seen it never. You're always polite, kind, thoughtful. I don't know. Maybe too much of gentrification."

"You think so?"

"I think, yes," Helmut said with a wink.

After a moment's reflection, "Any other personal flaws of mine that I might not be aware of?" Bill asked with a short smile, surveying the room at the same time. "Kindness? Honesty? Generosity?" he said, ticking off virtues and trying to deflect the more serious conversation.

"Yes, brother, since you ask. Sometimes you miss things. Big things. We all do."

Noting two British pilots sliding into the table nearest them, Helmut switched to German, lowered his voice, and leaned closer. "Berlin is a brutal place still. A hellhole. *Ein Höllenloch.* You underestimate the danger here. If Red thugs can grab Linse off his doorstep, they can grab anyone. You. Me. Our women."

Helmut indignantly snuffed his brown cigarette but kept the half-stub, dropping it in his apron pocket.

"I'll think about the gun," Bill said.

"Do more than think," Helmut said, rising and patting Bill on the shoulder. "I'd hate to lose my best customer."

The bulky German winked and stood. "Must go now. Think about what we talked of." He turned and went back to tend to his establishment.

The timing of Helmut's departure from Bill's side was evident. Bill did not take it as a coincidence that Helmut's daughter came jauntily through the front door as Helmut got to his feet. Elfriede was in a new dress, deep blue and calf-length, which fit her beautifully. She was always smiling, Bill had noticed, and was pretty, probably in the way that her mother had been.

Bill watched as her father approached her and gave her an embrace that was both affectionate and protective. She moved slowly to greet a few of the regular customers as she followed her father behind the bar. She spotted Bill and gave him a wide-smile wave. Elfriede had been working at the bar and eatery since she was ten. Helmut needed the help and her presence allowed him to keep a tight eye on her. Cochrane had finagled with some locale regulations to allow her to go to the American School in West Berlin. She excelled at English and music.

As had been the case for a few years now, she took a daily turn at the piano at Helmut's place and played admirably. She had begun on a rickety old stand-up that was crumbling, had loose keys, and had barely survived the war.

As a "thank you" to her father, of sorts, Cochrane had spotted a newer and better Eisenreich during the airlift and had bought it. Three burly American servicemen delivered it for him, their reward being a couple of cold beers each from the bar. Cochrane picked up the tab. It all came out of Cochrane's pocket or whatever rodent fund he had access to at the time. It was postwar microeconomics at its best. All parties were served well.

Occasionally, Cochrane snared some extra sheet music of American jazz or popular songs at the OSS and passed it along to Elfriede who often mastered it within a few days, much to the delight of her father and Helmut's patrons. Somewhere along the way, the local OSS had acquired a new piano bench and Cochrane had snared the previous one, sending it over to Helmut's place, also.

Recently, however, Elfriede's presence at the piano had taken an even more personal turn for Cochrane. On evenings when he and Laura came to the Bar Ritter, they naturally brought Caroline with them. At first, their daughter would wander over and watch the older girl playing the piano. Elfie always gave the younger girl a wink and a wide smile.

Then, as the days progressed, "Elfie" – as Caroline now called her – invited the smaller girl to sit on the piano bench with her. Eventually, impromptu, the German girl became a stand-in older sister for her new American friend. Rudimentary piano lessons began, with Caroline mastering "Chopsticks" at the keyboard amidst much laughter and much to the delight of her parents and the other attendees in the bar.

Elfriede, who was by now a very pretty blond, was strictly off-limits to the men who patronized the place, and Helmut had a truncheon behind the bar to prove it. But there was rarely any trouble at Helmut's place. For all the problems in Berlin, this was an isolated sanctuary of tranquility. With enough horrible stuff happening elsewhere on the city's streets, some hometown trouble had not found its way through Helmut's doors just yet.

Cochrane deeply hoped it would remain so, though trouble could never be locked out of any place forever. But for now, the evenings passed blissfully. Friends and students came and went; sometimes someone would come to Bill and whisper something in his ear. Sometimes he would have to excuse himself and go into Helmut's back room and listen to what someone had seen or heard.

Since a man could never be too careful, however, Bill occasionally sent some of his best contacts he knew into the Bar Ritter, often just to observe and listen. Bill also had his own anti-bugging team in Berlin, two corporals, Jameson and Torres, whom Bill knew from the Tempelhof. With Helmut's permission, he sent Jameson and Torres into Helmut's place to give the place a once-over. No one had found anything. Yet. They returned regularly overnight, never scheduled, so that no one would know when to expect them. So the place remained safe and sound, front room, backroom, bar, pantry, and bathrooms. So far. Cochrane was not given to prayer, but had he been, he would have prayed that it remained so.

In a way, Elfriede reminded Bill of a girl named Frieda whom he had escorted out of Germany to safety in America in 1943. Cochrane idly wondered if he would ever have to do the same for Helmut's daughter. He hoped not.

Nineteen forty-three. Bill played with the date. Almost nine years ago. Time flew by far too quickly, Bill mused to himself, not for the first time. A notion was upon him. Berlin was not so much a city on the rebound, but one in flux. The future could go either way. He didn't like the idea but could not dismiss it, either.

# Chapter 15
## West Berlin – July 1952

In General Albertson's former home, it was getting late.

Outside, there was a three-quarters moon, pasted like a wafer in the sky above the divided city. Its pale-yellow light flowed gently across near and remote rooftops and the top floors of several buildings, most of them in the American zone, but some in the Soviet sector. Bill gazed through the large window that afforded him the view of distant spots in the city, points a few hundred to several hundred meters away. He could see the skyline and the details of the buildings with his naked eyes. Day and night, it was a wonderful view.

Often Caroline would come to the window during the day, stand in front of it, and watch the city and its skyline. Her bedroom, while it was next to her parents' chamber, faced in a different direction and had a different view. Sometimes Caroline would watch the air traffic going in and out of Tempelhof and, more distantly, Gatow. The young girl was just old enough to understand that there had been a war. Her parents often talked to her about it and how they hoped there would never be another one.

Sometimes Bill stood next to his daughter, and they scanned the city together. Or he would stand behind her with his hands on her shoulders. Together they would study Berlin – in all its splendor and horror. Caroline noticed all the little details of what was there. Her father, on the other hand, sometimes saw all the things that were not there.

There had been a time, for example, in the thirties and forties when if a man scanned in any direction, he would see the steeples of churches. Most of them were now gone, victims of Allied bombing. A few had survived, many bent and broken – bent and broken just like several hundred thousand people who still roamed the streets, particularly at night. Bill

## REVOLT IN BERLIN – Part One       NOEL HYND

knew that most of the steeples were shaky: best never to walk on the opposite sides of the street, lest one become a victim to an avalanche of falling bricks in a strong wind. Even the rumble of heavy aircraft could bring down a weakened spire.

Sometimes as Bill and his daughter stood together, he would lean forward to get the widest angle on the city that he could manage. From time to time he would look toward Hermanplatz where the magnificent Karstadt Department Store had once stood.

Memories flooded back to him, not all of them good, when he leaned over his daughter and gazed in that direction. During Berlin's Golden Age, the back end of the 1920s, the Karstadt Group had opened the greatest department store in the world. The opening in 1929 had been an event in itself. The building, twelve stories high, was crisscrossed with speedy escalators, sturdy elevators, and departments for everything from bed linens to hunting equipment to ladies' purses to men's suits.

There had been fine eateries with small orchestras or string ensembles and a luxurious roof terrace where food and drinks were served and sometimes a "Negro band" played new music from New York, Chicago, and Paris. The place had been hailed as the future of retail consumerism. It drew enthusiastic Berliners and throngs of tourists from all over the world. When Bill Cochrane had first come to Berlin in the late 1930s, it was a difficult place to avoid and a perfect place to meet contacts. It was never too difficult to switch hats and jackets and disappear into a crowd if he felt he had watchers.

But also by the late thirties, the die was cast for the future of the enterprise. Nazis legally stole ownership from the Jewish merchant family that had built the business. Flags with swastikas boldly flew from a dozen locations along the roof; the building was a presence on the Berlin skyline and could be seen for miles. The party then put some of their doltish "businesspeople" in charge of the business – party lightweights from good Aryan backgrounds but who couldn't organize a catfight in a bag. They proceeded to run the company and its flagship store into the ground.

Then came the war, the big one the Nazis wanted. Within months of opening a front against England and the Soviet Union, Berlin itself was a bombing target. In 1945, when the leadership of the Third Reich realized that the Red Army was on the way, the Nazis packed the venerable old place with dynamite and blew up the building to make it more difficult for the Soviets to move and store food. The department store reopened after the war, but it had retained little of its old character, much like the city.

*Sic transit gloria*, Bill thought to himself as he stood behind his daughter, now looking toward Karlhorst and quietly contemplating the dismal end of Hitler and his henchmen. He might just as easily have entertained *Sic semper tyrannis* in his thoughts. Rumor was that the Russians had found Der Führer's body in the bunker. But they had never acknowledged as much, standard procedure since they never acknowledged anything. Bill wondered where they had stashed or burned or mummified the body, not that it made much difference.

Bill sighed. In a fatherly way, he drummed his fingers on Caroline's shoulders, gently teasing her and reminding her that he was there and loved her. For a split second, she touched his right hand with hers.

In a way, however, he was reassuring himself more than her. He had the propensity these days – the bad habit, he considered it – to be looking at the past more than the present or the future. The past was a bad place to get lost. Yet to understand the present and confront the future, he needed to make sense of it. Future and past, forward and back. A two-way street, he told himself, and often he felt himself going the wrong way.

Insecurity smacked Bill in the face. Yes, he was midway into his forties Too old for a game like this? Maybe. He'd reexamine all this after this teaching tour was done.

Then his worst thoughts roared up within him and his mind jumped to Walter Linse. Out there somewhere in the same city? Or had he already been bound, gagged, injected with God-knew-what and put on a Soviet military plane for Moscow?

Bill winced. Caroline reacted. Her father was still wallowing in the past, it seemed, gazing through the night to where he said some big store had been.

"Why do you always look over there?" Caroline asked tonight, pointing toward the area where the grand old shopping bazaar had been. Bill and Laura Cochrane always spoke English with their daughter at home. "Do you think that big store you liked is coming back?"

"No, sweetheart. Just remarking on how the city has changed," he answered.

"Is Berlin better now that the bad people are gone?" she asked.

That was a simple question. But the answer was complicated.

Bill had to think.

"Better in most ways," he said. "But there's still a lot of work to be done." Half a second passed and he added. "That's why we're here. To help," he said.

"Good!" Caroline said defiantly. "I want to help Berlin, too!"

"And just by being here, you will," he said, giving her a special hug. "But right now, it's bedtime for you."

Berlin fascinated Caroline. Sometimes she could see people on other rooftops, in windows, or on fire escapes. She would wave. No one ever waved back. She continued to wave, anyway. Maybe, she reasoned, she could make new friends. She did well in school, after all, and spoke English and German, much like Elfriede, the daughter of the tavern owner, Helmut. There were some French kids in the American School also, so she was picking up French, too.

Laura joined them at the window. Then the Cochranes put their daughter to bed.

Later, thinking through the events of the last two days, the abduction, his conversations with Kreitler and Helmut, Bill tossed endlessly in his bed, unable to sleep.

Then, considering the larger environment, he reminded himself – a nighttime security checklist, it had quickly turned into – that there was a pistol in the second drawer of his bedside table and the weapon was loaded. Much as he disdained guns in so-called "peacetime" and resisted carrying one, Bill Cochrane lived in the real world.

The weapon was a "Baby Browning," a small, blowback-operated, semi-automatic pistol manufactured in Belgium. The pistol featured a six-round magazine capacity. It was easy to fire. He had tested it at a range after it had been given to him by his friends Evelyn and Alan Conacher, his Canadian diplomatic friends in Paris. It was small, powerful, and easy to conceal.

He hated the weapon and loved it at the same time. He knew he needed it if a last resort were ever needed in his home or on the street or wherever trouble might emerge out of a shadow, a doorway, or a past too complicated to ever understand.

As sleep finally descended upon him, his thoughts drifted from the bedside table back to the city outside. The moon continued its journey across the dark sky. Its light now filtered through the stand of tall trees on the edge of their backyard. The stand of trees was just within the perimeter set by the high iron spiked fence that enclosed their enclave of five homes.

Against his better instincts, or perhaps on account of them, he had taken to checking the fencing each day, visually and with a touch of his hand to detect any tampering, any attempt to weaken the iron perimeter. He had found none. Similarly, he regularly surveilled with a critical eye the topmost points of the spikes, assessing them as ongoing deterrents against intrusion. They were fine. He also noted that the previous resident, General Albertson, no one's fool, had ordered several links of barbed wire strung around the entire enclave. So the iron spikes were topped with razor-sharp steel of an unpredictable pattern.

The wire wasn't pretty. But it worked. It could cut the flesh on an intruder's calf down to the bone in three seconds, arteries included.

There! His mental safety check was complete.

All of this gave Bill Cochrane a sense of security for himself and his family. It enabled him to close his eyes for sleep. But it didn't enable him to sleep.

Cochrane was rattled. The abduction of his old acquaintance Linse, and the account of the East German State security using convicts to kidnap people from the West, struck him to his core. It outraged him. He rose from bed, had a shot of whiskey, and returned.

How dare those people with their foul, oppressive system resort to common criminality to attain their goals? True, assassination and murder had long been a Soviet way of achieving goals. But where would it end, he wondered, if ever?

Already in the Balkans murder, extortion, kidnapping, and extrajudicial executions were *de rigeur*, a way of life and death. Was Berlin next?

And what would happen if the West fought back with similar tactics?

It took an extra hour and a second shot of booze. But eventually, he dropped off into an unsettled sleep.

# Chapter 16
## Berlin – July 1952

A week passed. Bill Cochrane continued to meet with his Tuesday and Friday classes while keeping a close eye on events at home and events in the city around him. He even met informally with some of his students after classes in a Rathskeller near the Free University. The talk over beer and pretzels often started on the subject of American literature of the twenties but quickly changed to that of crime and abduction in Berlin in general and the abduction of Walter Linse in particular.

Not surprisingly, the abduction of Dr. Walter Linse galvanized West Berlin and unleashed a public wave of resentment against East Germany and their Soviet mentors. The kidnapping also undercut the position of West German neutralists – and there were plenty of them – who had argued that the Soviet Union could be trusted to fulfill the terms of a negotiated German reunification settlement. It was a time of rising tempers and anger bubbling up in beer halls and cafés, offices and factories.

Within hours of Dr. Linse's abduction, spontaneous anti-Soviet and anti-Stasi demonstrations broke out across Berlin. Bill Cochrane attended a rally that drew twenty thousand people in Alexanderplatz. He mingled with the big, angry crowd and kept his eyes and ears open. His own fury was mounting. He had hoped for a peaceful summer but should have known better. There had been mysterious abductions before, dozens of them it seemed, but none could be so flagrantly attributable to either the Stasi or the Soviet Union.

After the protest rally in West Berlin on July 16, 1952, the Bundestag in Bonn also occupied itself with the case of Walter Linse. The Berlin representative, Willy Brandt, the delegate from West Berlin in the West German Bundestag, the federal parliament, spoke for the SPD fraction. Brandt demanded the immediate release of the attorney and as many as a hundred other Germans who, according to the federal government, have been abducted to the East since 1948.

Also speaking was Jacob Kaiser, the minister for All German Affairs. Kaiser raged in a shaking voice that the official figure of West Germans abducted by East German and Soviet agents since 1948 was more than a hundred. The large pro-Western contingent in the Bundestag rose in righteous anger, booed communist deputies, heckled them, and threw books and glassware at them. Most of the far-left deputies quickly fled the chamber.

Kaiser bitterly ended his remarks by bemoaning that the West German Federal Republic could not take any reprisals against the East except for tightening border control. Then he bellowed out a question that was to echo through Berlin for the days and weeks that followed, if not longer:

*Wo ist Dr. Walter Linse?* Where is Dr. Walter Linse?

The only traces that remained of Linse in Berlin, aside from his wife and family, had been the shoe that had fallen from the abduction car and the smashed eyeglasses that had been crushed beneath an abductor's boot.

*Wo ist Dr. Walter Linse?* The question would not go away.

American authorities bypassed the East German government and sent seven protest notes to the Soviets. The notes demanded a verification of Dr. Linse's safety and whereabouts, as well as his immediate return. Seven times, the Soviets refused to respond. The American High Commissioner for Berlin John McCloy appealed directly to his Soviet opposite number, General Vasily Chuikov, the twice-wounded hero of Stalingrad, who had been a brilliant wartime military tactician. Chuikov was currently in command of Soviet troops in Berlin.

Chuikov shrugged. He spoke vaguely of "a certain Linse" as though the name was new to him. Over and over, American diplomats inquired of Linse to any Soviet diplomat or military officer they knew. The U.S. repeated the question. *Where is Dr. Linse?*

The Soviets professed no knowledge. Not at once, anyway.

Privately, however, through back channels, the Soviet authorities gave the impression that the East German police had acted independently to snatch Linse off the streets. Now that they had him, they didn't know what to do with him. They had no idea the kidnapping would cause such a world furor. It was common currency that Linse could hardly be released under Western pressure. It was even questionable whether General Chuikov had sufficient authority over the Soviet intelligence goons MVD to release him.

"The best solution," Chuikov said to John McCloy, General Lucius Clay's successor, one evening over iced vodka, "would be if Linse would be permitted to escape, and if the incident would not be publicized by the West."

McCloy blinked in astonishment. "The whole city is looking for him, so is much of the free world, and you think he can just reappear, and no one will notice and publicize it?"

Chuikov made a gesture of exasperation. "The West has strange customs," he said.

Although Chuikov gave the impression that he would do what he could, McCloy was not very hopeful of Linse's release.

*Wo ist Dr. Walter Linse?*

By the third week of July, there were some conditional answers.

The Committee of Free Jurists informed the U.S. High Commissioner's office in Berlin that Walter Linse, the kidnapped West Berlin lawyer, was now being held in Lichterfelde barracks southwest of Berlin in East Germany. Lichterfelde Kaserne had once been a Prussian cadet training school. It had subsequently been the headquarters of Hitler's bodyguard regiment, the Leibstandarte SS Adolf Hitler until 1945. Later, newer buildings were built to serve as the headquarters for the Leibstandarte. The Stasi had now taken it over, but some Soviet army officers remained assigned there.

American and West German officials demanded to be able to visit. East German officials didn't bother to respond.

A week later, the answer became clearer.

The Stasi had snatched Linse and turned him over to the Soviets, who in turn imprisoned Linse under another name. This enabled them to say that they did not know of the whereabouts of anyone named "Linse."

U.S. authorities now knew Linse's prison name, and in what East Berlin jail he was held: Hohenschönhausen. Moreover, the U.S.-sponsored *Die Neue Zeitung* even published his prison number: 713.

The stories no sooner hit the newspapers and radio stations than the Soviets, in their usual fashion, denied it.

"Lies," responded the Soviet council, Sergei Vassiliev. "Western lies and propaganda. There is no truth to these reports. The government of the Soviet Union has no knowledge of Herr Walter Linse."

Somewhere in Moscow, or at least in the Eastern sector of Berlin, someone – or more than one someone – must have felt that the West was getting close to the truth. General Chuikov was now keeping himself unavailable, even for free vodka at embassy parties. American diplomats received no official response. But they did receive a querulous and ominous one in the East German Press. The official communist newspaper in Berlin, *Neues Deutschland*, mockingly asked the same question that West Berliners were asked.

*Wo ist Dr. Walter Linse?*

"Linse was mentally ill. He wandered off and got lost," said the propaganda sheet.

"But the world should be on notice," it continued. "Not a single agent of war-mongering imperialism will be safe, wherever he hangs out – be it West Berlin, Paris, Bonn, London, or even Washington."

# Chapter 17
## Eberswalde, East Germany – Summer 1952

Wolfgang Reymann sat under a tree with his eyes closed, catching sleep in small doses.

His hands gripped the long, heavy object in his hands. In his mind, he identified it as a rifle. Time spiraled. It was September of 1944. Or maybe it was October. He and his Wehrmacht unit had been sent to crush a rebellion of Slovakian people who were trying to break free of Nazi rule. They had signaled to the Soviet Union for help. Now the Battle of Dukla Pass raged on, the struggle for control over the Dukla Pass on the border between Poland and Slovakia on the Eastern Front. It was a meaningless stretch of land for the entire world, with the exception of the people who were native to it, and it was the site of the clash of World War II between Nazi Germany and the Soviet Union in September–October 1944.

Joseph Stalin, in all his wisdom, had ordered Soviet Marshall Ivan Konev to prepare plans to destroy Nazi forces in Slovakia. The plan: roll through the old Slovak-Polish border in the Carpathian Mountains via the Dukla Pass near Svidník to invade Slovakia proper. It was part of the Soviet East Carpathian strategic offensive.

But the Germans played an unpredictable card. Instead of withdrawing from a worthless piece of military real estate, as some commanders called the area, they sent fresh troops into Slovakia. They also reassigned a team of seventy-eight crack snipers to slow the advance of Konev's troops.

Wolfgang's assignment: Kill as many Red Army soldiers as possible. Get the officers as often as possible. Stalk the other snipers. The Russians had sent some of their best marksmen to this hellhole, also. Ivan Lidukis, for example, Lithuanian-born but now a Red Army bushwhacker. Oh, and work close to Konev if you can. Take him out with a bullet to the neck, head, chest, or back. If you come back alive, let us know. Heil Hitler!

Thanks to the snipers, the German resistance in the eastern Carpathian region was more stubborn than expected. The big battle which began on September 8, would not see the Soviet forces on the other side of the pass until October. A six-day march to Prešov, a mountain city of medieval churches turned into fifty bloody days to Svidník, a hick city miles to the east. Nearly eighty thousand dead. The battle would be counted among the bloodiest in the entire Eastern Front and the history of Slovakia. It barely made the English language newspapers around the world. It was an amusement park for snipers. Snipe or be sniped. One of the bloodier valleys in the pass – near the villages of Iwla, Kapišová, Chyrowa, and Głojsce – would acquire the well-merited nickname, "The Valley of Death."

Wolfgang twisted uncomfortably under the tree. His hands worked nervously on the tool he carried in his hands. He heard voices. He wondered if anyone saw him.

He was on the high ground, however. Was this his imagination or did he see one of the men he was there to kill? The Soviet sniper named Lidukis.

*Sehr gut jetzt! Lasst uns das erledigen!*

Very good now! Let's get this done!

Lidukis was the onetime Vilna policeman who had perfected his marksmanship hunting wolves. In one ten-day period, he had killed fifty Germans and his fame had spread into enemy lines. For a week, Wolfgang had stalked his adversary through a forest above the Dukla pass, looking for a spot from which Lidukis would snipe, knowing that if his enemy spotted him first, he would die instantly.

On the second day of the third week, Wolfgang retreated into the town of Chyrowa for water and bread. Lidukis had done something similar. As Wolfgang checked his foreground terrain through the scope of his rifle, he suddenly saw the man, fleetingly, for one second, maybe two.

Not three.

Then he disappeared back into hiding. It happened so fast that Wolfgang wondered if he had really seen what he thought he saw Lidukis. What did he see? A mirage? No one? Another German sniper? A different Soviet sniper?

For more than two hours, from a cover position where his back was against a tree, Wolfgang could not discern Lidukis's place of concealment. To the left of the area into which the Russian had disappeared, there were the charred remains of a bus. To the right was the rubble of a church. Where had he gone?

Between the bus and the church, there lay a sheet of steel covering a crater in what had once been a stone street. There was a small pile of broken bricks nearby. Wolfgang put himself into his enemy's thought process. Where else in this situation could a sniper hide? A shooter lying in wait only needed to create some firing space under the sheet of metal and then creep forward during the night.

Wolfgang waited till the sun rose the next day, dozing for a few minutes at a time overnight. By eleven the next morning, his rifle was in the shade, and the sun was shining brightly on the Russian's place of concealment.

At the edge of the metal sheet, there was a reflection. Something odd. A shard of broken glass? A wine bottle? A telescopic sight?

Wolfgang steadied his fire and fired. The Russian sniper lurched under the metal sheet and screamed. The rifle that had been concealed under the sheet of metal rattled forward into the street. It lay motionless with the dead Russian's hand still upon the stock.

Wolfgang steadied himself and fled. He didn't know if the man he killed had been Lidukis. The whole vision started to dissemble and fly apart as he was running…

Then came a hand on his shoulder, shaking him. The voice of a young girl.

*Onkel Wolfgang?...Onkel Wolfgang...? Bitte, Onkel Wolfgang…*

A heavy garden shovel slid from Wolfgang's hand as Gerda shook him awake. Over her shoulder young Hector, the son of the jeweler, was staring into Wolfgang's eyes. The boy smiled tentatively.

"We found it," the girl said.

Wolfgang shivered and shook himself awake. He regained his bearings. He had been asleep under a tree near the potato and onion patches in the village of Eberswalde. His war with the Russians had ended everywhere except in the darkest and most tortured recesses of his mind.

Wolfgang blinked awake rapidly.

"Found what?" he asked.

Gerda smiled ear to ear. Her blue eyes sparkled. She held up the silver chain with the Christan cross.

"We saw where it landed when those men yanked it from you and threw it," Hector said.

"We searched. We found it," Gerda said.

"She found it," Hector said. "I was going to give up. She kept looking."

Gerda handed the necklace and cross back to Wolfgang. Stunned, he also saw that the broken links had been restored. The tiny cross was in place and the chain was whole.

"I thought they broke it," Wolfgang said.

"We found it in pieces," Hector said. "My papa likes you. So he fixed it."

Gripping the recovered necklace in his hand, he embraced the two children. "Bless you. Bless you!" he said. "You thank your papa for me. I'll thank him again the next time I see him."

Wolfgang's young helpers had returned the repaired necklace just in time. And Wolfgang would never see Hector's father again when he could thank him, for two days later the two Stasi, Glienicke and Bauer, returned in the same battered vehicle they had arrived in before. Their state security handler, Vishinski, came along and also cast a critical eye on everything.

They drove to the end of the onion field where Wolfgang was at work. The two Stasi grabbed him, each taking one arm. They wordlessly marched him off to the retrofitted Jeep. No handcuffs, no shackles, no rough stuff. But it was obvious that Onkel Wolfgang had no choice. To attempt to flee, he knew, invited a bullet in the back. To drag his feet invited a shot to the back of the skull.

Some of the kids gathered and watched as those in authority led away their honorary uncle. It was more of an abduction than an official escort. In the middle of it, Gerda turned and ran back toward the village. Wolfgang watched her flee with empty eyes.

The adults stood and witnessed quietly. No one said anything. They had seen episodes like this before and knew that those who were ushered away like this never returned. Vishinski loitered behind the Stasi and eyed the crowd. If the people of Eberswalde were looking at the Stasi with dislike, they were glaring at Vishinski with hatred.

Someone called out, "Where are you taking him?"

None of the abduction team replied. Wolfgang turned and spoke in a voice barely audible. "Berlin," he said. "All paths lead to Berlin."

In response, Glienicke, the larger Stasi agent, pushed him and hurried him along.

Then other questions came forth from the adults. Angry questions. Demands for an explanation. But none of the Stasi team felt like explaining. Vishinski held the crowd quiet by drawing a pistol and holding it visibly at his side, glaring at the townspeople as he walked half sideways.

The stoic old soldier surfaced in Wolfgang. He said nothing further until he passed his young helpers. "*Sei mutig*," he then said softly. *Be brave.*

The Stasi forced him into the back of the vehicle. The Russian climbed in with him.

Wolfgang looked at the village and its people who had formed such a pleasant postwar interlude in his life. A goodbye was not possible. Goodbyes, Wolfgang knew, were never a good idea. He knew in his heart that he would never be back this way.

The vehicle turned on the dirt path and began to accelerate, as best it could. The vehicle ambled down the road. Suddenly there was movement.

Hector broke away from the pack of those left behind, impetuously picked up a medium-sized stone, and hurled it at the car. The throw had astonishing precision. It whacked the back end of the vehicle, causing a resounding clank, stone to metal.

The old Jeep slowed abruptly for a moment then continued. Then, as if prodded on by someone in authority within, it sped up and continued down the hill.

Hector's father appeared beside his son and placed a hand on Hector's shoulder. The boy was crying. He looked away, then looked back. But by that time the vehicle had turned a corner and was gone.

# Chapter 18
## West Berlin – July 1952

After his Friday class, Bill Cochrane was still pondering a question that a student had posed on Scott Fitzgerald when a large figure hulked into his path in the hallway outside of Bill's lecture hall, stopping him in his tracks. Startled, almost jostled, Bill lifted his gaze and found himself gazing into the uncompromising brown eyes of Dr. Kreitler.

"Got a minute?" Kreitler asked, his voice low, but amiable. The corridor resounded with the much younger voices of university-aged students. The din between classes was considerable.

"To talk?" Bill asked.

"Yup."

"Sure," Bill answered. "Your office?"

"No. Right here is fine," Kreitler said. "There's no way this hall could be bugged, and even if it were, there's no way the other side could hear over all these kids. I know a spot. Come along."

"Right here," was a malleable term. Kreitler put his chubby hand on Bill's left elbow and guided him along to an isolated rear section of the second-floor passageway. Kreitler's guidance turned into a grip as he moved Bill along.

There were two large potted trees, marble walls and floors, and no electrical outlets against the rear wall. "Right here" became a place that remained covered by student noise, and eavesdropping was not possible. The trees would deaden their voices while the gab of the students would echo around the walls as a cover. Kreitler pushed-led Bill between the trees, stopped, faced Bill, looked in all directions, and then looked back.

"So, what's this about?" Bill asked.

"I told you before that the Berlin office – I'm talking intelligence here, obviously, not academics – is getting a new boss in the near future."

"You did mention it," Cochrane said, recalling the encounter in Kreitler's office, the episode that starred the Yale safe and the smashed ashtray.

"I can now give you some surprising news, even though you might not like it. A name," Kreitler said. "William Harvey."

"You're kidding," Bill muttered in amazement.

"No joke, Bill. You know him?"

"We've met. And there's some backstory between us. He's a big, crude fellow. Farm-belt. His fans say he's brilliant. The old-time, Choate-Deerfield, Yale-Princeton guys think he's a big oaf. Heavy drinking, big-time womanizer."

"Just what we need here, right?"

"A bit of a windbag, too, if I remember," Cochrane said.

"That's the guy," Kreitler said. "Would it be safe for me to assume that you share my consternation?"

"That would be a very safe assumption, yes. And I didn't know Bill Harvey spoke German," Cochrane said, mystified.

"He doesn't," Kreitler said. "That's the real kicker."

After a moment's thought, "Where did you get your information?" Bill asked.

"The usual channels."

"If it's accurate—" Bill suggested slowly.

"It is," Kreitler interrupted quickly.

"If it's accurate it's a damned unusual hire," Cochrane answered. "Or promotion. I guess that's what it is. Must be some change of strategy against Moscow or some big project. I'm shocked, really."

"Join the club," Kreitler said, who looked and sounded genuinely pained. "Tell me honestly. What do you think of this guy?" Kreitler asked. "Idiot savant? Or just a garden-variety idiot, much like the many we already employ?" He paused.

"I've heard some tittle-tattle from people whose opinion I trust and there's a prevailing opinion that Harvey's a rude, Midwestern pig and is going to trample the china shop in a place like Berlin. What say you, Bill?"

"Honest?" Bill asked.

"Of course, for Christ's sake."

"I don't know," Bill said, his perplexity still apparent. "It can go either way with William Harvey," Bill said. "I've seen him be a boorish clown and I've seen him come up with more good instincts and analyses in an afternoon than other agents have in a lifetime. How do you explain table manners when a man flashes sparks of genius from time to time?"

"You don't," Kreitler said. "But maybe you'll get a chance to tell me."

"Why me?"

"Harvey's making an off-the-record trip to Berlin. He's not due to start for several weeks, but the Linse abduction, or something, spun his head around. There's a short list of people he wants to talk to. You're on it. Must be something in some file somewhere. Maybe it's those very personal networks you have. Don't know." Kreitler remained adamant and flummoxed at the same time.

"And tell me again where you got all this," Cochrane said.

"I told you all I could. The usual channels. Oh, all right. An embassy contact."

"Official? Unofficial?"

"She has two feet. One on each box," Kreitler said. "I got the distinct impression that it wasn't just that the name Bill Cochrane was on the list, but the list wasn't complete without the name of Bill Cochrane. Is that enough for you?"

"Very much so," Cochrane said.

"My thoughts, also, Bill," Kreitler said. "Well, you've been apprised, my friend. Or should I say 'alerted'?"

"'Alerted' would be a fine way to put it," Cochrane said, letting the terminology lie between them for several seconds. Bill looked away, distracted by two attractive girls nearby bantering and laughing in Czech. When he looked back to Kreitler, the latter's eyes were still on him, waiting perhaps for more.

"Anything else?" Bill asked.

"You said there was some backstory between you and Mr. Harvey."

"That's correct," Bill said.

Kreitler waited.

"You want to hear about it?" Bill asked.

"If you're able to tell me, sure."

There was a stretch of silence between them that ran several seconds. Then Bill answered. "This isn't the place for it," he said. "I know a better one."

# Chapter 19
## West Berlin – July 1952

Cochrane and Kreitler met again late that same afternoon, at quarter past five on a warm, sunny day. The venue was the Bar Ritter; the bar was lively, and Elfriede was working the bar with her father, charming the aviators who came in from Tempelhof and the various men and women in uniform, mostly American and British, who patronized the place.

Bill arrived first. Helmut had reserved a table for him in the corner of the main room. When Kreitler came in, Bill gave him a wave and summoned him over. Helmut, who rarely missed anything significant concerning the arrivals and departures of his patrons went to Elfriede as Kreitler lurched onto a bench that was at Bill's table, whispered something to her, and she went to the piano and started to play. The music, plus the level of voices, created the perfect background of sound that Bill liked. It was even better than one of those noisy, new, indoor fountains that many venues were now using.

"So, it's safe to talk in this place?" Kreitler asked casually.

"Right now it is," Bill said, thinking of Jameson and Torres, the anti-bugged corporals from Tempelhof who regularly checked the place.

"Ever been here before?" Cochrane asked.

"Never," Kreitler answered.

Cochrane motioned to the bar. "Helmut over there owns the place. He's been in business since the airlift. Good man. He's a friend."

"A friend or a special friend? From our universe?"

"You could say that."

Liesel, one of Helmut's new hires, turned up at the table with two one-liter steins of beer, plus a plate of pretzels, the latter being as large as a workingman's fist. After some small talk, and when no one else was near the table, Kreitler focused on Cochrane and addressed him.

"So?" he asked. "Backstory? You were going to talk about previous contact with William Harvey?"

"More or less," Bill answered. "I assume the name Kim Philby is familiar to you?"

"It is," Kreitler answered. "You knew Philby, too."

"We've crossed paths. Or more accurately, crossed swords. Never liked the man all that much. Mutual dislike. To get back at me two or three years ago, or maybe just to throw me off his trail, he attempted to seduce my wife in New York while I was out of town."

"That sounds like Philby," Kreitler sniffed.

"To put it mildly, I didn't appreciate the gesture, nor did my wife. To make certain that Kim understood my lack of appreciation, the next time I saw the man, I threw him down two sets of concrete steps at the British consulate in Washington."

Kreitler began to laugh. "Sounds like you took it personally."

"An attack on me is one thing. An attack on me via my family is quite something else."

"I understand."

"That brings us to William Harvey," Cochrane said. "Let's say we had some shared experiences there, too."

Cochrane began to recount the major points where his life had intersected with Harvey's. As it happened, both Cochrane and William Harvey had been with the FBI in Washington at the same time. They were posted on different assignments involving national security and never worked together on the same case. But they passed each other in the same office, knew each other's name, and had been nodding acquaintances at least. For a while in 1944, they reported to the same boss.

Harvey had his own way of doing things, however, and frequently treated firm orders from his commanders as mere suggestions. Cochrane, his mind in overdrive, recalled that during the war William Harvey had done commendable work.

"Through a few moves that I can only describe as 'nefarious,'" Cochrane said, "Harvey had recruited an agent within the German consulate in New York. The operation ended with the arrest of more than three dozen Abwehr agents in Manhattan." The tale took several minutes.

"Grade-A stuff," said Kreitler.

"Indeed, it was," Cochrane said. "Hoover was delighted with Harvey's outstanding work, so much so that he made it a point to take as much of the credit for the operation as he could."

By this time, Kreitler's tankard was exhausted. He signaled to Liesel and a refill arrived.

Bill continued to talk. He explained how J. Edgar Hoover had eventually turned on Harvey and fired him due to his habit of running operations – most of them – by himself and without the director's blessing or oversight. The new intelligence community in Washington had snatched him up even before he had hit the sidewalk in front of FBI headquarters. Dulles liked odd characters, after all, and in Harvey, he had one of the oddest, at least by espionage standards.

"I must say, I lost track of Harvey around this time. It must have been 1947 or '48. Not that there were any reasons why I would have been following his career. Again, we knew many of the same people, so eventually his name would come up in conversation. I sensed he was doing covert stuff in Europe. I had a friend named Irv Goff who knew all the office chatter. He told me, I think, that Harvey had sidled up to Jim Angleton, who was running black ops for the CIA at the time. I got the further idea that Harvey was turning into a pretty solid cold warrior. I rarely asked questions about him. Didn't want to send the wrong message."

"Of course," Kreitler said.

"Now let's jump forward a couple of years," Bill said. "For whatever reason, Harvey turned up in Washington a couple of years ago. I was back from Berlin, commuting between New York and Washington, and Laura and I received an invitation to a party in D.C. Very official, the type of thing you want to go to just to run into people and hear what's going on. No harm in that, is there?"

"Not usually," Kreitler said with a chuckle.

"Bill Harvey was there with his wife, Libby. Kim Philby was there with his consort if I might call him that: Guy Burgess. It turned out to be quite an evening," Bill said.

"He's a raging homosexual, isn't he? Burgess?" Kreitler asked.

"That's what people say."

"Cambridge is infested with them," Kreitler continued. "Disheartening, really."

Cochrane ignored his drinking partner and forged ahead.

"Burgess, drunk as a skunk as usual, took an odd focus on Libby while Harvey had drifted off to another room. Burgess could barely stand up. I saw this myself. Libby had knocked back more than a few drinks, herself. If drunk is 'three sheets to the wind' I think she was six sheets and Burgess probably nine."

Kreitler was leaning forward, intrigued and amused. Bill kept his voice just below the din in the room. Elfriede was still at the keyboard. Cochrane knew her pacing and knew she would wrap up shortly. He glanced at his watch. She had been playing for thirty minutes. Bill had kept track of the time, always a clever idea.

"One thing led to another, as we all knew it would," Bill said. "Libby knew that Burgess was a talented artist and had worked as an illustrator for a time. She produced a tablet of paper. She giggled a request that Burgess sketch her. 'Oh! With pleasure,' Burgess replied. 'Sketch you as you are or the way I see you?' Burgess asked, rising to the task, and talking much too loudly, the way drunks do. 'Either, my dear Englishman!' Libby said. 'Or both.' 'Of course,' Burgess said. 'The real you in all your glory, Libby'. Those were his words as I remember them. 'All your glory.' By now the whole damned room was watching them."

"How many people?" Kreitler asked.

"Forty. Fifty. Laura, my wife, came over and stood next to me. She knew that there would be fireworks."

Kreitler laughed again, took another quaff of Helmut's best pilsner, and wiped his mouth with his sleeve.

Cochrane leaned back. "Well, Guy went to work. Within a few minutes, he had produced a recognizable sketch of Bill Harvey's wife. It was a fine piece of work, but pornographic. In it, a woman easily identifiable as Libby smiled lasciviously and, her raging libido out of control, held the hem of her elegant dress hiked up to her waist, her undergarment dropped to her knees. Libby saw the artwork and began to howl, not with laughter but with indignation. Someone equally drunk snatched the oeuvre away from her and it disappeared, quickly circulating around the diplomatic salon to riotous laughter even as Guy Burgess lay collapsed on a nearby sofa."

Eventually, Cochrane explained, the sheet of paper landed in the hands of Bill Harvey. Harvey's wide porcine eyes lit up. Harvey charged around the embassy like a wounded bull, looking for the perpetrator. He found Burgess half-passed out, lifted him up, and, when Burgess's eyes flickered open and he tried to kiss Harvey, the latter – Harvey, the CIA's top cold warrior – attempted to strangle him.

In Bill's recounting of the incident this evening at the Bar Ritter, Kreitler was beside himself with laughter, his eyes watering, as he washed back half a pretzel with the final half a stein of beer.

"I'm surprised Harvey didn't kill him," Kreitler said.

"He damned nearly did," Bill said.

Burgess came to consciousness, fought back, kicked at Harvey, and tried to gouge his eyes with a key, Bill recalled. Harvey might easily have been successful and killed Burgess, but an impromptu team of British and American diplomats spent the next few minutes pulling the hulking Harvey off the lissome Burgess.

"They nearly needed a crowbar," Bill laughed.

"I'm sure," Kreitler said. "Must have been a howl."

"It was," Bill resumed. "But the diplomats separated the combatants, herding Bill and Libby Harvey into a side room, amidst ripped suit pockets on suits, destroyed ties, and facial scrapes and bruises all around. Jim Angleton came in from the sidelines, intervened, and marched Harvey out into the freezing night, his hand in a death grip on Harvey's belt from behind. Took him out onto the embassy's back lawn to cool him off, while a trio of American wives huddled around Libby and tried to calm her. When Bill Harvey's temperature had dropped below the boiling point, he rounded up his wife, and a chauffeur took them home.

"Must have been quite a scene when they got there."

"I'm sure," Bill said. "But the big loser of the whole intrigue was not Burgess. It was Philby. Quietly on his own time, Harvey began to prowl into the greater picture of Philby, Burgess, and another man in their orbit, one named Donald Maclean. Harvey, ever suspicious, saw Philby as the nucleus of a Moscow-centered cabal. He poked into some rarely read files in Virginia about the three men and the times they had spent at Cambridge.

Harvey nosed around Philby, Burgess, Maclean, their interlocking relationship, their friends, and their past – particularly Philby's as a journalist during the Spanish Civil War and how every operation that Philby touched had eventually blown up for the West. Harvey began to see Kim Philby as an agent of the Soviet Union. And Jim Angleton, once he got past his rage, started to listen."

Recent events had told the next act of the story.

Philby, seeking to quash rumors, nonetheless warned the Maclean team that Harvey, among others, was onto the Soviet connection in Washington. Burgess and Mclean began a circuitous trip to Moscow, arriving in May of 1951 while Bill and Laura were in New York.

Harvey's report landed on Angleton's desk in June of the same year. The case escalated. The Americans demanded that Philby be recalled to London and London did so. Shortly thereafter, Philby resigned from MI5. If Harvey hadn't throttled Burgess over the obscene sketch of Libby joyfully hoisting her dress, who knew how long Philby's charade might have lurched along? Not long afterward, he was dismissed from all government service, though he continued to deny that he had acted as a Soviet agent.

*

Bill Cochrane glanced at his watch. Almost seven-thirty. It was midsummer, so when he paid his bill at the Bar Ritter and walked to the street outside with Dr. Kreitler, it was still daylight. Nonetheless, both men knew that evening travel in Berlin was safer before dark.

The men parted, both feeling that a freewheeling conversation had created some bonding between them. There was one taxi available, and Cochrane allowed Kreitler to take it. Bill was in better physical shape and was carrying his Browning.

Additionally, he had one other errand.

He turned and went back into the Bar Ritter. Helmut, who always had his eye on the front entrance, frowned vaguely when he saw Bill return. Was this trouble? A forgotten or lost item?

Bill engaged him with a smile, then beckoned him to lean over the bar so they could have a word. Bill spoke.

"The fellow you just saw me with," Cochrane asked. "Ever seen him before?"

"Never," Helmut said.

As it happened, Elfriede was passing behind her father. Helmut turned and asked her the same question. She smiled and shook her head.

*"Niemals,"* she answered. "Never."

She went on her way.

"Why?" Helmut asked.

"I work with him at the Free University. He seems like a good fellow. He said he'd never been here before. I'm just checking."

"Suspicious bastard these days, aren't you?"

"Sometimes," Bill said. "Just following your friendly advice and being careful."

Bill gently patted his pocket and the gun it contained. Helmut understood and nodded.

# Chapter 20
## West Berlin – July 1952

The rain that began to fall the next afternoon came out of the sky in fat, heavy drops. Bill Cochrane had not expected the change in weather, so he had no raincoat and no umbrella, just a summer-weight suit that was quickly drenched when the rain intensified and shoes that were as porous as one of Switzerland's finest cheeses. He had listened to the weather forecast on Radio Berlin, and the outlook had been for clear and warm from dawn to dusk. Not for the first time, they couldn't have been more wrong.

No matter, there was a bus stop a few blocks away, so he pulled his suit jacket close, held the German-language newspaper he was carrying over his head, and loped along at as quick a pace as he could muster, staying close to the dark, sooty bricks of one of the Free University's old administrative buildings.

His focus on getting to the shelter of the bus stop was so paramount in his mind, that it took a few seconds for him to process the fact that a pair of headlights had gone on behind him from a motor car that had been waiting, and another second to guess that it was not a coincidence that the headlights – and the car – were now moving in the same direction as he. From the vehicular sounds behind him, he realized that there were two cars, not one, and it further occurred to him, with a speed now faster than lightning, that this was how Dr. Linse had been snatched off the street.

Another second or two and he catastrophized: Kreitler was a double agent and had held him late at the university at an unimportant adjunct faculty get-together just so he would be vulnerable. Shame on himself, Bill concluded. This was another Stasi team, and he was the next one to be snatched off the streets of West Berlin. He gripped the pistol in his pocket, held the newspaper tightly to the top of his head and began to run.

The rain intensified. It fell in powerful sheets now. There was a clap of thunder, and a double flash of lightning. He picked up his pace. He looked for a doorway to duck into or an alley but found none among the new buildings constructed since the war. Everything was locked or fenced in.

The vehicle following him accelerated. It occurred to him to take a deep breath, whirl, and sprint back to the sanctuary of the university. He sped up, slowed, and sped up again, hoping to throw off his pursuers, while he desperately looked for an escape avenue.

There was none. The new construction since the war had resulted in larger buildings with locked doors to the outside and no passageways between. The first vehicle sped past him, slowed, snapped forward, and then jumped the curb, turning inward and blocking him. He heard the second vehicle come to a skidding stop behind him. He heard car doors explode open and he heard male voices, angry and insistent, and definitely directed at him. But the rain blinded him, and he couldn't tell whether they spoke German, English, or Russian, due to the rain. He heard the car doors slam. He heard laughter. Questions pinballed in his head:

Had Linse heard laughter when the East German thugs forced him into a car?

Would this team just shoot him on the spot?

Would his daughter remember him as kind and affectionate?

Bill stopped in his tracks. He drew the Browning from his pocket. But he held it at his side. Raising it would provoke an immediate retaliatory reaction. He wasn't at that point yet.

He half peeked behind him as he surveilled the situation: one dark figure on the traffic side of the second car. In front of him an American sedan that had jumped the curb and now blocked his path. Two men with hands in overcoats standing like sentries on the near side of the car.

Then the rear door opened. A large bulky man stepped out, took a few strategic steps, and blocked the rest of the sidewalk, facing Cochrane. Any escape was blocked.

The man was large and stocky, shaped like a giant turnip with a wide waist made wider by the fluttering flow of an open trench coat. He wore a hat on a thick head that made his upper extremity look like the top half of a giant mortar shell.

Cochrane squinted against the rain and from the harsh glow of a streetlight. The rain and the lights played holy hell with his vision. He shielded his eyes with his forearm as he struggled to keep the useless newspaper over his head. Then slowly, Bill could make out some key details as the man moved toward him.

"Bill Cochrane, right?" the man said. A flat accent. American Midwest.

*"What the hell?"* Bill thought. But he kept quiet.

Bill could see a smile taking shape on the man's face. Then he could see the rest of the man's face. Initially, he could see the big, bulbous eyes. The severe nose followed. Then the thin Boston Blackie mustache. That and the physique of a strong-armed, Midwestern state policeman and Bill Cochrane knew that William Harvey, the new CIA chief in Berlin, was the man in front of him.

More laughter from the men near the vehicles.

The man spoke again.

"What the hell, Bill?" Harvey said, approaching. "Put the fucking gun away. Drop the Jesse Owens-sprint routine, man We're here to take you out. Do some talking. I mean, what the goddamned, hell? Didn't frigging Bernie Kreitler tell you I'd be here?"

Harvey indicated that Bill should give a glance at the second car. Bill turned and scoped out a longer look. The rain slackened enough for him to recognize Kreitler, who gave him an open-handed shrug and a dumb smile. Bill turned back to the men in front of him. Peripherally, he recognized the driver of the car as the unidentified man who had been the intruder in his classroom. The second one was Larry DeWinter, grinning like a drunken gargoyle.

Then Cochrane's gaze returned to the large man on the sidewalk, positioned perfectly to block any move he might attempt.

"William Harvey?" Cochrane said, easing.

"No. I'm Hedwig of Fucking Poland," Harvey bellowed. "For Chrissake. Get in the car. I got to take you somewhere and talk to you. Goddamn, it's wet out here! You going to listen to me, or do we have to tie you the hell up?"

# Chapter 21
## West Berlin, July 25, 1952

The meeting turned into a boys' night out, courtesy of Bernard Kreitler, who had more local roots than Bill had imagined, as well as some downright strange ones.

Nightlife had returned to West Berlin, much of it aspiring to pre-Nazi heights or depths, depending on the customer's predilections. Kreitler was known at a place called the Neue Oklahoma Cafe. The place was down an alley around the corner from the Alexanderplatz and then through another alley until one heard American music and encountered a pair of swinging saloon-style doors. There Berlin reality ended, and postwar pro-West fantasy began.

Scantily clad cowgirl hostesses with German accents greeted patrons and led them to tables. In the case of William Harvey and his guests, the table was in a corner with no other table near it. A good place to talk amidst the noise and the music, much like the Bar Ritter

Tough-looking singing cowboys in black ten-gallon hats, red bandanas, blue jeans, leather vests, and boots worked the room as waiters, their order pads in their pistol holsters. They alternated as entertainment first with a five-piece, all-Black "Chicago" jazz ensemble and then with a chorus of more scantily-clad cowgirls who shimmied on a cramped stage and sang the latest American pop hits – soft stuff from Rosemary Clooney and Teresa Brewer to Nat "King" Cole and Eddie Fisher.

Astonishingly, they weren't bad.

Around Bill and his new best friends was an armada of Western people, mostly men but with the odd female here and there. Uniforms galore: middle-range and senior officers, Yank and Brit, all with an eye on the cowgirls in boots, bodices, and buckskin.

"Great place," Harvey said admiringly, as his entourage took its place at a table. He already had the first of the evening's many cigarettes in progress. "I like it already. Look at them females, huh? Good choice, Bernie," he said to Kreitler.

"I figured you boys would like it," Kreitler answered.

"Ever been here, Cochrane?" Harvey asked, turning to the other Bill.

"Never," Cochrane said. "Never even knew it existed."

"Bill's pretty much a family man from what I hear," Kreitler said.

A cowgirl arrived and took a drink and food order. She departed. Harvey took out a silver flask from within his jacket, took a long swig of something presumably alcoholic, and remained tuned into the conversation.

"You hear right," DeWinter said, returning to Kreitler's remark. "Straight-arrow type Bill is. That's not a bad thing, though. Come on guys. Give Bill a break."

"Thanks," Bill said, mildly irritated.

"Family man, huh?" Harvey snorted, taking his gaze away from the cowgirls for a moment and looking at Cochrane. The conversation rambled for a few minutes, during which two cowgirls arrived and served drinks – beer and bourbon.

Then, "You a subversive?" Harvey asked Bill. "What the fuck are you doing in our line of work when you'd rather be home playing pinocle with your missus?"

"Teaching a literature class and trying to survive," Bill said. "Keeping an eye on a city I care about." Then, before anyone could send the conversation in an accusatory direction, and to turn the question back on William Harvey, Cochrane continued. "But let's face it. I have something you fellows want. Otherwise, none of us would be here."

A silence followed, which DeWinter ended. "You got that, right, Bill," he said.

More back and forth, the first cowgirl returned with steaks and burgers. Harvey gave her a 1000-watt ogle. She smiled at him and vamoosed.

Then, "Okay, let's gab," Harvey finally said, smoking non-stop and speaking through his own white cloud. "This is all classified stuff, so you don't go telling your fifty best friends and you don't blurt it out to your beddy-bye partner, either. Understood?"

It was understood.

The Linse abduction was a horror in its own right, Harvey said, but there was worse to come. First, the destination of the report that Linse was concluding when he was abducted was intended to go first to Dr. Kreitler, who was acting as a cut-out for Washington. A big new Yale safe had been dropped down and bolted in at his office, just for the safekeeping of such stuff before it could be transcribed, coded, and sent back to Washington and Langley.

"There's a special room on the top floor of one of the university buildings," Kreitler said. "Super-secret."

"Second," Harvey said, "the content itself."

"Linse gave me an advance scoop," Kreitler said. "Nothing in writing. All verbal. We met here two weeks ago. The Russians and Stasi don't follow us in here; they'd stick out like infected thumbs. Don't know how to dress. Most of them know how to make a pipe bomb but can't do a necktie." He paused. "Plus, those bums you saw in the alleyway? A couple of them are our watchers. They spot the Stasi and Russians if they try to come in here."

"I like that," Harvey said from within his cloud.

Chuckles around the table.

Then, "Let's get to it," Kreitler said. "Apparently the Soviets have been working on new forms of dissuasion and deterrents to suppress political dissent in the unlucky satellite lands: Poland. Hungary. Albania. Czechoslovakia. Falls from windows in mental hospitals are going the way of the troika. Same with abductions in those countries. The new thing is marksmen. High-caliber ambush. Bang, you're dead. The rifle experts from the war. Rediscovered and repurposed."

"Snipers?" Bill asked.

"Correct," Kreitler said.

"So why didn't they snipe Linse?" DeWinter asked.

"May I take a guess at that?" Bill asked quickly.

No one said no.

"It's obvious, isn't it?" Cochrane said. "If Linse was carrying his report, the Russians or Germans didn't want him lying dead in the street," Cochrane said. "They would have wanted to get those papers before they landed in Western hands. So they needed to grab him. Get him and his papers. Plus, they could then keep him as long as they wanted and squeeze out the names of any of his informants. How am I doing?"

"I think you got it, smart guy," Harvey said.

"Are the snipers Soviet?" Bill asked. "War veterans?"

"The Russians authorities in the Eastern satellites want to get the best. So they seem to have been looking at Wehrmacht veterans, also."

"That's the back-channel info we're getting in Langley, too," Harvey said.

"Some of those Wehrmacht snipers hung at Nuremberg for shooting civilians," said Cochrane. "I remember General Clay signing off on some of the execution orders."

"And some of them only shot enemy combatants," Kreitler said. "Bad luck if you were one of them, right?"

"Let me get this clear," Cochrane said. "Is this a Stasi operation or a Soviet?"

"Was Lend Lease a British operation or an American one?" Kreitler asked.

"There were enough fingerprints to go around," Cochrane answered.

"There you go. Same old, same old. East Germany models itself on Stalin's Russia," Kreitler said. "Erich Mielke models his Stasi operations on Beria's MGB. Not too hard to follow, that part of it."

"No," Cochrane said. "It's not."

Dinner plates were empty, so were glasses. Two German cowgirls arrived, cleared the table, and refreshed glasses as requested. William Harvey pulled out a stack of American twenty dollars bills and flirted shamelessly with the girls. The cowgirls seemed to be simultaneously fascinated with him and scared of him. They disappeared again.

Harvey turned to Bill Cochrane.

"I'm told you have your own network of people in and around Berlin," Harvey said. "Are they available?"

"They might be."

"Can you tell me about them? Names? Location?"

"Not a chance," Cochrane said.

"And why is that?"

"They work for me with whatever budget you provide. I'm concerned about betrayals and leaks in the larger agency operations. So I run the show and keep my own house in order."

"What if we bought it from you. Cash."

"Don't even try. The answer is no."

"We're talking significant money here."

"My answer hasn't changed."

"What would convince you to allow some oversight?"

"Nothing. And I'm leaving this table if you ask again."

Harvey, not used to being stonewalled, growled. He looked at Kreitler, then at DeWinter.

"Bill means what he says, Mr. Harvey," DeWinter said.

Harvey growled again, then spoke. "I read a vague and cryptic report that you filed to the agency in 1950, following a previous operation in Berlin. It mentioned, and you wrote it I believe—"

"If we're thinking of the same one, yes, I wrote it," Bill said.

"It alluded to a woman you have in your stable who had access to Erich Mielke's homes. Sex parties or something. Ring a bell?"

"It does."

"The woman was unnamed. She still alive?" Harvey asked.

"I have no reason to think that she is not."

"Would she care to snoop for us?"

"I'd have to inquire."

"Of whom?"

"Of the woman we're talking about."

"Is she in Berlin?" Harvey's eyes were bulging, his gaze narrowing.

"Abroad," Cochrane said.

"Ah. Clever," Harvey said.

"Common sense," Cochrane retorted. "You read the report."

"More than once," Harvey said, dragging a gold toothpick from somewhere near his belt. He used it thoughtfully for several seconds on the back teeth on the right side of his lower jaw. Cochrane knew Harvey was trying to get him to say more. So he clammed up.

When the tidy-up by toothpick was complete, Harvey spoke again.

"The travel. Distant? Near?"

"A day maybe. I can arrange it out of Tempelhof," Bill said.

"Okay. Good," Harvey said. Several seconds passed as Harvey calculated and processed, then, "Listen up, Mr. Cochrane. I'm putting several quiet personal networks to work on this. Setups same as yours. I'm hoping someone creates some luck real fast before we're all dancing away from bullets in the Western zone. You know, like in those dumbfuck Tom Mix movies."

"I get it," Cochrane said.

"Comrade Mielke's got to get his ass kicked! He needs to know that the snipers are a nonstarter in Berlin! Hear me? Fucking commies are all alike. You can tell them something all you want and the only thing they understand is when you bust them hard. So, understand me, man, I don't care if we have to pay your mystery girl to chop his nuts off in person to do it. I just want the message delivered. No snipers. Clear?"

"Very," Bill said. "And I agree with you."

A moment, then, "Good!" Harvey said.

Harvey took a long look at Bill. The pudgy eyes narrowed. "So who's this mystery bitch?" he tried again.

"Sorry. Her identity, like all my agents in the field, remains with me."

Through the haze of tobacco smoke, "What makes you think she'll be successful, Mr. Genius?" Harvey continued.

"An instinct," Bill answered calmly.

Harvey laughed. "Oh, fuck that!" he said.

"No, no, I assure you," Bill said. "Instinct is an all-encompassing concept. An elusive one, maybe. It's something you develop after working with people, depending on them for your survival and vice versa, knowing them, how they think, what their capabilities are, and what sort of situation I'm dropping them into. If you think about it, espionage is more philosophical than mathematical. Ever thought about it that way?"

Bill paused. No response. Instead, Harvey's gaze was boring into him, a vague frown framing it. The man didn't twitch a muscle.

"I've also been in Germany much of the time since 1938," Bill continued. "I bring a wealth of knowledge of the people and the country into the equation."

Bill went quiet. He was afraid that he'd sounded too preachy, too sanctimonious, too professorial. "And God help me if I err and send the wrong agent to the wrong place and I end up with a mortality on my conscience," he thought but didn't say.

Up on the stage, five cowgirls were now entertaining everyone with an admirable and heavily accented rendition of "O Mein Papa", one of the best traditional German nostalgia songs ever written by a Swiss citizen.

Harvey checked out the stage, gave a slight grin in that direction, and then came back to Bill, by which time the grin had departed.

"So you think your Kraut spooks can get this done?"

"That is my hope."

"Fucking fast!"

"My hope, also."

"Okay," Harvey snorted.

He settled back.

"I'll set things up. Talk to Bernie here on Monday. You'll get the operation dollars and anything else you need. Good luck." Then as an afterthought, "This girl who might have access to Mielke, do you bed her?"

"No."

"Good idea," Harvey said. "Smart. Not till later, anyway, right?"

Bill smiled noncommittally, which both DeWinter and Kreitler recognized as another *No*.

## Chapter 22
### West Berlin to Cambridge – July 1952

It was almost eight o'clock on a quiet Wednesday morning. "Trips I have taken and survived," Bill Cochrane thought to himself as he looked around the empty sidewalks outside the iron gate in front of the lodgings he had taken over from General Albertson. He could make a list of such trips and then he ticked them off in his head.

A flight to Portugal in 1943 during which his plane was forced down by the Luftwaffe.

A train trip from Berlin into the militarized German hinterlands in 1938, during which he had discovered a troop movement that was a prelude to the invasion of the Sudetenland.

More rides that he could count in veteran C-47s during the Airlift, rugged, tough-minded, arial warhorses with blue rings around the American logo.

The morning was already warm. It occurred to him that it was on a morning like this only two weeks and one day ago that Walter Linse had been kidnapped, not to be seen alive since his abduction. It had even been around the same time in the morning. Who said that the worst crimes occur at night? The Linse snatching had been in the brightest of morning sunlight.

Absurdly, Bill wore a light raincoat. It gave him extra pockets and rain could always be expected in England. If it weren't raining one minute, Laura always said, it would be the next. But that was why English ladies had such beautiful complexions, he had always retorted.

Sgt. Jimmy Pearson was supposed to pick up Bill Cochrane between eight and eight-fifteen this morning and take Bill to Tempelhof for a flight to the U.K. So far, no Jimmy. Bill dropped his right hand into his raincoat pocket and placed it on the Browning. Not only did he now carry it, but he also carried it where it would be quickly accessible.

Paranoia or caution?

Both, he told himself.

He turned. Laura was watching from a window in their downstairs dining room, the curtains pushed to the side, Caroline standing by her, also looking out. Bill gave them a smile, a nervous one he feared, and tipped his hat. Caroline waved, assuming her father was invulnerable. Laura looked apprehensive.

Bill shrugged. Still no Jimmy.

Cochrane knew that he was better served to watch the sidewalks and the streets. He turned back. A few feet behind him, he had left the iron gate carefully unlatched. He could bolt back within if he had to. After Jimmy had picked him up, Laura would emerge and push the gate shut. They had prearranged the move. They had used it many times.

So far, so good.

Where the hell was Jimmy? It was 8:08 AM. Not like Sgt. Pearson to be late, Bill reminded himself.

Bill feared that the stress and anxieties of aging were catching up with him. Recently, his mind, which he had once assessed as being unnaturally sharp, was taking off in strange directions, just flying away by itself into strange new vistas of irony, deceit, danger, and defeat.

It did so here. The world, he decided as he stood on this threateningly empty sidewalk, was changing too quickly for him. He was not feeling as comfortable here as he had in the past. His mind, out of control now, explored why.

For a moment he thought he had it. The prevailing Western mood in postwar Berlin had changed.

When Bill had been here previously, two of the most important Americans in postwar Berlin were General Lucius Clay and General Frank Howley. Bill Cochrane had met both men during the Airlift and afterward. These two men – Clay and Howley – set the tone of the city in the first years after the war.

Clay had graduated from the U.S. Military Academy at West Point, New York in 1918. He ranked high academically in his class. He had spent most of his life not in command but in administrative planning jobs under the New Deal. He was well acquainted with President Roosevelt and with Roosevelt's inner circle. FDR's people respected him and his work. He rose to the rank of colonel by the time of Pearl Harbor. His assignments involved a close liaison with and understanding of politicians and political processes.

Following the American entrance into World War II, Clay became his country's foremost production and supply specialist. During the war, he commanded the army procurement program. After the fall of Berlin, Clay was the first director of civilian affairs in defeated Germany after World War II.

Clay was a quiet, thoughtful man, unpretentious and inauspicious. He preferred to get his job done quietly and without fanfare. Colonel Howley, often referred to by his men as "Howlin' Mad Howley" was the opposite several times over.

Howley had first arrived in the city on June 17, 1945, in a Horch 853 Sports Cabriolet convertible that had sped westward on the one highway open through the blighted countryside of East Germany toward the fallen capital, then occupied by the Red Army. Behind the luxury German auto was a parade of one hundred thirty-five American Jeeps and military trucks. Every inch of each vehicle had been waxed and buffed to a high sheen. Each Jeep or truck bore at least two American flags. Among the convoy were two supply trucks carrying ten thousand bottles of whiskey and wine to celebrate the liberation of Berlin. Howley rode in the backseat of the convertible, smoking a cigar. Howley had commandeered – or blatantly confiscated – the automobile from a Nazi general.

"It was my intention," said Howley later that day after arrival in Berlin, "to make this advance party a spectacular thing."

Spectacular it had been.

But looking around as he contemplated Brandenburg gate, Howley had spotted suggestions of things to come. There were two enormous banners with the faces of Lenin and Stalin glowering down at him: a bold challenge for the coming days and years. Later the same day, Soviet Army officers informed Howley – on behalf of The Great Stalin – that the negotiated terms from Yalta were no longer valid and the Americans should leave Berlin.

Howley was having none of it. He told the Russians to "go to hell" and that his soldiers "aren't leaving." He said all this with a smile. Then he saw what the Soviets in Berlin were presiding over.

He stopped smiling.

The city was in ruins, having been reduced to rubble by American and British bombers. This had been followed by close-quarter, German-Soviet street combat as the final resistance of the Reich was defeated. Later, the Soviets carted off all the vital infrastructure they could, plus any German who knew how to operate machinery. The Germans who remained were sick, starving, mentally pulverized, and helpless. Colonel Howley then ordered the men under his command to set up billets and relief stations overnight for German people – food, clothing, and shelter if needed. The Soviets awoke the next morning, blinked, and realized that the American occupation of West Berlin had arrived.

Eventually, Howley developed a technique for dealing with his Soviet opposite, General Kotikov, the commandant of that period. Howley would take issue with the Soviet position and the outright falsehoods attached to it. He would put forth his own line of reasoning.

"*Of course,* I do not expect you to tell me the truth. You're a liar," he would say. "You always lie, and no matter what you're going to tell me, it's not going to be the truth." The Russians thought this was highly amusing and they respected Howley. They knew that he never lied to them, including when he was telling them that they lied.

Everyone in Berlin knew who Howley was. The Soviets even gave him a special distinction. Soviet radio played what passed for cowboy music on Radio Berlin every time they mentioned him. "Howley, the Rough Rider from Texas," they called him. Even here, the official Soviet line was at odds with the facts. Howley was actually from New Jersey, where many men could be even tougher than those from Texas.

Both Howley and Clay, in one way or another, were charged with maintaining civic order in a Berlin that still had its ugly moments of postwar lawlessness. Both men made mistakes, the same as any man would. But they had also succeeded in governing the unruly city. This had been no small accomplishment. When Bill Cochrane had last been in Berlin, he could still sense their spirit, even among the men who had replaced them.

Now it was gone.

Two mayors. Two police chiefs.

Gangs of postwar thugs on the ascendant. Kidnappings and killings.

The city was more turbulent than ever because the lousy Soviets were constantly stirring the pot. Military rule had ended, and civilian rule had begun. Against his more rational judgment sometimes, Bill missed the wise, practical, old soldiers. He missed Howley's efficient, cynical, hands-on view of the enemy. He missed Clay's noble tenacity. Clay had ordered and maintained the Airlift and refused to leave his post until the Soviet blockade of the city had been lifted in September of 1949.

As Bill simmered on the sidewalk this morning, he hoped he could live up to the standards set by those two men. Whatever he needed to do to confront or thwart men like Ulbricht and Mielke, by God, he would do it.

Unconsciously, he pressed his palm against the Browning in his pocket.

He looked around. His anxiety went into overdrive.

*Christ, where is Jimmy?*

Bill jerked back the cuff of his raincoat and looked again at his watch. Eight fourteen and thirty-eight seconds.

Then he heard the unmistakable sound of an American Jeep approaching. He turned toward the sound and saw the vehicle whiz around the corner and turn onto his street. He calmed immediately. He heard the gentle double beep that Sgt. Pearson always used, then the squeal of tires. The vehicle sped toward him and came to an abrupt halt. There were two men in the vehicle, Pearson at the wheel and the same marine companion as last time, Lazzia.

Eight-fifteen. Right on time. Never in doubt.

Bill turned and gave Laura a nod. She was still watching him and so was Caroline.

The front door to the Jeep opened. Lazzia hopped out sharply, M-1 in hand, and held the door open for Cochrane. Cochrane slid in and sat in front. Lazzia quickly accessed the rear area from the back of the vehicle.

"Morning, Sir," Jimmy said. "We'll get you back to Tempelhof in a few minutes."

"The plane is in a special section, Sergeant," Bill said. "It doesn't leave till I'm on it, Jimmy. Just drive safely. Watch out for Russians."

"Will do, Sir. Should I hit a few on the way if I see them?"

"Not this morning," Cochrane answered. "Maybe some other day you can run over their toes."

"Very good, Sir. I'd like that."

"So would I, Sergeant," Bill said. "But let's keep the international 'incidents' to a minimum, okay?"

"Of course, Sir," Sgt. Pearson said.

Jimmy pulled the Jeep smoothly away from the curb. Cochrane waved to his family again. As the drive began to the airport, he watched the gate to the compound. Laura quickly emerged from the house and pulled the gate shut, locking it.

Bill breathed easier when he saw her disappear into their house. After all these years, these things should have become easier, more routine, he told himself. Instead, they were becoming more challenging. It was not his inclination to allow anyone to know that though, even Laura.

If she asked, he would admit it. But until she did, he wasn't admitting.

*

The Jeep trip to Tempelhof was bumpy – there was no shortage of potholes on the highway out of Berlin, and there wasn't one that Sgt. Pearson didn't seem to challenge. Oddly, however, the flight was smooth. July was thunderstorm season in northern Europe, some of them extremely violent. A pilot named Glenn Taylor, now a USAF lieutenant, whom Cochrane knew and recognized from the Airlift, was Bill's chauffeur in the sky. Two other Americans were hitching rides to the U.K., also, using Cambridge as the backdoor to London.

The day was clear. Bill always enjoyed the low approach. He watched through his port-side window as the aircraft descended, his eyes on the vital landmarks – the university, Kings College Chapel and its spires, and the murky, narrow, blue-green-brown River Cam that snaked through the city.

The plane took an approach to Molesworth to the northwest and passed above the American cemetery where a brigade of white gravestones – crosses and stars of David – spread in a circular pattern across several dozen acres of green grass. The men and women who lay there were mostly crew members of British-based American aircraft who fought in the skies over Europe during World War II plus many who lost their lives in training areas of the U.K., in the waters of the Atlantic, and during the invasions of Normandy and North Africa.

Then the vision of the cemetery was gone. The C-47 touched down four minutes later.

"Good day to fly, Mr. Lewis," Lt. Taylor said as Bill was disembarking. "Nice weather, soft clouds. Do you know when you're returning?"

"Not yet, Lieutenant."

"Keep your ear on the radio," Taylor said. "Storms in the Atlantic. Might hit England in a few days."

"Thanks for the warning."

"See you soon again, Sir," Taylor said. "Always a pleasure."

A special taxi and chauffeur were waiting for Bill on his arrival at Molesworth Airfield in Cambridge. It dropped him at the University Arms hotel by two in the afternoon. A rented car, arranged by one of the murkier departments in the embassy, was waiting for him. He slipped into his old Lewis identity for the visit, registered accordingly, and spent the evening at The Hero of the Thames pub, listening to his friend Edward, the barman, for any pertinent news or rumor.

Some nights the chatter and polemics at The Hero of the Thames were lively, some nights they were not. This was one of the latter, probably for the best, Cochrane figured. He returned to his hotel at a sane hour, slept well, and got a solid start on the trip westward that lay ahead of him for the following day.

\*

By the next morning, Bill Cochrane was ready to renew acquaintances with some old contacts and put himself on a path that he had been on before. It had always paid off previously, so he asked himself why it wouldn't pay off again this time.

In the old days, he would have had a quick, positive response to such a question.

This time he had none. But he went to his rental car and set out.

# Chapter 23
## England and Germany – July 1952

On the same afternoon as his arrival in Cambridge, Bill set out to visit Laura's increasingly dotty Aunt Beatrice. It was at Beatrice's modest estate where two members of Cochrane's tight ring of special friends, Alyssa and Stefan Cerny – formerly Anna Schroeder and Heinrich Roth, for whom warrants were still out in East Berlin – worked as caretakers.

After a polite hello to Beatrice and a dose of trite, small talk, Bill wandered out to Anna and Heinrich's cottage in the early evening. It was midsummer, so daylight was still evident. Cochrane spent more than an hour over a fresh bottle of German brandy, Asbach Uralt, that he had purchased at a wine retailer in Cambridge and had brought along for the occasion.

He was pleased to learn in person that there had been no ominous developments for Anna and Heinrich. The horrors of the war and the immediate postwar years had receded, at least for them. They seemed to have fallen off the East German radar. But they also knew better, as did Bill. One false move, one informant, one vengeful little snitch, and their lives in shrouded exile could be compromised.

Bill had always insisted that Anna and Heinrich, along with all his other émigrés, routinely use each other's fictional new names, even between each other. No reversion to a past life, not even the smallest reference or term of endearment should be made, lest a killer cat escape the bag. Bill's private network was even urged to minimize their use of German, even though it was their native language.

These were "standing orders" for all of Cochrane's refugees, as well as the conceit that he was still "Mr. Lewis," their American social friend. The odd part of the charade, to Bill at least, is that while he addressed all his team members by their new names, in his mind he thought of them by their original, or "real" names. It created an odd bit of mental gymnastics sometimes.

Then, this evening, "That weird little man came to see us the other day," Roth said.

"Which one?" Cochrane asked. "I know several."

"Mountain Hawk," Roth said. "Isn't that what we're told to call him?"

Anna rolled her eyes.

"Ah," Cochrane said. "How is the old sea dog these days?"

"Fine," Anna said. "He inspected our place, if 'inspected' is the right word for it."

"It is. Did he find anything that bothered him?"

"Fortunately not," Roth said.

"Spent too much time prowling in my clothes closets," Anna said.

"Anything unusual there?" Cochrane asked. "In your closet, I mean?"

"The usual thing for a proper lady from Berlin. Leather. Chains. Whips. Stockings. Unnamed devices of pleasure and pain. What do you think? Of course not, 'Mr. Lewis!'" she laughed. "What are you asking me that for?"

"Much like extracurricular sexual apparatus, since you evoked the image, *listening devices* turn up more in women's closets than men's," Bill said. *"That's* why I ask. Happy?"

"He didn't find anything," Roth said, with a grin. "Not in Anna's things. Not in mine. Okay?"

"Well, we should drink to that, yes?" Bill suggested. "Good news, right?"

They all agreed. Yes. There was good humor about the visit.

*Mountain Hawk.* To ensure a safe landing for his special group of émigrés to Britain, Bill had employed a technical specialist whom he had known for many years, a certain Nigel Page. Bill had given him the code name of

Mountain Hawk because he had nothing to do in any way with hawks or mountains.

Page had been Laura's discovery, actually. Page had been in the Royal Navy for two and a half decades, including the war. Chief Petty Officer Page had twice been on ships that had been sunk – one in battle, the other torpedoed. He had been picked up and rescued twice, unscathed each time, and, as he recalled it, barely rattled. He had, Bill noted with steadily growing interest, an innocent air of invincibility around him, as if horrible things happened to everyone else, but not him.

Not Nigel.

Page was a small, thin man, no more than five feet five and a hundred thirty pounds, "barely heavier than the shadow he cast" as Bill's old friend Irv Goff might have said. Goff always liked to collaborate with small, dangerous men because they could slip in and out of places with greater ease than a big, lumbering brute. They made smaller targets for any enemy and just plain looked less threatening, even if they were not.

Nonetheless, Nigel had retired from seafaring in 1947 and had settled as a pensioner in the tiny village of Caxton, just west of Cambridge, a town noted for an eighteenth-century gibbet that still stood. Now, in his frumpy sixties, Mr. Page survived as an old-fashioned jack-of-all-useful trades. He performed carpentry and plumbing. He was a skilled exterminator. Laura had first found him when he was installing a new electrical grid in a friend's farmhouse. The friend had compounded the problem by losing the key to the farmhouse.

"Then how did you get in?" Bill asked.

"Oh. I learned to be a pretty fair lockpick in the navy, Sir," Nigel said with a wink.

"Where and under what circumstances, may I ask?"

"Singapore," Nigel said. "Hong Kong. Australia. Our dumb sailors were always leaving stuff behind in whore houses and grotty hotels. We'd have to go in and retrieve it after sunrise when no one was home."

"Of course you did," Bill said. "How did you happen to have the tools?"

"Same tools as a commercial locksmith, Sir. My old man was a locksmith in Brighton. Tools for locks are small, Sir. I always kept a set. Never know when they could be useful. After that, it's just a matter of knowing when no one's home and how to work quiet. Break-ins are usually easy."

Bill Cochrane knew raw talent when he saw it.

Bill fell into a conversation with Nigel. One wondrous thing led to another. Bill learned that the man was always appreciative of new work. "New style even, Sir," Page had said. "I've never stopped being a student."

"That's good to know, Nigel," Bill said. "Useful."

"That's me, Sir. 'Useful.'"

"It certainly appears so," Bill said. "Let's talk further sometime."

"Very good, Guvnor."

Further conversations ensued at Bill's public house of choice, The Hero of the Thames, on King Street where Edward, bartender and proprietor, arranged a private room.

There, over the course of several evenings, Bill introduced his new student to the brave new world of modern eavesdropping devices, how to plant them, how to spot them visually, how to detect them electronically, and more.

Fine wire kits, introduction to telephone taps, belt buckle microphones, microphone pens, and bugs in shoes. From a CIA hardware dump in London, confiscated samples of the current opposition's best work, Bill brought along a fine collection of the newest things. His favorite and one of the most nefarious: a long, thin listening device, the size and shape of a child's six-inch ruler, microphone and transmitter included, that could fit down the spine of a book, causing no suspicion because its use called for its insertion into the spine of a book that was already in a room. All one needed to do was break in, plant the device in a book, and scat. Therefore, a man who could pick a new lock was always useful.

The *new* student, Nigel Page, soon became a *star* student, quickly graduating to visual or camera surveillance, receivers, and surreptitious entry, the latter of which built on Nigel's skills as a lockpick. Graduation came one weekend when Cochrane planted seven bugging devices in The Hero of the Thames with Edward's permission. Nigel entered at three AM, picked the lock, and, using a tiny flashlight, retrieved all seven, helped himself to a bottle of ale, and relocked the place by four AM. He turned the devices over to Bill the next day when the pub opened.

"What if I told you that you missed one?" Bill asked.

"With all due respect, Guvnor, I'd say you was pulling my winkie and you could fook yourself. There were only seven. Not eight, not six-and-a-fooking-half. Seven, Sir."

"You're hired," Bill said.

And so out of nowhere, Bill had his first "technical officer" for his small brigade in exile. Despite having little formal education, Nigel Page – or Mountain Hawk – was brilliant. Bill might have coded him as "the ancient mariner," but – his admiration for Samuel Coleridge notwithstanding – he knew better.

"They seem to forget, but they never forget, do they, Sir?" Roth asked over the German brandy, the Asbach Uralt, the evening when Cochrane visited. "One day one of them will find me, won't they?"

Anna, or Alyssa, sitting next to him, rested her hand on her husband's.

"Let's hope not," Cochrane said. "Better than that," he added quickly, "let's do everything in our power to prevent something unfortunate."

"The past is complicated, no?" Roth asked, musing onward. "One day I walk into a store and the wrong person sees me, someone from the dark past, eh? And then, of a sudden, the hiding is all over. Bang, bang. Some night. They will come for me. Right, Sir?"

"It always pays to be careful, Stefan," Cochrane said.

"Any chance of getting me to America, Sir?" he asked.

"I can talk to my superiors on your behalf," Cochrane said. "We'd like to keep you here on our team for a few more years, though, and I think that's what my higher-ups will tell me."

Stefan nodded stoically.

"I can play along for a while," he said. "A few years maybe. It's not bad here with that old hen who owns the place. My wife and I, we are not to be here forever."

"I understand," Bill said. He thanked his hosts and rose to leave. All seemed good with Alyssa and Stefan. Bill was not disposed to upset the equilibrium.

# Chapter 24
## England and Germany – August 1952

Bill Cochrane spent a day with Laura's Aunt Beatrice in Bath, then drove back toward London. From there it was on to Cambridge where Bill checked back into the University Arms Hotel, his usual place. The hotel was already on its evening schedule. He knew the man who was on the desk, Jessup, from previous stays. Jessup: Bill didn't know if that was the fellow's first name or last and it barely mattered. It was what he went by. Jessup had an easy smile and walked with a limp. Cochrane assumed it was from the war; Jessup was of that age.

He had dinner that night at The Hero of the Thames pub where Edward greeted him warmly.

He checked in the next morning with "Frau Swenson," whom he had once known as Bettina in Berlin, dating back to 1943 when she had lodged him and a young woman who were trying to flee the Nazi regime and escape to the United States. Now she lived quietly under her pseudonym with a man known as Horst, her paramour from the war.

They, too, were living peaceably, Bill was happy to learn.

"All of which leaves me with a young lady of our acquaintance. Sarah. Sarah Vogel. Our aspiring artist friend. Any news of her?"

"No."

"Seen her recently?" he asked.

"No."

Sarah Vogel, who had until 1950 been known as Lotte Meidner, was Bill's most recent German exile whom he had smuggled into England. She was also the most troubling and the loosest cannon in his arsenal, always a threat to come off her moorings.

Lotte had been involved in a dicey shooting in East Berlin two years earlier. A couple of malefactors who would never be missed were dead, and the entire Stasi brigade from Comrade Mielke down to the lowliest street enforcer was apoplectic. Worse for those who played for the East German police team, Lotte had from time to time played musical beds with some of the higher-ups in the Stasi power structure, possibly even with Erich Mielke if Lotte's version of things could be believed.

Hence, she was a young woman of interest to all sides.

On an inspired afternoon, Bill Cochrane and a few of his usual enablers, including Otto Kern and Sgt. Jimmy Pearson, had come up with a devilishly inspired idea. From a military contact in the French zone, Bill came up with a spare female corpse of a young woman of about Lotte's age and buried it with public honors at Friedrichsfelde Central Cemetery, where proper Marxists were often laid to rest. For whatever reason, the funeral service turned into a brawl with Bill Cochrane suffering a fractured wrist during the proceedings.

As the East German police tried to sort things out, Sgt. Pearson had hustled Cochrane and a very much alive Lotte Meidner out to Tempelhof. In the weeks that followed, in the aftermath of her funeral in East Berlin, she had been set up under a new ID with an official new British passport in her new name: Sarah Vogel.

"I saw Sarah maybe three weeks ago. Maybe a month," Bettina said.

"And?"

"Doing well. A chip on her shoulder as always. But doing well. Your stipend keeps her going. I believe she also works as a waitress in a dreadful little rathskeller on King James Street near the university. Imagine that. Ten years ago the Luftwaffe was dropping bombs on the neighborhood, now someone opens a German beer hall. Short memories, right?"

"Very," Bill agreed. "I assume she's still painting," he said. "Indulging in her artistic streak, as opposed to her libidinous or homicidal streaks. Would I be correct?"

"That's how it appeared to me," Bettina said. "She's even sold a few canvases. Can you imagine that?"

"Oh, I can, indeed," Bill said. "Her work was actually quite good. I imagine with instruction it has developed a bit."

"Only seen it once," Bettina said. "I suppose it's all right."

"You're passing along her monthly stipend, correct?" Bill asked.

"Of course. She wants me to leave it under the door if she's not there when I call," Bettina said. "Or if she's just in too crabby a mood to come to the door."

Her partner, Horst, quiet as a mausoleum, sat across the room, saying nothing but possibly listening. Listening and maybe understanding. His head was drooping, and his attention was lagging. He sat with arms folded and ankles lazily crossed.

"I bring the money along in a small brown envelope. Sometimes I see her, sometimes I leave it under the door. I didn't hear from her after my July visit."

"So, arguably, our girl could be dead on the floor," Cochrane suggested.

"Could be, but isn't," Bettina said. "I've learned a few things from you over the years, Mr. Lewis. There's a widow lady that lives downstairs by the door. Big, heavy woman. Bleachy blonde. Her name is Charlotte. She's always in sleepwear, even mid-afternoons, boobs practically tumbling out. 'Charlotte the Harlot,' I call her in my own mind, but don't you tell her if you ever meet her."

"I wouldn't dare. How does 'Charlotte the Harlot' figure into this?" Bill asked, mildly amused.

"I slip the lady a few shillings when I visit. Told her Sarah was my niece. The Harlot sends me a postal card to confirm that she's seen her. Lost her own daughter in the war during the blitz, poor woman. I hate to lie to her, but I bring her tea and cakes sometimes, too. Nice lady even though she doesn't seem to bathe."

"I don't suppose you'd have one of these cards handy?" Bill asked. "The most recent one, maybe?"

A quaint, fake pout, then a laugh. "Don't believe me, huh?"

"Certainly, I believe you. But I'd like to see the correspondence anyway. I have a boss to please, too, after all, and he'll ask if I saw a card or just took you at your word."

"Uh-huh."

"His name is DeWinter, and he can be unpleasant. Should I put you in touch?"

"Ha!" she said, suddenly with a smile. "Of course, I have the cards, all of them. I knew you'd ask. Got the whole bloody stack of them don't we, Horst?"

Horst jumped a trifle at the sound of his name.

"Give Mr. Lewis the stack of cards, darling," she said. "They're in the top-left door of my desk."

Horst blinked himself awake and hauled himself up onto his feet. His knees creaked. His breathing suddenly seemed labored as he moved. The desk was on the other side of the room. Without speaking, but breathing noisily, Horst lurched forward and somehow arrived safely on the other side of the room. He retrieved about a dozen postal cards from the drawer that Bettina had indicated. They were bound by a rubber band. Horst's gnarled fingers dropped them in Cochrane's lap. He trudged heavily back to his armchair into which he sank.

By the time of Horst's return to his chair, Cochrane had already broken open the pack of cards and was lightly examining them. Postmarks checked. Messages were cheerful. A valid red one 2½d *Festival of Britain* postage stamp and a real postmark. All of the postmarks were within the last four months. The most recent was in late June.

The handwriting on the front of the cards was distinct from the handwriting of the message on the reverse side. The messages pleasantly said little, obliquely acknowledging the receipt of some undesignated item.

"You pre-addressed these and applied the postage stamps, I assume, Frau Swenson," Cochrane said.

"Correct."

"And this would be Charlotte's writing on the reverse?"

"Correct," she said again without hesitation. Her eyes narrowed as Cochrane stood, crossed the room, and handed the cards back to her. Her eyes narrowed. "Don't fool with me, Mr. Lewis," Bettina said with a smile. "You know my handwriting and you know I wouldn't lie to you."

"You've learned the game well, Frau Swenson," Bill said.

"Took lessons from the best," she said. "Just kept my eyes open. Been observant. The game is never tricky until it is, right?"

"Too true," Bill said. He paused. "But all this suggests that Sarah's address is different from when I returned to the United States," he said.

"That's correct, also."

"How and why did that come about?"

"Her landlord where you installed her made a ruckus about the smell of oil paint coming out of her flat," Bettina said. "She was starting to get into verbal fights with the man. I heard of an available place out on Mill Road. Near Romsey. Do you know where that is?"

Bill laughed. "Romsey? Yes, all too well," he said.

Bettina shrugged.

"All right," he continued. "Could you give it to me? Her address. Where I'd find her?"

"Of course." She wrote it out on a page from a small notepad. She handed it to Bill.

"It all happened fast in a weekend. The move."

"You might have advised me," Bill said curtly.

"I might have, yes. But do you know how fast flats get filled in a university town? Even dreadful little twisted ones like the one she has. No time to contact and ask for permission. No harm done, I don't think."

Some blood came to her face. She reddened.

"Let's hope not," Bill said. "I'll have to have my eavesdropping specialist visit her also."

"Oh, Lord, I should have told you, shouldn't I? And I didn't. Oh, I blundered badly, didn't I? I just was, uh…"

"Trying to manage it yourself?" Bill said with an air of conciliation covering any suspicion.

"Yes. Mail is so slow, and you never know who's reading yours before you do. Telephone and telegraph are equally undependable."

"In any case, I should soon find out if there is any lapse in security," Bill said. "Let's hope her new place isn't bugged. I'll have to have our Mountain Hawk visit. I guess I should have asked. He's been here recently, right?"

"Friday of last week. One of us – Horst or I – has been home at all times since then. No one else has been in or out. I can't account for the street outside but we're clean as a new penny in here."

"Solid," Bill said.

There was an awkward pause. For a moment Bettina looked frightened. "Am I on your down staircase? Tell me honestly."

"Not at all," Bill said. "Honest mistakes happen. I'll assess the situation today and alert you if there are problems. I don't expect any."

"You're going calling on her?"

Bill glanced at his watch. It was half past four PM on a Thursday afternoon.

"Yes. It's a bit late today," he answered. "But I'll follow up tomorrow morning."

A tiny pause, then, "Does she still hate me?" he asked. "Sarah? For taking her from Berlin? For dropping her down in England? God knows I gave her a new lease on life. If I hadn't interceded, she would have been dead from a bullet, the only question being whether one of our rogue people had done it or one of Mielke's."

A thoughtful moment. Then, "Not so much that she hates you," Bettina said. "She hates what you do."

"Sometimes I hate myself, also," he said.

"Is that true?"

"Yes. For exactly the same reason. But I keep doing it. Where's the logic to that?"

"I have no idea," she said.

"Nor I," Bill answered. A silence hung in the room. Bill's eyes jumped to Horst. The old German was now gloriously dozing and starting to snore.

"Don't get garroted by a Bolshevik when you visit Sarah," Bettina said. "God knows who her group of friends are over there. I can only imagine."

"I'll be careful," Cochrane promised.

"I don't know what you see in that crazy girl," Bettina said, with a slight shake to her wise, middle-aged head. "She seems erratic to me. Unstable. Loopy. Wait till you see what she's taken to painting. I think she's a Sappho. Like one of those girls you'd see prewar at the Auluka-Lounge on Augsbergerstrasse. You planning to recruit her?"

"I don't know if I even could, Bettina," Cochrane said. "The thing is," he said, "sometimes one puts a 'loopy' agent on an assignment, then he or she makes a brilliant decision in the field that the control agent could never have made. Then you have a success for which he takes credit but might never have otherwise earned."

"Or you have a dead or missing agent on your hands," she countered.

"I got you and Horst to England, did I not?"

"That you did," she conceded.

"But thank you for your insights," he said.

Cochrane concluded the visit five minutes later. He returned to the University Arms Hotel. There remained only one more port of call in Cambridge and it was the most important. Fortunately, Bill had completed his homework.

# Chapter 25
## Cambridge – July 1952

Bill Cochrane drove from the hotel to Sarah Vogel's new neighborhood the next morning after breakfast. He arrived shortly after nine o'clock.

The morning had become overcast during the drive and a fine rain fell. He found the house number where Sarah was said to be renting, drove past it, and parked about a hundred feet past her door. He locked the car and walked back down the quiet street. An old man with no right leg and two crutches hobbled past him – a war veteran no doubt, but possibly a civilian casualty – and gave him a warm smile. Cochrane found Lotte's address again. Her building was of white wood with a dark brown roof, nestled between a pub on the right side and a watch and clock merchant on the left.

Mill Road was one of the busier thoroughfares in southeast Cambridge. Its northwestern end stretched to Fenner's, the cricket ground of the University of Cambridge. Its southeast end led out of the city. In between was a business hodgepodge of quirky shops, pubs, grocery stores, and merchants. Bill could also quickly see the presence of a small creative community, artists, craftsmen, small press printers and publishers, and booksellers. He could see why the young woman whom he had known as Lotte would like to live there.

He was also aware of the history of the area. Most of the people who resided on Mill Road were attracted to the area by its alternate lifestyle air. To many, it felt more authentic than the nearby stodgy university. But many were also drawn to Mill Road by its history, and especially by the ways in which it seemed to convey the sense of civic identity and pride that existed independent of the university.

This was nowhere more evident than in Romsey Town, where trade unionism and Labour politics had put down their deepest roots between the wars, helping to fuel the vivid stories of "Red Romsey" that some of the neighbors could still recount fifty years later: stories about local working men giving their free time to help build the Labour Club on the corner of Coleridge Road or about the celebrities of Labour politics who had visited the ward.

These were stories that resonated with pride about having carved out an identity for Romsey that owed little or nothing to the colleges and university that had dominated the wider city for hundreds of years. Gordon Fraser, publisher, lived at 274a Mill Road during the late 1930s. Dylan Thomas attended a notorious, week-long drunken party there in 1937 after coming to Cambridge to give a pre-binge poetry reading.

Cochrane stepped into an alcove through an unlocked door to Mill Street. Faced with a second lock and no buzzer, he tried the knob. The door opened with a slight hesitation and click.

He entered the building and stopped short. To his left was a Dutch door, open on the top, closed on the bottom. On the other side of it was a plump woman with blond hair, which was dark at the roots. She was looking at him critically with tired, reddish eyes. She wore a rumpled housecoat above what appeared to be a frayed negligee. She held a cigarette between her thumb and forefinger and had frozen at the sight of him.

"Yes?" she said. She spoke in a tone of challenge, as opposed to one of greeting.

"You must be Charlotte," Bill Cochrane said.

"Depends who you are, love," she answered. The words were warm. Her tone was chilly.

"An old friend of Sarah Vogel," he said. "I believe she lives here."

"Oh. Well. Yes," Charlotte said. "Maybe."

"Flat two zero three. If I'm not mistaken," he said.

"Maybe," she said again.

"Why don't I go up, knock, and see if Sarah is receiving company this morning?" he asked.

"Why *don't* you?" she answered. "Would solve a problem for both of us, wouldn't it?" Charlotte said.

"I didn't know I had a problem," Bill said amiably.

"Course you didn't. Your type never bloody does."

She made a harrumphing noise and gave him a second look that was even more discourteous than the first. She pushed the top half of the door shut before Bill could ask what type he was, though he was more inclined to keep such an inquiry to himself.

When the top half of the door did not latch, she swatted it hard from within – Cochrane could hear the blow – and the half-door swung back hard, slammed shut, and latched. By that time, Cochrane was on the steps, taking them more quickly than he otherwise might have.

He ascended. The stairs squeaked. He arrived at the door to 203. There was no bell. He knocked. From within he could hear a scurrying sound, followed by footsteps approaching the door. No vocal reply. Then, after a pause, footsteps, and a female voice with a slight Germanic accent called out, "Coming," turning the word into three syllables.

Bill assumed she was pulling clothes on.

The footsteps stopped abruptly on the other side of the door. Lotte, or Sarah, or whoever she was busy being these days, had at the last minute cautioned herself about throwing open the door at random. Cochrane looked down and could see the shadows of her two feet on the other side of the door.

There was no peephole either he noticed as his gaze rose to eye level.

Then, "Who is it?" she asked sharply. There was something in her tone which, from long experience, told him that she sensed trouble. He recognized the voice. Time flew apart in his memory and suddenly they were in Berlin again two years earlier, him visiting and urging her to cooperate in a murder inquiry and then her reluctantly fleeing the city as he ushered her to the apparently unappreciated safety of Cambridge.

"An old friend," he replied gently.

Stillness from the other side of the door. He assumed she was trying to decide whether to open it or not. Then a bolt clattered from within, and the door swung open.

Then there they were, *Angesicht zu Angesicht*, face to face, for the first time in two years. She wore a garment that was half-robe and half-smock. It stopped somewhere mid-thigh and showed ample leg. It was loose. It was equally clear she wore nothing underneath. Much the way that Bill and the former Lotte Meidner had not been face to face for many months, the grungy, grimy, paint-speckled smock had not been face to face with a washday in many months, also.

"Hello, Sarah," he said.

"Jesus goddamned Christ!" she snapped. She quickly retied the sash on her robe, tightening it. "Thought it was you. Go away."

She tried to slam the door, but Bill's foot was too nimble. He blocked the door with his foot and his arm. His arm gave a twinge where it had been broken on the day of her fake funeral.

The door flew back toward her. He was ready for her to charge and try to push him out, and he watched her hands to make sure she didn't pick up a knife or smash one of the wine bottles that littered her counters to use as a weapon.

But, no. Instead, she went to a table, angrily grabbed a pack of Players cigarettes, sucked one from the pack with her lips, lit it, stood with her arms folded, blew out a long stream of smoke, and turned.

By this time, Bill Cochrane had entered the flat and closed the door. He stood pleasantly before her. A hybrid aroma of oil paints, tobacco smoke, and dirty dishes accosted him.

"Nice to see you, Sarah," he said. "I sense you're in your usual foul mood. How's life? Good, I hope."

"Fuck yourself," she said. "Just fuck yourself. How's that? That's how I am. Fuck yourself!"

Undeterred, "Mind if we have a conversation?" he asked. "I think it might be a good idea."

"For whom? You or me?" she demanded.

"Ideally both of us," he said. "Thank you for asking."

"The hell," she muttered.

Her English had improved considerably since Bill had last seen her in person, now giving her the ability to be equally churlish, dismissive, profane, and obnoxious in two languages. Not for a moment did he take it personally.

"Jesus Christ," she muttered again.

"You've been receiving a stipend from us," Cochrane said. "I assume you've been spending it and surviving on it. Not surviving too badly, I might add, because I know how much it is. So I don't think I'm out of order in asking for a few minutes of talk. No harm in that, is there?"

"Depends," she said. She stood facing him. "Why are you really here? You want sex? Is that it?"

"No."

"Then what?"

"Just talk," Bill said.

*"Leck mich am Arsch,"* she muttered, turning and glaring at him. Then something in her eyes changed as if she had ridded herself of her first wave of anger and wondered what might have brought him there after so many months.

She turned and went to the corner of the main room where there was a sink and two cabinets on the wall. There was a battered hot plate on the counter near a cluttered sink. She pulled two glass mugs from a shelf and started boiling water, all this while Bill stood quietly and watched.

She muttered something to herself in German about the past not leaving her alone, sprinkling her thoughts with profanity, but said nothing directly to Bill. From a drawer, she pulled two tea bags, dropped one into each cup, and stood waiting for the water to boil.

Bill interpreted this as an invitation to stay.

*"Vielen Dank,"* Bill said. He began to look around her place more carefully as she waited for the water to boil.

# Chapter 26
## Cambridge – July 1952

Around the room were the plates that Lotte had used for the last few days and the bottles and cartons that she had finished. There was a garbage bucket in the kitchen area near the sink, but it was untouched by human hands.

Still standing in the same place as when she had begun to make tea, he quickly scoped out her living quarters. Bill had been in more than a few homes of artists. In his experience, no two were alike. He spotted an array of her canvases as well as her easel and workspace. He took the tools of her trade as an opening for conversation and, dare he even consider it, future cooperation.

"May I take a look at your canvases?" Bill asked. "And perhaps talk a little as I do so?"

"It's not like I can stop you," she conceded.

"I'll take that as a yes," he said. "Thank you, Sarah."

Indignation. Self-righteousness. Mystification. Belligerence.

Lotte, or Sarah, clung to all these elusive states of mind, using them as social and psychological barriers. Meanwhile, Bill plunged his hands into his coat pockets and under her censorious, slow-burning glances, guided himself on a brief tour of what passed for her gallery.

Her flat was oddly configured, it was difficult to tell where her creative part – the artist's studio segment – began and where the living quarters ended. Everything was pushed together. As his memory came back to him, the arrangement of clutter – the essential mixed in with the irrelevant – reminded him of her flat in Berlin, in a dicey location in the bombed-out Eastern zone. He didn't dare ask, for fear of setting off any dangerous emotions. She smoked another cigarette aggressively as she watched him on his tour.

The Berlin set-up had been boxy, very Germanic, with two square rooms linked to each other like a pair of crates adjoining each other. Here things were very different.

Her front room had a large bay window from which she could watch the street. The wall curved. There was a seating area before the window and shutters that had no pattern to them: some were shut, some were open, some were in between. One was missing. Very Romsey.

The rest of the room was straightforward. A long blue divan was the centerpiece of this room. It looked as if it had been rescued from a second-hand store: the material was tattered at the edges and the legs didn't match. There had been bombing of Cambridge during the war and it wouldn't have surprised Bill to learn that the divan had been in a house that had been destroyed. In some areas, more household effects had survived than people.

The back area was long and narrow, irritatingly so. It was wide for a corridor and cramped for a room. There were paintings, hers, leaning across both sides. Where there were no paintings, there were books. Stacks of them, including art books. They were in English and German.

He scanned the titles. Interesting. American authors and British. Pearl Buck. Steinbeck. Elizabeth Bower. Some German. Dostoyevsky in German translation. A little bit of Russian; all in English translation. *Anna Karenina,* also in English, the book that the great Tolstoy referred to as his first genuine novel.

Conspicuously absent: Lenin and Marx. So far so good.

Bill blinked and continued onward. She did nothing to impede his movement. When Cochrane saw some Gertrude Stein, he concluded she was doing most of her reading in English. And since Lotte had arrived here bereft with little more than a canvas suitcase with clothes and undergarments, everything was a recent acquisition.

Bill next looked carefully at her paintings. He noticed that Lotte had experimented with portraits, landscapes, and full-length body works, all of them women, mostly nudes and semi-nudes, all of them slightly erotic and seductive. She had signed each work in the lower right with her new name, *Sarah*, plus what appeared to be the year. *Sarah 50*, or *Sarah 51*, for example. To the best that he could recall, her artwork here was very different from what she had painted in Berlin. The style was looser and freer.

Coincidence? He wondered.

He was pleased with her use of her new name. She wasn't fighting the new identity.

Bettina had mentioned that she had been set up with a good instructor here, an Austrian-Jewish émigré named Schorgl, who had fled Vienna in 1939 and who now was a teacher in the British school system. "Someone who can be trusted," Bettina said of Herr Schorgl. "And someone who, of course, will keep an eye on our problem child and report back."

Sarah 52, more recently, read the signatures on her most recent works.

Bill completed his circuit and came back to where he had begun. There was an easel, a strong whiff of fresh paint, and a half-finished female nude, the model coyly turned at a three-quarters angle – an unsmiling, mournful but beautiful face, a young body, long flowing black hair streaked with white. Bill glanced back at the array of other paintings and realized that most were of the same young woman. Not unusual, but noteworthy.

"Tea is ready," she said.

Lotte carried two cups to a sitting area, a ragged chair, and a large cushion on the floor. Bill sat in the chair. She sat on the cushion. He set the tea on a small side table, and she set hers on the floor after sipping.

"Work in progress?" Bill asked about the half-completed work. He began the conversation in English.

"None of your business." She paused, eyeing him again with anger. "What do you think? Junk, eh? That's what you're thinking."

"Not at all. I rather like your work. I see a strong style developing."

She was quiet for a moment. Then, "You still have a wife?"

"Yes, I do."

"You like the naked females?"

"Why wouldn't I?"

"A lot of Americans are puritans. Prudes."

Bill laughed. "I'm not 'a lot of Americans.'"

"But you work for them."

"It's complicated, Sarah," he said. "Or Lotte. I try to do what I think is right."

"And so you're an art critic now, too?" she challenged, going back to the painting.

"Isn't everyone?" Bill said with a smile.

Silence. Then, "Somedays," she said.

"If you wish to know the truth, I like your painting. I see similarities with Moïse Kisling, the Polish-French artist. A genius with the female form, with a heavy dose of the surreal layered in. I like that. Real life plus an extra dimension."

More silence. She lit another cigarette. Then, "You know Kisling?" she asked.

"I don't know the man personally, but I know his work. I met him once. That's why I happen to be familiar with his output. He lived in America for a while. California."

She smoked. She listened.

Still on Kisling, Cochrane doffed his professorial hat and kept talking.

"Under the Vichy government, certain critics suggested too many foreigners, especially Jews, were diminishing French traditions. Their comments were part of a rise in anti-Semitism during the German occupation, resulting in French cooperation in the deportation and deaths of tens of thousands of foreign and French Jews in concentration camps. Kisling returned to France after the war and defeat of Germany.

"The Nazis deserved what they got," she muttered.

"See? We agree on something," Bill said.

"*Vielleicht*," she said. *Maybe.*

"I saw some of Kisling's work in New York with my wife after the war," Cochrane continued. "He was present at the exhibition. The gallery owner introduced me. I wish I had bought one of his works, but he was already too expensive for me."

Bill hadn't lost her yet, so he kept the conversation going.

"I think he had an exhibition in Washington, too," Cochrane concluded. When the French Army was discharged after the surrender to the Germans, Kisling emigrated to the United States. He rightly feared for his safety as a Jew in occupied France. And even more paramount, he feared for the lives of his sons. He got them out of the country, first to friends in America, then he and his wife joined them. His wife was a model for him, you know."

"I know about him," she said.

"So you know his work?"

"I like it," she allowed.

"The Kisling family lived next door to Aldous Huxley and his family in Southern California. Ever heard of Huxley? English author. *Brave New World*."

"No," she said. "Don't know that one."

"*Brave New World* warns of the dangers of giving the state control over new and powerful technologies. One illustration of this theme is the rigid control of reproduction through technological and medical intervention, including the surgical removal of ovaries, the Bokanovsky Process, and hypnopedic conditioning. Frightening stuff. The type of thing we're starting to see in East Germany and East Berlin. The students at Humboldt rebelled last year. The Russians arrested thousands. Some were executed. Did you know that?"

"I heard. Thanks for the lecture. I didn't need it."

"Horrible, isn't it?"

Then, "Why are you here?" she asked again.

"I see that's the blue divan in the painting. Who's the model?"

"A friend."

"Nice that you have one."

"I have many."

"That's even nicer. She's quite pretty. What's her name?"

A long pause.

"Oh, come on," Bill said.

Then, "Victoria," she said.

"Handsome name. Same as the queen," Bill said. "Very English."

"And same as the rail station. Stop playing games. I'll tell her you said you liked her body. Why are you here today?" she asked again.

"Have you been back to Berlin since I brought you here?"

"No."

"Interested?"

"Maybe to visit. Never to stay."

"Still have friends there?"

"I don't know. I'm dead, don't forget."

"I recall. I was at your funeral and was attacked by your former paramour. Surely, you remember that part."

"Too well," she said.

"So Cambridge suits you?"

"Did you ever receive a list of complaints from me or that fat lady who works for you?"

"If you mean Frau Swensen, she's not fat, she's stout. And she doesn't work for me, she's a friend. And no, I didn't receive a list of complaints."

"That's because I don't have any, all right? There's no list."

"Glad to hear it," he said. He switched to German. "Look, it's no secret to you as to what I do. Occasionally I need people capable of gathering information in the Soviet zone. I won't lie to you: it can be dangerous. I have my own small network of people I use. Only I know who they are.

They're well taken care of and paid well, even when they don't work."

She was silent. But she was listening.

"Interested?" he asked again.

"Depends."

"If I remember, when you were moving around East Berlin two years ago you had some contact with some people in power. Am I correct?"

"Yes. Get to the point."

"Erich Mielke was one of them if I remember."

"You remember," she said. She finished her tea. Bill's remained untouched. He had taken his eyes off her as she brewed it. Who knew what was in it?

"You once told me that you had been to his home."

"Correct,"

"Which home? The one for the public to see and know about or the other one, farther out in the countryside?"

She was silent.

"The one where the *hübsche junge Mädchen*, the pretty young girls, got 'invited.' Or 'rounded up and taken,' if that's a better term for it," Bill said. When Lotte opened her mouth to protest, he continued. "Oh, I know what the procedure was. They'd grab a bunch of young girls from a socialist party function. Round them up and take them to a private spot. Such as Mielke's private residence or residences." He paused. "Lucky you weren't killed."

More silence.

"Come on, Lotte," Bill said, breaking his own rule about the use of former names, but firing a clever shot. The use of her birth name, he hoped, would get past any armor she was wearing and get closer to whoever was inside. Lotte not Sarah.

There was a longer stretch of silence. He indulged it for several seconds, Then, "It's an easy question, Lotte. It has a *yes* or *no* answer."

"Maybe."

"Come on. I want to be able to justify to my boss the money you receive. I don't want him to call it into question."

"*Jawohl*," she said. She had been to both of Mielke's homes. She suddenly found it easier to talk about. No one even bothered to learn the girls' names. The men just pounced on them and enjoyed them, a one-way orgy in most cases. Once Lotte had even fled to Mielke's private study on the second story. The study overlooked a wooded area and a game preserve. There was a magnificent Fabergé oil lamp on Mielke's desk, ornate, deep blue with gold. It was hard to miss: the centerpiece of the chamber. A prized possession, she was told by one of the other girls who was taken there regularly. The tsar had once owned it and Stalin had given it to Mielke, who now loved to show it off to official visitors.

"He's like a crazy man about that lousy tsarist lamp," she said. "Treats it like it's his kid or a prized bull. He has fire extinguishers all over his workspace and won't even let the servants touch it."

"Servants?" Cochrane asked, surprised. "A socialist leader of the people in the DDR and he has *servants?*"

"Yeah," she said. "A staff. Mostly D.Ps from the war. A bunch of Turks, I think."

"Women? All of them?"

"Some men, mostly women."

"I'm not following how a socialist has household servants," Bill said with a grin. "Isn't that against—?"

"It's against a lot of things," she said sourly. "Listen, he's a bad man. Ulbricht is, too. I never liked what I saw there."

"You never told me that before."

"You never asked. And if you did, I would have told you to shut up. You would just have given me the 'see-I-told-you-stuff', right?"

"Maybe," Bill allowed. A moment, then, "If I gave that impression, I apologize. I shouldn't have."

"Doesn't matter," Lotte said.

"Do you think you could find those places again?" he asked. "Mielke's homes? His houses?"

Telepathically perhaps, she seemed to know what he was thinking – or in a larger sense, asking.

"Maybe," she said.

"Why 'maybe' again, Lotte?"

*Maybe*, Bill wondered, in the sense that she actually couldn't remember, she had blocked it out? Or *maybe* in the sense that she wanted more money?

"They've taken down the street and road signs in the neighborhoods. There is no address."

"In Berlin or out in the country?"

"Both."

"Then how would you know them?" Bill asked.

"I lived in Berlin. The Berlin home, I know from the walking path from the S-Bahn. The rural place, the one with a stretch of woods behind it, I was driven there three times."

"Alone?"

"With other girls. Six. Eight. It was a transport bus. No markings, but you could tell it had also been used for prisoners. Guards on both sides. Windows covered. I memorized the route in case I had to escape and come back alone."

"Did that ever happen?"

"One time."

"Bad experience?"

"Yes."

"Mielke and his inner circle? The higher-ups?"

"Yes. Very high."

"Stasi and army?"

"Yes."

"Which army? Soviet or East German?"

"Both," she said. "They were out of uniform. We were not supposed to know. But the Germans spoke German and the Russians spoke Russian, as if you couldn't tell anyway. God in Heaven! I hate even talking about it! I was young and it was repulsive."

"Could you understand the Russian?" he asked. It occurred to him that he had never asked her about her proficiency in the language of Mother Russia. So many questions left unasked, he ruminated. *"Shame on me,"* he thought. He inquired now.

"I've picked up some. You know. From listening and hearing."

He nodded. "Who was worse? Soviets of Stasi?"

"Whoever was touching you."

"And these higher-ups? You recognized them?"

"Too well! I could tell you the tattoos, the private ones," said snapped with a flash of anger.

"I'm sorry."

"Why? You didn't do anything."

"But it must have been frightful."

The silence gave an affirmative response. Then, *"Ja,"* she said, speaking volumes with a single word.

"How did you see the route if the windows were covered?" he asked.

"I sat behind the driver."

"That was careless of them."

She managed her first smile of the visit. "There was a young Stasi man next to me. He put his hand under my skirt. It was summer. I put mine under a blanket on his lap. He let me watch through the window."

"You're clever," Bill said.

Another trace of a rueful smile. *"Vielleicht ist es so,"* she said.

For a moment Bill sensed a small return to tranquility. He let her ease into it.

"This is helpful," he said. "Final thing. Did any of these officers, Mielke and his friends, did they talk in front of you?"

"About what?"

Bill shrugged. "Anything. The new currency? The Allies? Abductions? Snipers?"

"Not that much. They'd get drunk. But they knew better than to talk."

"What about the abductions? There was just one the other day. A gentleman named Linse."

"Don't know anything about it."

"But even the girls knew it was going on," Bill suggested.

"Sure. But you knew better than to ask. There were always abductions."

"What about assassinations? Long range? Some of the marksmen from the war? *Militärische Scharfschüzen?*" he asked.

"Russian things, those," she said. "Mielke wouldn't want his people doing that. If they used Germans, they'd have the Russians recruiting." She shrugged.

Cochrane could tell she was talked out. She finished the cigarette she was smoking and snuffed it out. She shook the pack, found it empty, crumpled it, and tossed it toward the kitchen waste basket. It missed. While she was looking around for another pack, Bill reached into his pocket and pulled out a fresh pack of Players.

"Here, Lotte," he said.

He tossed it to her when she turned back. She caught it and opened it. She broke it open, lit one, and inhaled.

*"Gern geschehen,"* Cochrane said.

*"Danke,"* she answered.

It suddenly became a conversation that had collapsed under its own weight. It was effectively over, Cochrane could tell. He had lost her attention and her focus. He started to pitch bringing her back to Berlin to advise him on a project he had in mind, one that would entail rediscovering the location of Herr Mielke's lairs.

But she was hearing none of it.

"I would submit that you'd earn more in a month's visit to Berlin than you would in a year at the rathskeller. Follow the math?"

"I follow it."

"We'd get you in and out of here by air. We have routes and ways. I'll accompany you if need be. Or you'd be on your own. We'd arrange something. Will you think about it?"

"I just did."

"And?"

"I'm not going back to Berlin," she said.

This went back and forth for several minutes. Her resolve solidified. He sighed. A partial success, this visit, but an overall failure, at least for the time being. At least, he told himself, he had managed to thaw out the relationship a little.

He eventually found himself back at the hallway and picked up his hat. "Thank you for your time," he said. "I'm glad you're doing well."

There might have been more. Bill might have added something crucial. But their time was cut off by a knock on the door. She apparently recognized the knock.

"Victoria?" she called out.

A woman's voice answered in English in the affirmative. Lotte, reverting back to her Sarah persona, sprang nimbly to her feet.

"That's my friend who models for me," she said. "You should go."

"May we talk again?" Bill asked.

"Yes."

"We should," he said. "I'll be at the University Arms hotel for the next day or two," Bill said. "It depends on the weather. I'm not partial to flying in thunderstorms. If you change your mind—"

"I won't," she said.

"Of course not. No one ever does, do they?"

"No. No Berlin again for me. You should go," she said. "Now."

Lotte went to the door and opened it. She gave a jerk of her head toward the exit, strongly suggesting that Bill should use it.

The door opened and there was, presumably, Victoria.

Bill graciously tipped his hat to the young woman. As in her portraits, Victoria was blessed with a pretty but mournful face and her hair was flecked with grey. The model looked at him with surprise, assumed the worst, and gave Sarah a smirk as she eased past.

With that, the visit with Lotte had ended.

Outside, the rain was falling steadier. Bill looked at the sky; it had turned darker. There was a flash of lightning and then a resounding boom of thunder, followed by more of both and then a drenching downpour. He pulled the collar of his raincoat close to him, checked the pistol in his pocket that he had almost forgotten about, and quickly stepped to his parked car.

DDR Propaganda Poster: Party Conference of the South,
July 1952, Forward For Peace, Freedom and Democracy

# Chapter 27
## Cambridge – August 1952

For two days the rainstorm stalled over East Anglia and unleashed a watery torrent from the sky, "bucketing down," as the locals explained it, as the precipitation was nonstop, sweeping sideways, and washing small streams through the public parks, across the old gray university buildings, and raising the waterline of the river.

Molesworth closed to incoming and outgoing air traffic and even one of the new motorways between London and Cambridge closed from flooding. Bill managed to phone Laura and assure her that he was safe and sound and missing her at the University Arms. Another call to Dr. Kreitler's office at the Free University in Berlin brought Kreitler up to date on the weather. As one could never be too sure how many people were on an extended line – the Soviets and their German understudies were known to be perfecting their surveillance arts these days – there were few specifics Bill could report other than that he was stranded in Cambridge and would need Kreitler to cover his class on Friday.

"Who are you reading?" Kreitler asked.

"Fitzgerald. *Tales of the Jazz Age*."

"Oh, that piece of crap. Not too taxing," Kreitler said.

"You don't care for it?"

"Not my favorite. But I don't need to be excited about it to talk for ninety minutes. Good luck with the family matter. See you next week."

"I hope so," Cochrane answered.

Bill filled his two days at Cambridge by browsing through bookstores and prowling through the public library. He took lunches in small student and faculty brewhouses at the foot of King Street.

Evenings he spent at The Hero of the Thames, where he liked to chat up Edward and keep his ear to the ground for

*REVOLT IN BERLIN* – **Part One**       NOEL HYND

political rumors, particularly the pink ones. All this time, Bill kept an eye open for Lotte, hoping she might have a change of heart and mind and track him down at the hotel. He had a growing hunch that she might, but the hunch was based on nothing more than wishful thinking.

But there was no appearance of her. None.

On the first night, Edward's place was quiet and nearly empty. Even Edward's hardiest patrons had chosen to stay home, sober and dry, as the drenching rain continued. But the skies began to clear early evening on the second day. The rain stopped and there was even a glimmer of sunlight flickering through the clouds. Then the clouds themselves lifted.

Edward's place was suddenly full and animated. Toward nine in the evening, Edward and his patrons at the bar ventured into a long harangue on British politics, giving Bill the definite impression that the feeling in Britain was as gloomy as it had been in Berlin.

Bill sidled into the discussion to see where it would lead, keeping his remarks tight and polite, not losing sight of the fact that he was a visitor in the United Kingdom. Bill offered the opinion that England had "won the war" and the citizenry had that to be proud of and might need to give the government a longer leash for returning Britain to prosperity.

His remarks were not favorably received.

"George VI, Mr. Lewis," Edward said. "His Highness's tobacco habits plus the politicians have left this kingdom in a bit of a mess."

"As an American," Cochrane said, "I recall the late monarch as a noble man who held the Atlantic Alliance together."

"Maybe," said a drinker named Murphy who sat to Bill's right. "But we're in a bit of a pickle now, aren't we?"

"This is 1952, mate," Robbie Davis, another regular at Edward's bar chipped in to Bill. "War's been over for seven years. Country's not got any bloomin' direction. Communists will take over eventually. Damned Bolsheviks are already all over the trade unions."

Bill listened carefully.

Cochrane was aware of the quirks of recent history and the distress of the Cantabrigians at Edward's bar. It had been no secret that the late king's health had been in a free fall for years. Then in 1950 while Cochrane had been back in New York, there had been a general election in Britain.

The Labour Party of Clement Attlee won but only with a slim majority of five seats. Twenty months later the same Labour Party called a snap election for Thursday, October 25, 1951, with the hopes of adding to the party's parliamentary majority. But there was also an underlying motivation for the second election in twenty months. The king, though ailing, feared that since the government had such a slim majority, and he was to leave the country to go on his planned Commonwealth tour in early 1952, there was a possibility of a change of government in his absence, something that would have an unseemly air to Britons as well as the Crown. Thus Prime Minister Clement Attlee had decided to call an "early" election to address that concern.

The move had repercussions that could never have been expected. Despite winning the popular vote and achieving both the party's highest-ever total vote to date, Labour won fewer seats in Parliament than the Conservative Party. The collapse of the vote for the nearly extinct Liberal Party had enabled the Conservatives to win several uncontested seats by default.

During this low period, the number of Liberal MPs was in single digits. It was often joked that Liberal MPs could hold their party meetings in the back of one London taxi. Nonetheless, the election unexpectedly marked the return of seventy-seven-year-old Winston Churchill as prime minister, who was now doddering when visible in public.

The stress of his older brother's abdication in 1939 plus the war had taken its toll on the health of King George VI, exacerbated by his more-than-a-pack-a-day cigarette habit, which resulted eventually in lung cancer plus a raft of other severe ailments, including arteriosclerosis. By his mid-fifties,

*REVOLT IN BERLIN* – **Part One**　　　　　　NOEL HYND

he was old and haggard also, much like Churchill. His elder daughter and next in line for the throne, Elizabeth, assumed an increasing amount of royal obligations.

The Commonwealth tour was reconfigured. Princess Elizabeth and her new husband, Philip, Duke of Edinburgh, would take the place of the King and Queen.

On September 23, 1951, the king underwent surgery to remove his entire royally cancerous left lung. Rumors were everywhere, but much like Franklin Roosevelt's deteriorating health during World War II, the health of the monarch was a state secret.

On January 31, 1952, despite advice from those close to him, George VI went to London Heathrow Airport to see Elizabeth and Philip off on their tour to Australia via Kenya. At half past seven on the morning of February 6, the monarch's household staff found him dead in his bed at Sandringham House in Norfolk. He had passed away during the night from coronary thrombosis. He was fifty-six and had been king for sixteen years.

"His daughter went to Kenya as Princess Elizabeth and flew back a week later as Queen Elizabeth II," Edward said as most of his drinkers stared somberly into their pub glasses.

"Victoria reigned for sixty-three years, Mr. Lewis," Edward said. "Gladstone and Disraeli spent most of thirty years in and out of the PM's office. It shouldn't be happening this way."

"Now there's a "new" prime minister who's too old and a queen who's too young," Murphy said.

"And it all happened in a hundred days," Edward said. "It's not right."

"Only thing keeping the Russian tanks at bay is the English Channel," said Murphy.

"They have nuclear power now," Davis said. "They'll drain the fooking channel and the tanks will roll from Berlin to Brighton Rock to Buck House."

Cochrane felt compelled to enter his two farthings' worth. "The Russians get no farther than Berlin," he said.

All the heads at the bar turned toward Bill and his conspicuous American accent. Even Edward looked skeptical.

"How's that, mate?" Davis asked.

"The Soviet Union gets no farther west in Europe than the East German border," Cochrane elaborated.

"Who's going to fooking stop them?" Murphy asked.

"The United States," Bill answered.

During the laughter that followed, Bill – in a quiet fit of pique, with the images of the rows of graves at the nearby American cemetery in the forefront of his mind – politely paid his bar bill and exited.

## Chapter 28
### Cambridge – August 1952

The hotel was approximately a ten-minute walk from the pub, depending on how angry or distracted the walker was. The content of the discussion at The Hero had left him temporarily without words when he hit the cobblestone streets by the public green that lay between the pub and the hotel. All this was good because no one would have wanted to hear what was on his mind. In any case, he purposefully forged ahead, keeping one eye alert for any strange cars or trucks that could have been some sort of surveillance. It was no secret that Soviet and Eastern European spy rings had targeted the United Kingdom. The opposition was as active here as anywhere else.

But there was no evidence of trouble. By the time he arrived in front of the hotel, he had calmed, not the least reasons for which were the bright moon above and a galaxy of crisp stars. Tomorrow promised good weather for flying. He could report back to Kreitler, DeWinter, and Harvey that his network wasn't going to be much help.

He was to some degree relieved. He was in a battle that he had not sought with a minute army that he did not wish to use. He could return to teaching, and no one would be the wiser.

Then the image of Walter Linse tapped him on the shoulder and yanked him back to reality. Linse was probably being tortured somewhere in a Red prison. And here was Bill looking to cop out, his gut filled with a couple of pints of lager, and his psyche irritated by some tiny minds in a tap room.

He went through the sturdy glass front doors of the University Arms Hotel, feeling the shame weighing on him like the anchor of an eighteenth-century man o' war. He took half a dozen steps into the lobby and the front desk clerk rescued him from his shame.

"Sir?" the voice called. It was Jessup. Before Bill could speak, Jessup moved his head toward the pub at the far end of the lobby. "An unaccompanied lady asking for you, Sir," Jessup said. "Been here for an hour, Sir," Jessup continued. "With a travel bag and waiting."

Bill approached the desk. "You're sure she's here for me?" Cochrane asked. "I'm not expecting anyone. Very few people even know—"

"The lady is here for *you*, Sir," Jessup said.

Bill turned and walked toward the pub. The visitor wasn't in the pub exactly, she was in the far end of the lounge, which was a continuation of the lobby, not far from the breakfast room, currently dark. Without a gentleman escort, single ladies could send the wrong message. But the individual was in a Queen Anne chair, positioned sideways. She wore a dark kerchief and a sensible cloth skirt, hemmed at the knee. There was a beige traveling coat folded neatly across her lap. Two legs were casually crossed and protruded from the chair. A small suitcase lay on the floor by her side.

Bill approached the woman and froze as she leaned forward. He frowned in confusion. It took a moment before the shock of recognition grabbed him by the lapels.

"Sarah?" he asked.

"I changed my mind," Lotte said, looking up at Bill when he arrived in front of her. "What time is our flight tomorrow?"

She had cut her hair and dyed it. She sported lipstick, deep red with a greenish tint. She wore a heavy pair of glasses. Short of wearing a party-trick-style fake nose and a mustache, she couldn't have looked more different.

"*What* flight?" he asked.

"Berlin," she said sotto voce so that no one nearby could hear, even though they were alone in the lounge. "Isn't that where we're going? To Berlin?"

Flummoxed, he felt awkward and strangely outmaneuvered.

"It might be where we're going if you tell me why you reconsidered and why you think you can help," he said, keeping his voice low. "Otherwise, it's where I'm going and a fairly insane place for you to go."

"You can't stop me," she said. "I have an English passport and I know it's good because you got it for me."

Looking suddenly for a place to talk further, Bill glanced at the empty breakfast room. The lights were off but through the open door he could see that the tables were set for the next morning.

"Come with me," he said. "Bring your bag."

He reached toward her and took her arm to guide her. She bounced to her feet. He led her into the breakfast room, flicked the light on, and sat her down at a table.

"You should be pleased. Why aren't you?" she asked.

"Why do you think you can help?"

"I know some people," she said.

"What people?"

"In East Berlin."

"Most people, if they knew you at all, think you're dead."

"They know I'm not," she announced quietly,

"*Who* knows you're not?"

"A few friends. They hate the communists now, too."

"How many is 'a few'?"

"Three. Maybe four."

"Boys? Men?"

"Girlfriends. All of them. They're jealous that I got out."

He waited.

"No man. No men. I swear it," she said, answering the question that he had not yet asked. It was not the first time she was one inquiry ahead of him.

"And how do they know? These 'girlfriends'?"

A long pause. "I visited once."

"You did *what*?"

"You heard me right, yes?"

"Yes. When did you visit?"

"About a year ago."

"Why?"

"I got lonesome."

"You never told me that you visited," Bill said his displeasure growing, as he carefully watched her face.

"You never asked," she said.

He leaned back in exasperation. He had this nervous habit of tapping with the fingers of his left hand on any available surface when he was annoyed. He was tapping now, and she read it.

"Well, damn it!" she said, suddenly furious and defensive, "What do you expect of me? To be a nun all my life? I love Berlin, too, like you say you do. I don't mind being away, living in England, but I don't like exile."

Cochrane tried to settle down. "How do you know I'm not going to beat the daylights out of you?" he asked.

"You won't. You're a gentleman."

"What makes you so sure?"

"Frau Swenson tells me. You rescued her, too. I know this."

He sighed. He shook his head. He was so exasperated that he nearly laughed. "Visiting Berlin could have gotten you killed, Sarah."

She shrugged and smiled. "Okay, so, yes, I know. But it didn't. I'm sitting here in front of you."

"You got lucky," he said.

"That or I'm careful and smart. Like you, maybe. How's that?"

Cochrane sat without speaking for a few moments, looking out into the empty lounge and hearing a few voices and the console radio from the bar. One part of him wanted to know what Lotte might be up to, whom she may have communicated with in the last twenty-four hours. The other part of him, his gut, told him that he had nothing to lose by letting her loose in East Berlin and reporting back. There was a spy for every ruined building in the city, hundreds of operations, wheels within wheels. He wasn't part of one that could be readily damaged.

If an operation with Lotte ran aground, not much would be lost. If she struck paydirt, could get some penetration into the advent of snipers, so much the better. In the end, she was at greater risk than he.

"I'm packed and ready to leave," she said.

"It will take a day or two to set up," he said.

"I should go home and wait?"

"No," he said. "You should stay here. Remain prepared."

"We will share a room?"

"Not in a hundred years," he said.

"See? A gentleman," she said.

No, but not looking for avoidable complications either, he thought to himself. But his next words went elsewhere. "I'll talk to Jessup at the reception desk. I'll get you a room here."

"For me at this fancy hotel?" she asked.

"Yes. Is there a problem with that?"

She shook her head and smiled widely for the first time for his entire visit.

"No," she said. "No problem with that." She looked around and continued to smile.

"Wow," she said.

"Sure," Cochrane said, standing.

Tired, he wandered over to the man at the front desk. There were three singles available. Two were luxury on the front of the building. The third was smaller, overlooking the garden in the back but with a private bath. That one was cheaper.

It was also the one Cochrane booked for his recruit. The American taxpayers were paying, after all, whether they knew it or not.

# Chapter 29
## East Berlin – August 1952

In the United States and England during World War II, snipers had usually been volunteers. But the Wehrmacht had often taken a solid marksman from the front and sent him back to Germany for specialized training. There, at special ranges bedecked with swastikas and portraits of Hitler, these elite soldiers learned the finer points of assassination from a distance, in addition to deception and concealment.

Wolfgang Reymann's three months of official sniper training followed this pattern. Yes, he had learned to shoot accurately in the forests of Bavaria, but during the war, he had sharpened his riflery skills with the guidance of experienced snipers who had returned from the eastern front and mastered the concepts of patience and perseverance.

At a special range in the forests near Hanover, he learned how to estimate distances with his naked eye, making the best use of the buildings and terrain around him, and even employing dummies that could be moved about with ropes and equipped with rifles that could be remotely fired with wires, thus drawing fire from enemy snipers that he would then quickly return for a kill.

One aspect of the "shooting academy" amused him endlessly.

There was a stretch of land with a replica of a Soviet village, complete with stores, homes, and churches. Students were required to shoot the enemy, represented by dummies and cardboard cutouts, as quickly as possible – men, women, and children alike – with hunting rifles as they appeared in windows, doorways, and behind trees.

His time spent on the frontlines added to his experience bringing down quick, agile game in forests, and he excelled at these exercises, though shooting representations of women and children gave him pause. Throughout the training, the instructors revised and rebuilt the landscapes to make them more challenging.

Now as Wolfgang returned to Berlin in August 1952, the training – much as he quietly hated it – did not seem so strange. The big difference here was that the Soviet village had been reimagined as an urban battlefield. It was located in a casually secured stretch of bombed-out rubble and crumbling buildings in northeast Berlin, half a kilometer north of the administrative enclave at Ruschestrasse in Friedrichshain.

Wolfgang's new instructors were primarily Soviet – tough, battle-scarred men who had served in south-central Europe. They were contemptuous of him and even contemptuous of the Stasi officers, Berg and Glienicke. The only person they showed any deference to was Mikhail Vishinski, the MGB officer who seemed to be running the urban sniper academy as much as anyone.

Comrade Reymann was assigned a room with two untalkative roommates named Kregg and Poulgar in the GDR government complex. The other men were in the sniper academy, too. Kregg was a tall, thin, blond man with a boyish face. He was from Berlin North, he had grown up there, "two minutes from Alexanderplatz", as he explained it. He was twenty-seven and somehow looked twenty. Poulgar was bigger and darker with wide shoulders and big arms. If Kregg resembled a stork, Poulgar resembled a bear. He was from the farm country of Schleswig-Holstein, in northwestern Germany near Denmark. His home area was now in the British zone.

It was a given that they were supposed to keep a close watch on each other and report any sign of hesitance or "subversion" in their new roles to the proper higher-ups. This, even though it was assumed by everyone that the "sniper recruit barracks" were electronically bugged. It was a drab, punishing life, with a morning rising bell at forty-thirty AM and a nighttime return to barracks and silence at seven PM. Frequently Wolfgang wished he had died in the war.

But training continued for three weeks. His ability to shoot sharpened, even if his desire to shoot was absent. Gradually, he began to regain his astonishing abilities with a sniper's rifle.

One day Vishinski moved Wolfgang and his bunkmates to their next stage of training. A Stasi guard took the four men by closed vehicle to what was known as the "proving grounds." This was an area of several dozen blocks that were still rubble from the war. They were not legally inhabited by anyone, but homeless squatters could occasionally be seen darting from building to building.

Vishinski led the three men up five flights of crooked stone steps in a former factory until they arrived at a large empty area on a cluttered top floor. There were gashes in the walls on all sides, big open spaces that had once been windows. There were smaller gashes, Wolfgang noticed, between the windows. He correctly guessed they were rifle portals. There were other Stasi men there in uniform and a squat, balding man of about fifty. Wolfgang saw that everyone was being deferential to him and someone addressed him as Herr Comrade Mielke. Wolfgang instinctively didn't like the looks of him, without even knowing that he was the number two Stasi commander in East Germany.

Mielke said little and when he did, it was to the Russian and the two German instructors. He let Vishinski, Berg, and Glienicke do the talking and small-time organizing. Mielke stood to the side with his arms folded behind his back and observed carefully. As Vishinski pontificated and spoke, Berg distributed Karabiners to all three of his students, plus a small leather ammunition pouch carrying twenty rounds.

"Urban sniping is different than battlefield sniping," Vishinski announced pompously. "You will not be on the move, you will have little foliage for concealment, your slip-away path will be among rubble and concrete. You will sometimes have as targets individuals on the street, sometimes individuals or their family members in their homes. You may shoot from some buildings that are prearranged and designated. Or you can find your own lair for a more efficient shot. Remember that the first round is the most important. Shooting a second or third round is a recipe for failure. Failure can mean escape for an enemy of socialism and a labor camp for the failed sniper. Clear?"

It was.

Much as Wolfgang tried to remain focused on what the batty little Russian was yelling about, he was already working up a hatred of the man. Hadn't Wolfgang been a warrior long enough? It was one thing to fight on the Russian front to defeat the Bolshevik hordes marching toward the Fatherland. But now to perform *for* them, along with contemptible, turncoat stooges like Berg and Glienicke? Ludicrous!

Then his eyes shifted to the pudgy little Kraut who was some sort of high-ranking Stasi – the man someone had addressed as "Mielke." Wolfgang's eyes narrowed on him, but he carefully hid any facial reaction. If he could have plugged a little traitor like that with a bullet in the stomach during the war, he would have earned an Iron Cross.

Well, he reasoned, if he could have crawled within three hundred meters with a Karabiner, he sure could have——

*"REYMANN! COMRADE REYMANN!"* exploded a voice near him. "Eyes front!"

In an instant, Vishinski's lecture had disappeared into the ether. The Stasi Berg, four inches shorter than Wolfgang, was in front of him in a fury, hopping up and down like an Australian kangaroo he was so mad, demanding to know where Wolfgang's mind had been.

"On the weather, Sir. Heavy heat and atmosphere today, Sir. Part of the calculation of a shot, Sir."

"Eyes, *front!*" Berg snarled again. "Or you'll go to the clinic for castration before the labor camp! Would you like that?"

"No, *Sir!*"

"Damned Bavarian swine!" Berg growled, stepping away. "Worse than a filthy gypsy or a Jew!"

Wolfgang riveted his eyes on Vishinski. They didn't waver. But he could see peripherally very acutely, a skill he had learned on the edge of various battlefields. The little sack of cow manure named Mielke was chuckling at him: an aggressive, stump-sized, fake socialist in a grey suit, necktie, and luxurious sheepskin coat!

How dare he? Had that little turd even lain in wait for four days in subzero tundra to whack a bullet through the throat of an enemy tank commander?

Probably not.

Glienicke was babbling away now. The Stasi man was adamant that a sniping team should not position itself in trees despite the fact that the significant elevation would improve the view of the enemy.

"Such a position in a tree will easily be identified and isolated, preventing a sniper from slipping away to fight another day."

Wolfgang again suppressed a smirk and kept a lid on his inner thoughts. He had once seen the Soviet enemy try exactly that in a battle in the Balkans. A dozen men in an advancing Wehrmacht company were sniped within five minutes by well-aimed head and chest shots. Then the company commander, a colonel, went down when he popped his head up from cover to take a peep through his binoculars. It was quickly apparent that the Germans were facing a double team of Soviet snipers, two sets of three, something they had heard about but had never before seen or encountered.

Efforts to dislodge the snipers from a thick line of forest proved fruitless, and worse yet resulted in the deaths of several German machine gunners. The unit lacked artillery or even heavy mortars to dislodge the enemy, so everyone hunkered down for several hours. A call to a different location summoned Wolfgang to the area.

Reymann assessed the situation. He knew he had to get closer to better assess the situation. He found five grenade bags and filled them with grass, adding helmets and using grease and oil to create what would appear like faces through distant sniper sights. faces. He left those behind with assistants while he carefully crawled forward during the night.

At dawn he was ready. When Wolfgang gave a prearranged signal, his assistants raised the dummies. They drew fire. Wolfgang identified where the enemy snipers were lodged as the upper branches of several trees swayed from the pressure waves of the gunfire. Wolfgang returned fire, as did several rifle teams supporting him. Soon the Russians were falling out of the trees like plump partridges.

Now here he was in Berlin in 1952, his eyes fixed like a rifle sight on another Russian whom he took to be an adversary. It hadn't taken much to rekindle the hatred that he had felt during the war.

Now Vishinski explained the day's exercise.

On all four sides of the building, there was a cityscape of rooftops in each direction. A crew of workers was stationed in four places. They had posted four wine bottles in various places at distances of two hundred to five hundred meters. Then the setup men had taken cover. Each of the three shooters would have two minutes in each window. The objective: hit as many as one could with the allotted sixteen rounds. The supervisory team stood in witness.

Vishinski held a stopwatch. He started the watch and signaled that the exercise, or competition, should begin. He and the two Stasi officers held binoculars and watched over the shoulders of the shooters.

Poulgar, who had served with the Wehrmacht's Third Mountain Division in Norway, went first. He hit a dozen bottles with sixteen shots.

Kregg, who had served with an SS division in Poland and Hungary, shot second and hit nine bottles with twelve bullets. He might have hit more but he had trouble finding the bottles.

Wolfgang approached the assignment with the skill of an accomplished expert. The Karabiner suddenly felt good in his hands – an extension of his body. He had a keen eye for the details of what lurked far away. He found his targets faster than the other men and used only five minutes and fifteen seconds to shatter all sixteen bottles.

The shooters broke down their weapons and cleaned them as their supervisors conferred over what they had seen. There was a special assignment to be had for a sniper in Berlin. The supervising team had intended the competition to go on for the rest of the week. But now there was a change.

Comrade Mielke was enthusiastic at what he had seen. The Bavarian peasant seemed gifted and oafish at the same time, skilled and malleable. Mielke approached Wolfgang when the weapons were turned over to a Russian armorer, a bullyboy, overweight MGB man named Mikho who had been waiting on the stairs.

The assignment was "offered" to Wolfgang.

With the runner-up prize being an assignment to a labor camp, he feigned gratitude and readily accepted. Several minutes later, their whole team was on an informal march back to the barracks a kilometer away. Kregg, the Berliner, fell into step with Wolfgang on his right side while Poulgar kept pace behind them, making sure everyone else was beyond earshot.

"We hate it here, too," Kregg said.

Wolfgang, fearing a trap, said nothing.

"Want to leave?" Kregg continued.

"All hail the socialist revolution," Wolfgang said.

Then he was startled. Poulgar had come up on Wolfgang's left side and was practically shoulder to shoulder, comrade to comrade, veteran subversive to new subversive, and disaffected soldier to disaffected soldier.

"One night this week, Comrade," Poulgar said. He had a low voice that seemed to come up out of the cratered asphalt. "We go out for beer? Or vodka?"

Some instinct within Wolfgang – boredom, fatigue, desperation, hope, or maybe all four – told him to take a chance. "Sure," he said. "How do we do that?"

Kregg smiled and made a sound that passed for a laugh.

"Same as always, *Scheisskopf*," Kregg answered. "We bribe the idiot guards. Then we go to a street place and drink."

# Chapter 30
## Cambridge and London - August 1952

Cochrane took Lotte to London the next day, not to Berlin.

There was an American special-operations office not far from the United States Embassy on Grosvenor Place. There Bill guided her to the care of a Mr. Nigel Samuels, a former engraver and silversmith in Vienna, who now worked with the embassy in London to assist certain individuals with new identification. Pictures were taken, as were fingerprints.

After a short conference among the three of them regarding her new name, the decision on her new name became counterintuitive. She would be Lotte again, this time with the last name of Schaaf.

Her only friends in Berlin, she said as they waited in a private room in Mr. Samuel's atelier, were a pair of German girls she had known since just after the war. She could stay quietly with them and prowl some of her old haunts.

"How far away are they from your old neighborhood?" Bill asked.

"They have a basement flat about five blocks south of the Schlesischer Bahnhof," Lotte said. She had lived all over Berlin before that, she reminded him, never more than a month or two at any one place, the longest being a single room on Chausseestrasse in the north of the city near Orienburger Tor, which was now a defunct U-Bahn Station.

"There's a border crossing right there, isn't there?" Cochrane asked.

"Yes. I used it when I visited a year ago."

"And you stayed with the same two girls?"

"Yes."

"They won't betray you?" Bill asked.

"They didn't last time," she said. Then, since he looked as if he wanted a better answer, she added. "They won't."

"What are these girls' names?"

"Why do you ask?"

"In case either one gets in touch with me," he said. "I think that's a fair question."

"Hana and Sonya," she said. "They're nice."

"How do you contact them?"

"They have jobs in the British zone," she said. "Hana works for a food company."

"In an office?"

"No. She's a shopgirl. In a store."

"And the other?"

"In a café," Lotte said. "She serves tables."

Bill drew a breath. One part of him was in open revolt with the other. Suddenly, her answers were too easy, too facile. Was it just that her personality was so different than his because she was so much younger and her war experience was different?

Was there something larger that he was missing?

Or was she completely untrustworthy and playing him along?

His gut remained on her side, but he had a growing number of misgivings.

Even her mission now seemed vague to him, and he had concocted it himself. Go back into your old stomping grounds, snoop, talk to people, see what you hear.

Simple, right? No, preposterous. Life wasn't that easy, and neither was espionage.

Or was it?

Then again, it wasn't that different from many other covert operations, looking for intelligence that was readily available but only for someone in a specific area and with feet on the ground and eyes on the street.

*Go. Look. Snoop. Ask questions. Listen. Report back.*

Sometimes the best espionage was the result of a simple, stultifying, daily routine.

"There are a lot of soldiers in the area where my friends live," Lotte had said earlier.

"What sort of soldiers?" Bill had asked.

"East German. Some Russian."

"Officers? Conscripts?"

"Both," she answered readily.

He continued to calculate as they sat in Nigel Samuels's office. Calculate and question.

"When did you see them last, Lotte? Your friends?"

"About six months ago."

"Really? Where?"

"Cambridge."

*"Cambridge!?* You never mentioned that."

"You never asked," she said, explaining this away the way she had dismissed another of her questionable activities.

"Did they visit you where you live?"

"No. They had friends at the university. They slept on floors in the dormitories."

"Where did they get the money to travel?" Bill asked.

"I told you. They work."

"And where did you get the money to travel to Berlin?" he asked.

"From you," she laughed. "You pay me."

"Of course," he sighed. She lit a cigarette, one that he had paid for one way or another.

"Can you tell me where they live?"

"No," she said. "It's in Friedrichshain. But I cannot give you an address. That would be betraying them."

"I understand," he said. "Don't turn up in the park with an easel and paints either," he said.

"Most of the people I knew when I was growing up in Hamburg are dead," she reminded Bill. "I have no family. All my friends were killed in the bombings. Berlin? I knew a few people, but it's been two years. My appearance is different. I will be fine."

"And former boyfriends?" he asked.

"Easy to avoid," she said. "And I have no desire to resume anything."

"You make it sound easy, Lotte."

"And you make it sound difficult," she said. "Complicated."

"That's because it is."

She laughed and stuck out her tongue, then laughed again.

He might have blown up, but the door opened. Nigel Samuels appeared, sat down next to them, and introduced Lotte to her new official identity, the official blue citizen identification card of the German Democratic Republic, hot off the forger's presses. Samuels had even worked some magic on it to make it appear weathered.

"Sorry to take so long," he apologized. "I needed to be sure the ink had set."

"Of course," Bill said.

Cochrane took it in his hands and examined the card. It was, indeed, an excellent product.

# Chapter 31
## Cambridge and Berlin – August 1952

Cochrane and Lotte spent the night at the University Arms again, separate rooms to be sure, and departed for RAF Molesworth the next morning. They caught an RAF freight flight early in the afternoon, one that had no passenger manifest, and which would ease past normal customs. The aircraft, a battered cargo Dakota, took them on the usual bumpy ride to Berlin.

On the flight, over the drone of the engines, he laid out his expectations and enough basic tradecraft so she could find her way back if everything blew up or even if everything didn't.

He handed her a small copy of *The Great Gatsby* that he had been carrying with him. Small pencil marks under certain letters in Chapter Seven spelled out the address of the Bar Ritter. In an emergency, she should find her way there, ask to see Helmut, and ask him to contact Dr. Kreitler at the Free University. Kreitler would be acting as a cut-out and contact Bill. In the odd event that Helmut was unavailable, she should talk to the piano player, a girl named Elfriede. She would be forewarned and know what to do. Bill's own backup in case something – ranging from abduction to garroting – had happened to him, would be Laura.

In case of an absolute disaster, such as Bill's death, Laura would contact the U.S. Embassy and the latter would contact a gentleman named William Harvey. Harvey would be in charge of damage control. He was rumored to be good at it.

If all was going well, and there was always the possibility that it would, she was to phone the number at the Bar Ritter every three days, ask to speak to the aforementioned Helmut, and inquire if a Frau Witte had been by. Helmut would say no and pass the word along to Bill that there was no problem. The check-in was recommended but not essential.

"I realize there are times and places when such a thing is impossible," Cochrane said.

"I get it," Lotte said.

"Does all that make sense?" Cochrane asked when the Dakota finally began a descent into Tempelhof. Most RAF flights went into Gatow now but this one, for so many reasons, was different.

"I suppose," she said.

"You 'suppose'?"

She nodded.

"Great," he said.

He handed her enough money in West German marks, British pounds sterling, and East German marks for her to navigate for two months. She was free to play the game for the full two months if she needed to, but they should arrange to meet after one and a decision would be made on how or whether to continue.

When the plane was on the tarmac and taxied to a stop, Bill made one more decision. He pulled the Browning out of his pocket along with a small packet of bullets. "Do you know how to use a pistol?" he asked.

"Yes."

"You don't have to take this," he said. "But I think it would be a good idea. A lot of women carry something in the Soviet zone. There's no implicit guilt in having protection."

She looked at it hesitantly and took it.

"Danke," she said.

He nodded.

Cochrane's man Kurt would be there to meet the aircraft. He was the perfect person to escort Lotte to the Eastern zone and drop her within a block of her destination. He was a physically powerful man, honest, loyal, tough as hell, and had an address in Friedrichshain, also, so he could not be accused of being suspicious if he were out of his neighborhood. Since he also normally worked in freight management at Tempelhof, there was nothing questionable about his presence at the airport.

Kurt was waiting by Cochrane's small, occasionally used office when he arrived with Lotte. Cochrane handled the introductions, then followed at a discreet distance as they left the airport and walked to the tram stop to travel to the East.

Cochrane felt there was a swarm of butterflies in his chest as he watched them leave. He stopped at Helmut's for a drink, said nothing about the operation being in progress, and went home. He remained by his home phone that evening and was relieved when it rang a few minutes past seven.

A gruff voice, Kurt, asked in German for a Herr Vincent Impellitteri concerning some lost shipments at Tempelhof. Bill politely responded that the caller had the wrong number. Kurt apologized and hung up.

Bill breathed easier. The call, using the name of the current mayor of New York City, meant that Lotte had arrived safely at her destination. Had there been a problem, Kurt had been instructed to use the name Wendel Wilkie and Cochrane would have rushed back to the airport.

Bill settled in with his family for the evening. There was even a set of lecture notes to prepare for his next class. It was tough going. He was convinced he was presiding over a disaster.

# Chapter 32
## East Berlin - August 1952

As a divided, nearly-obliterated Berlin climbed back to its feet after the war, informal little corner pubs called *Kneipen* came to life. At some West Berlin intersections, one could stumble across one on almost every corner. They were part of an underground economy that snaked very quickly into the "accepted but unofficial" everyday economy. They often emerged in the bombed-out remains of storefronts of which the owners had been killed. Residents who frequented the Kneipen tended to know each other. They chatted, conversed, had friendly and not-so-friendly arguments, and recovered from the stresses of daily postwar life.

But since all property had been turned over to the state in East Germany, the state was the owner of these properties in East Berlin. The state would have cracked down on the squatters setting up businesses, but bribes went up and down the line. The same people who were in charge of cracking down liked to go out for a drink now and then. So the Kneipen survived.

In the grayer areas, near the government installations and the secret military barracks, they flourished. It was dreary stuff at first, but Germans liked to drink and laugh and curse even in the worst of times.

They also liked to, and sometimes needed to, drink at all hours. For these circumstances, certain Kneipen remained open late, catering to a tougher clientele, and were located in seedier areas. These places served stiffer drinks, encouraged prostitutes, and were operated by black marketers who had links to the East German Communist Party.

It was one of these unnamed places that was frequented by newly recruited "special soldiers" who were bivouacked in Friedrichshain.

There was a place known as Der Rote Stiefel, The Red Boot, which was one of these late-hour joints. Karl, the barman and guiding genius, had hung a blood-stained Soviet army boot out a second-floor window using part of an old flagpole. This was his way of creating a sign and an unofficial name for the place. Here was a highly existential piece of sign-making: it could be interpreted as respectful of Red Army men who had fallen or a wish to see a greater number shot to death. Karl was occasionally asked about the meaning of the boot, its significance. But when asked, he responded with such a cold glare that no one ever asked twice.

Karl, a bald, three-hundred-pound, black marketer during the day, operated the place each evening from behind the bar. On summer nights he wore no shirt, only a vest, maybe to show off the Iron Cross that was tattooed on the upper left side of his chest, just above the heart. On his belt at the center of his back, he wore a Mauser. His place served vodka and more vodka, cheap Polish stuff that wasn't as cold as it should have been, but which served its purpose.

The three would-be Stasi snipers – Poulgar, Kregg, and Wolfgang – entered The Red Boot around nine thirty PM. The clientele was mostly men, most with East Bloc military haircuts, though there were a few working ladies around the back room.

There was a short bar on the right-hand side and a row of ten stools, four of them occupied, before the bar. Behind the bar, there were two broken mirrors pieced together and a row of bottles – no more than a dozen, no labels.

At the bar. a quartet of heavy men, some with missing limbs, were slumped toward their drinks, lost in gloomy silence, perhaps refighting battles, deaths, and losses that had long since been finally tabulated except for in their minds.

The Kneipen was long and narrow, brick walls exposed on both sides, areas of fresh plaster visible. On the left-hand side, there was a row of tables by the walls, some with two chairs, some with three. At the far end, the room broadened out. There were larger tables where groups could sit.

There was no music in the room. If one wanted music and a younger, less somber crowd the place to go to was the one across the street, the one called Die Edelweiss where congregated the dissatisfied students who barely remembered the war and the air raids. Over there at that more ebullient place, a kid with a harmonica played seditious American tunes every night. The conversation was livelier, with conversation on the present and the future. Here at The Red Boot, attention was on the past and any way to beat it to death or escape from it.

The conversation in the room dropped to nothing when the three young snipers entered the room. Karl stared at them through narrowed eyes. But Karl had seen Kregg and Poulgar before and knew they behaved and probably were not Stasi or MGB. They looked like special ops recruits because that's what they were. It was pretty straightforward.

Kregg gave a nod to the hefty German at the bar. Karl nodded back. A quick jerk of Karl's massive head indicated that the three new arrivals should sit in the front room near the wall. Since the three new arrivals were okay with Karl, they were okay with everyone else.

Kregg led his party in the direction Karl had indicated. They pushed two small tables together and shoved away a third, leaving a space so they could talk. Each of the men put some coins on the table. Kregg somehow had an American dollar bill. He added that to the pile.

Karl arrived with a bottle of vodka and three shot glasses. He scooped up the money. He lurched back to the bar.

Kregg poured generous shots all around at their table. The war veterans knocked them back.

Then Poulgar poured a round. They quickly one-gulped those down their throats, too. The vodka was rough and primitive. It felt like gasoline going down. That did not stop Wolfgang, however, from breaking into a grin with his two new friends and pouring a third round within the first ninety seconds at the table.

They leaned back. The vodka gave a quick buzz, a liquid blitzkrieg.

They felt better. More talkative. They looked at each other.

"Lousy Stasi," Kregg grumbled.

"Filthy Russians," Poulgar said.

Wolfgang's circumspection was gone. "I hate Vishinski," he said. He kept his voice low as did the other two men at the table. "He tried to shoot German children in the village where I was."

*"Peacetime?"* Kregg asked, mildly astonished.

"About two weeks ago. I hit his arm to stop him. You don't shoot children!" Wolfgang said. "I never shot children. Either of you?" he asked.

"Never!" said Kregg.

Poulgar was adamant in agreement, even proud. "I zipped enemy soldiers," he said. "Combatants. Men in uniforms with weapons who would have killed me!"

"Vishinski is a bastard son of a whore!" Kregg said.

"Worse than those two Stasi queers," Poulgar offered.

The three men poured another round of vodka. It wasn't Warsaw's finest, but it was among Warsaw's most effective. They sat quietly and considered the situation for several minutes.

"Vishinski was talking about hurting men and their families the other day," Wolfgang said. "You heard him. I won't do it. Either of you want to murder families? Wasn't there enough of that during the war? Now they want to continue during peacetime?"

"Refusal gets you sent to a labor camp. Or a gulag in Siberia," said Kregg.

Finally, the same thought came to all three.

It was Kregg who spoke first. "I'll be damned to hell before I work for the bloody Russians!" he said. "Let's kill all three of them and get the devil out of Berlin!"

"How do we do that?" Poulgar asked as Wolfgang listened intently.

"I know the routes. I grew up here," he said. "Passages between buildings. Sewers. Cellars."

"Is that the vodka talking or you talking?" Wolfgang asked.

"It's me talking, plus *this!*" Kregg said. With a speed of his right hand that astonished even the other two men, Kregg came up with a small compact pistol, a Mauser, which had been concealed somewhere within his clothing. He spun it around as a magician would, then it was gone, stashed away until he needed it next. "I didn't fight a war to be a prisoner of the Red Swine for the rest of my life," he said.

"So? Who's with me? We do what we need to do, right?"

Neither Poulgar nor Wolfgang said a word. But their agreement hung in the air over the table as final shots of vodka were poured around the table.

# Chapter 33
## West Berlin – August 1952

*Wo ist Dr. Walter Linse?*

Five weeks after the brazen abduction of Dr. Linse, the question of his whereabouts continued to resonate in diplomatic circles in Berlin as well as police stations, diplomatic events, bars, and rathskellers. Students at the Free University continued to ask the question as well as agitate for a response.

*Where is Dr. Walter Linse?* Since July 8, West Berliners had never stopped inquiring. A courageous anti-communist journalist, he had within a few weeks become Western Europe's most prominent casualty of the Cold War: every few weeks a dissident or someone suspected of being disloyal to Stalin disappeared, turned up floating in a polluted river, or went out a high-story window of a mental hospital – "jumped or pushed," as the saying went. Linse was merely the most recent victim, but he was also the most prominent.

American diplomats in Washington and Berlin continued to send protest notes to the Soviets. Moscow and East Berlin never missed a chance to decline to respond. Cochrane admired the way the French had just gone ahead and dynamited their Radio Berlin antenna. The Russians understood the debris that remained from the antenna more than they had understood the polite requests.

West Berlin's Police Chief Johannes Stumm had set his best men on the case. By mid-August his men had come up with some explanations of what had happened and why.

"Come into my office and take a look at a piece of crap that I just received from our friend with the cigarettes, big, bulging eyes, and fondness for cowgirls," Bernie Kreitler said to Bill as Cochrane exited his class the following Friday. "You'll hate it."

"Sounds like I have no choice," Bill answered.

"That's correct," Kreitler said.

Kreitler had locked his office door. He opened it with a key he kept on a gold-colored chain attached to the belt loops on his pants. When he stepped in, the door of the Yale safe was a quarter open, just the way he left it. Kreitler reached into the safe without looking, angrily yanked out three pieces of paper that were stapled together and handed them to Cochrane.

"What's this about?" Bill asked.

"You'll see. Sit over there and take a look at this," Kreitler said in a smoldering, level confiding murmur that suggested an alliance between them. He indicated the armchair adjacent to his desk as what he meant by "over there."

"Won't take long," Kreitler said. "Will take even less time to get the essence and then several weeks to get the taste of bile out of your mouth. You're to read it once and then I'm supposed to get rid of it. "Ready? Go."

Bill, not knowing what to expect or even what this was about, said nothing.

He sat. He read.

Kreitler returned to a spot behind his desk, stood with his arms folded, and glowered as he watched Bill read.

It was the Linse case again, Day One to Yesterday. There had been warning labels and handling instructions, Bill could see, but they had been torn off. When Bill's peripheral view hit Kreitler's desk, he saw a sturdy new ashtray with a crumpled paper in it that looked as if it had been exactly those labels.

Bill dug in, hoping for something positive but knowing both from gut feeling and long experience that it would be just the opposite.

There was nothing in the file that was a challenge to understand, but not much to like, either. There was, in fact, much to hate. Bill hadn't gone two or three paragraphs into the communication before feeling his own anger rise.

West Berlin's Police Chief Johannes Stumm had assigned sixteen of his best agents, fourteen men and two women, to the Linse abduction case within hours after the kidnapping occurred. Now here it was mid-August, and his team had produced many unpleasant answers.

On the previous day, Chief Stumm had reported confidentially in German to Mayor Reuter what he knew and what he didn't know. Reuter had sent the report along a classified chain that included U.S. High Commissioner Walter J. Donnelly who directed it to William Harvey, after one of the ladies with a high-security clearance, a Bryn Mawn graduate named Bess, who worked as a security translator under the initials *BGF*, had translated it into English. Harvey had sent an English-language copy as well as the original to Kreitler, who read both, just in case there had been a variance of meaning.

There hadn't been.

The report had arrived during Cochrane's Friday morning class. Kreitler had read it with outrage in both languages, admired the translation despite the content, and then loitered like an angry, caged bear outside of Bill's lecture hall until the day's discussion of F. Scott Fitzgerald and *The Great Gatsby* had serenely glided past its many green lights.

The three-page report declared that four East German criminals had done the kidnapping. They had been recruited while in prison and specially trained by the Stasi for the assignment.

Bill waded through the muck of the document.

**"This sweeping inquiry, conducted by scores of Berlin's most skillful police officers, represents a combination of exhaustive effort, the study of hundreds of leads, and the application of all modern police methods. The investigation has disclosed not only the names of the four principal kidnappers but also of thirteen other hand-picked and professional outlaws and gangsters who played important roles in one of the most brazen and repugnant crimes in the history of Berlin.**

**"The four East Berliners who had been convicted previously of charges of murder, burglaries, embezzlement, and safecracking are:**
   **Harry Liedtke, 22, whose most recent address is 17 Barnim Strasse, Berlin-Friedrichshain.**

Erwin Knispel, 50, who has many addresses in East Berlin.

Herbert Nowak, 27, whose most recent address was Heidenfeld Strasse, Berlin-Friedrichshain, near the Zentralviehhof.

Josef Dehnert, 22, who has changed his address frequently in East Berlin.

**THESE FOUR men are identified as part of a criminally organized and criminally subsidized ring of kidnappers approved, sponsored, and directed by the DDR Ministry for State Security which has become widely known as the dreaded MSS, [Editor's note: colloquially "Stasi" – *BGF*] which not only is modeled after the MGB, the Ministry of State Security of the Soviet Union, but is an integral, thriving organ of the Russian police state.**

They were aided in the planning and execution by thirteen other East Germans, Chief Stumm's report concluded. All were members of a covert East German ring whose code name was *Weinmeister,* which Bess, or BGF, was helpful enough to translate as Wine Master, for anyone who might have missed it.

"Weinmeister is sponsored, directed, and financed by the East German Ministry of State Security," the report said. "Participants earned five hundred to a thousand "East marks" for each kidnapping. They are allowed a profitable sideline: the black marketeering of cigarettes, silk stockings, and coffee.

Stumm offered a 5,000 DM reward for each of the kidnappers. He also announced the arrest of three minor accessories to the crime. One, described as the mistress of a ring member, had been caught just as she was plotting the abduction of another prominent anti-communist in the British zone.

Onto the conclusion went the report as Cochrane read carefully, keenly searching for any small detail that might be of use in the future. He reacted with extreme distaste to the laundry list of accessory lowbrow felons who had trailed and tracked Walter Linse and set him up for the strongarm gang that snatched him.

Many frightened Berliners witnessed the abduction from beginning to end. More than five dozen citizens have come forward to assist West Berlin police in the identification and arrest of the perpetrators. This crime, of which the Soviet authorities have repeatedly denied knowledge, was aided and abetted by the following thirteen accomplices, all of whom have criminal records:

Paul Liebig, 38 to 42. This man, an official of the MSS in charge of the Unsichtbar-Gruppe Weinmeister. It is not even known whether Liebig is his correct family name.

Fritz Phielmaier, alias Paul Schmidt, aged 31, last known to have lived at 10 Weinmeister Strasse, Berlin-Mitte. He is an assistant to Paul. He is also a drug addict and claims to be a physician. In 1946 he, Phielmaier, was tried, convicted, and sentenced to three years in prison in the British zone for illegally using the title "Doctor." Later that same year Phielmaier was declared to be not completely sane and was committed to a Schleswig sanatorium for observation. He escaped May 20, 1947.

Hans Richard Kleinman, alias Bauer, aged 30; many addresses, the most recent of which was 13 Lottum Strasse, Berlin-Mitte. Kleinman, a pimp and professional criminal, is wanted for the theft of $220 and DM 20 from a Swedish tourist couple, the crime committed on August 18, 1950, in Berlin-Steglitz. Subsequently, he was arrested by Soviet sector police and later released.
Sonja Hofman, 23, who has relatives at Rigaer Strasse, Berlin-Friedrichshain. Sonja has lived with Harry Liedtke at 17 Barnim Strasse. She is engaged to the criminal Liedtke. Occasional prostitute.

Else Kleinman, wife of Hans Kleinman, 25 or 26 years of age, often pimped out by her husband Hans. ARRESTED.

## REVOLT IN BERLIN – Part One         NOEL HYND

Dagobert Knoblauch, 22 to 23, formerly of Anklamer Strasse, Berlin-Mitte, another paid gangster known to have been held in the Dirkenstrasse prison in February 1950.

Fritz London, 26, last known to reside at 24 Immanuelkirch Strasse, Berlin-Prenzlauer Berg with another adult male. Surname assumed to be fraudulent. Trafficker in stolen Czech handguns. Crossdresser and possible homosexual. ARRESTED.

Walter Werfel, [personal data unknown] but whose records show an arrest more than two years ago by East sector police in Berlin-Treptow for stealing and fencing automobiles. Sentenced to ten years in Barnim Strasse prison, recruited, and released by Stasi after seven months.

----- Leiser, first name unknown, 35, Pistorius Strasse, Berlin-Weissensee. Thief. ARRESTED.

----- Skrolek, first name unknown, {female} 30 to 35, sister of Wladimirowicz Feder.

----- Saurag, first name unknown, 35, address unknown. Pickpocket.

"The West Berlin police have formal evidence that this MSS-sponsored and protected kidnap organization is financed by the sale of great quantities of cigarettes, coffee, and silk stockings on the black market," the report added.

"These then are the sort of people – all of them paid, guarded, and supported by the Soviet-controlled and dominated Stasi of East Berlin and the GDR – who assaulted and kidnapped the unfortunate Dr. Linse. Arrest warrants have been signed. Those named who have not yet been apprehended will be arrested and prosecuted if they are ever seen in West Berlin.

As for Dr. Linse himself, his precise location and physical condition are the subject of an additional report. Suffice it to say that we know that he is in Hohenschönhausen. He is being held under a false name. For a month this enabled representatives of Soviet Russia and communist East Germany to maintain the fiction that they did not know "officially" any details of Linse's whereabouts.

It was signed,

*- Johannes Richard Reinhold Stumm, Polizeipräsident in Berlin an der Spitze der West-Berliner Polizei.*

Cochrane looked up. He handed the report back to Dr. Kreitler.

"The Russians have a genuine respect for the methods of diplomacy and a cynical contempt for its use," Bill said sourly. "Don't they?"

"You're given to bouts of understatement today, aren't you?" Kreitler said.

"Your three pieces of paper rather knocked the wind out of me," Cochrane said.

Kreitler, still standing, extended his hand. He took the pages back from Cochrane. "You need to see this again?" Kreisler asked.

"No. But may I see the original German if you have it?"

A beat, then, "Sure," Kreitler said. He gave it to Bill. He stood and waited as Bill checked it.

The translation matched the original. BFG had done an excellent job. Bill handed the German copy back to Kreitler who crumpled them. He placed them in the ashtray, his new document incinerator, and set them ablaze with a lighter.

The two men watched the flames rise, Cochrane in the armchair, Kreitler standing with arms folded. Neither said anything. Each man was alone with his own thoughts yet had a pretty solid guess that the other man was on a similar path and letting his mind flow in certain directions.

Cochrane kept his eyes on Kreitler. Finally, the flames ebbed and the smoke dispersed. Kreitler's gaze went to Cochrane and their lines of sight smacked right into each other's.

"How's your wife?" Kreitler asked.

"She's good. Thank you," Bill answered.

"Your charming little girl? Caroline?"

"A joy. Fine and dandy," he said.

A slight hesitation followed, enough for Bill to know the question that was on its ominous way. "What about this 'other' young lady of yours?" Kreitler asked in a lowered voice. "*Sarah?* Isn't that what we're supposed to call her?"

"She's been gone for a week," Bill said. "Eight days, actually."

"There was a safety signal, wasn't there?" Kreitler asked.

"There was one, yes," Bill said. "But so far, no signal, no word. Nothing," he said.

Several more seconds passed between them.

"Wow," Kreitler said, still in a hushed tone.

"Yes," Cochrane answered. "'Wow' is right."

The next day the report was released to the newspapers and magazines published around the world.

The next day, also, Lotte – or Sarah – continued to be missing, much like many other women who disappeared into the East and were never seen or heard from again.

# Chapter 34
## East Berlin – August 21, 1952

For more than a week, Lotte had wandered her old neighborhood and those adjacent in East Berlin, sometimes in the evening with her girlfriends, sometimes during the day by herself. She purchased a gray cap to wear and a long summer dress at a used-clothing store. She tried to blend in. There was an irony to what she was doing. The more she wanted to break out and break free, the more she needed to go drab, gray, and gritty and blend in with the city around her.

At a coffee bar on the Kommandstrasse one afternoon when she was alone, she bought three cigarettes and drank a sour coffee. The counterman was a short, scarred man with both outer ears missing, probably from the war since he was wearing an old military hat with all the insignia removed. He introduced himself as Peter and said that he had been to Moscow with the Wehrmacht during the war. He showed her his left hand. There were two missing fingers.

"Russian frostbite," he said. "You alone?" he asked.

"I'm joining friends in a few minutes," she answered.

"Here?"

"At a friend's flat."

"Want to earn some money?" Peter asked. "I lost my ears. I lost my fingers. I have the rest of me."

Lotte finished her coffee and hurried off.

There were even more military and police uniforms in the area than she remembered, a signal perhaps of more unmarked barracks and installations. Bill Cochrane had frequently advised her that much valuable intelligence was right out in the open. One only had to be observant.

Her girlfriends said there were military institutions nearby, but they were often unmarked. The new German soldiers were undisciplined, they warned her, and they paid off their commanders so they could go out at night and carouse.

Women were safe if they were with a soldier and not safe if they weren't.

"That's how life works here now," Hana told her.

Yet oddly, after she had spent several days in East Berlin, she started to better understand how it survived and how much it had changed in two years. Lotte looked carefully at her immediate surroundings, the streets that were still in rubble, and Friedrichshain's old run-down streets, the twisted prewar lampposts that had survived. But she also sensed the melancholic vitality of some of the regulars in Berlin's bars and cafés. The people she met may not have looked happy, but they seemed resigned to being there. Maybe, she concluded, they were happy to have just survived the war, like she was.

While looking for links to the military that she might exploit, she could barely ignore the misty, cobbled corners in the morning, the people in bars, in clubs, at work, and on the street. East Berlin captured the essence of the culture and survival that was the way of life on the other side of the internal border, including the brazen lawlessness and oppression.

There were hungry, swooping pigeons on brooding, battered streets and the occasional new Skoda, driven no doubt by a member of the Communist Party. There were handsome teenage boys with fake Princeton sweatshirts – all of them aspiring to emigrate – and there were sultry, reflective women deep in their own thoughts in cafés, sipping ersatz coffee as she had. They smoked and waited for some man to miraculously deliver them to the other side of the country. Or even farther.

Frequently, she would look at people and wonder how they had landed in this place. She knew her own backstory but didn't know anyone else's. She carried the pistol, the Browning, that her mentor had slipped to her. She wondered how many other women in East Berlin carried a weapon out of the daily fears they endured. She equally prayed that she would not have to use it. She kept having the urge to paint or sketch but suppressed it.

She sighed. She was getting nowhere with Mr. Lewis's assignment. She had even been unable to find a secure telephone to call in. Well, she decided to herself, she would give this the rest of the month and see what she could unearth.

*

In the private room where they sat, a small restaurant two blocks from the Bar Ritter, Bill Cochrane and Helmut could hear the occasional taxi or truck rumble by. Bill had been back in Berlin long enough now so that he could tell the military vehicles from the civilian and the American from the British or even the occasional French. Russian vehicles had their own grinding socialist-paradise sound, every motor seeming to be the first cousin of a tractor on a Bulgarian wheat collective. Out of caution, however, every time a vehicle stopped, and footsteps emerged, and a door slammed, they held their conversation.

Of the two tables and eight chairs in the room, there was one unifying constant: nothing matched. Then again, why would it?

There was a long pause. "Did I ever tell you about her mother?" Helmut asked, looking up from his drink with tired eyes. "What happened to her, I mean?"

"No."

"Raped and murdered. Probably tortured, too. Russians," he said. There was something hideous about the way Helmut just blurted it out after years of knowing Cochrane. Only seven words. They told the whole story, or at least enough for Bill to understand. There was suddenly a heavy strain upon Helmut's face and a line of sweat across his forehead, even though the room was far from hot. His eyes looked half-dead as he turned them back to Bill Cochrane. Bill thought he saw a deep sorrow in them, one that might never lift. To their left, a curtain rustled in an evening breeze.

"You want to know more?" Helmut asked.

"Only if you wish to talk about it," Bill said.

"Not much to talk about, is there?" he confided with a grunt. "She, her name was Marta, disappeared in May of 1945, about a month after the Red Army came to town. Went out for bread one morning. Never came back. I went through hell, Bill, and so did my little girl. Police didn't do much." He paused. "Her body was found in some debris in the Eastern zone three weeks later when some rubble women were clearing a street." There was a long pause. Helmut's two hands met on the counter, and he turned toward Bill with eyes that were now moist. "Just because it was Marta's body doesn't mean there was anything that even I could recognize," he said softly. "Know what I mean?"

"Dear God," Bill said. He put his arm across Helmut's shoulder. "Yes, I know."

"That's all there is, Bill. Honest. Maybe there's more, but I'm determined not to remember, see?"

"I see," Cochrane said.

Helmut never drew the smoking gun connection which tagged his wife's final horror and death to the Russians, but Bill had no desire to pursue it. It was what it was and when talking about an abducted woman's death in the Soviet zone, even if a conclusion was wrong, it was usually at least partially right.

A bittersweet smile returned to Helmut. He continued in English. "You know the thing is, I'm going to tell you, Elfriede is a little spirit of her mother. A ghost. I look at her and she resembles Marta. Eerie but beautiful, you know? So this is with me every day." A pause, then, "She talks to me more and more about going to America someday. I'd miss her so bad that it would hurt. But maybe someday, if we continue to work together, you can pull a string. That's the phrase, isn't it? Pull a string. You know?"

"Maybe two strings, and yes, that's the phrase. But I can't promise."

"Yes, sure, I know this."

Then quickly, in less time than it would take to tie a shoelace, Helmut's suppressed anger was back. The image of his wife's death kept revisiting him, over and over and over.

"I don't forget, Bill," he said, talking straight on as he poured himself what remained in the bottle. His voice stiffened and so did his shoulders. "And I don't forgive, neither. I've been biding my time, Bill. Laying low. Watching. Making notes on the people I see. I've been waiting for the moment that I can really hurt them, those Russian bastards. I'm out for blood if you want to know the truth. I'll bide my time, but in the end, I'm going to hurt those bastards."

"I understand," Bill said.

Cochrane fell silent for a moment, then made a critical decision. He grabbed a paper napkin that was on the table and wrote his home address on it, although with a variation. He handed it to Helmut.

"What's this?" Helmut asked.

"Where I live. In case of extreme emergency. Get me. Pound on the gate, scale the wall, kick the door in, but get me if ever the need arises. Okay?"

"Okay."

"I reversed the three digits of the street address," Cochrane said. "Memorize the address correctly then destroy the napkin. I did it that way so even if there's a mess-up, the address stays secure."

Helmut looked at it and nodded. "Nice neighborhood."

"Thanks. The house belonged to some big-shot Nazi who stole it from the rightful owners. The army seized it in 1945."

Helmut snorted. "Yeah. Sure. Why not?"

They laughed.

Helmut grabbed the glass and finished his whiskey. His gaze went far away, then came back again. He turned to Cochrane. Their eyes met in silence.

"Hey, Bill," Helmut asked. "I can ask you something?"

"Of course."

"This girl you sent into the East zone? The one who was supposed to give signal calls to me? I don't know her name."

"I haven't heard from her," Bill said, correctly anticipating the eventual question.

Another several seconds. Not a word from Cochrane.

"And that's why you give me this address?"

Cochrane nodded.

Then, "Worried?" Helmut asked.

"Damned right I am," Cochrane said. "I'm responsible if she's in over her head. Want to know the truth? I was a damned fool to send her! Crazy kid but I liked her. Thought she'd be good at this filthy game. I should have stuck to Sinclair Lewis and Scott Fitzgerald, Helmut. I'm *very* worried, Helmut. Believe me."

Helmut nodded thoughtfully. "Yeah," he said. "Russian butchers with their inbred bastard Stasi lapdogs!"

He slammed his whiskey glass down so hard that the table shook. Abruptly, Helmut stood. "Come on, friend. Let's get out of here before I see a Russian or one of their lackeys and kill him."

# Chapter 35
## East Berlin, August 1952

Two evenings later, Lotte and her friends happened into a dingy drinking spot in Friedrichshain. It was called Die Edelweiss. It drew her in because there were lively sounds emanating from it, the sound of some sort of cool music, and the voices sounded young. It was a far cry less than twenty meters from a sinister place across the street that had a blood-stained red boot hanging out of a second-story window as a sign. She had glanced into Der Rote Stiefel, as the locals called it. She found it full of frightening men, crazy dangerous war veterans, men who sometimes ground females to a pulp. She knew better than to enter a place where a single woman might never reemerge alive, much less unharmed. Die Edelweiss felt much more receptive.

"Give it a shot," she told herself. Lotte and her two friends went in.

In a cramped and cluttered room, lit by candles on wine bottles and furnished with battered tables and chairs, they encountered a young man named Oskar. Oskar said he was happy he had visited East Berlin, but he had no intention of staying. Lotte and her friends were at a set of long, narrow, crowded tables, a dozen people at each: students, workers, sinister types, and even a few men with neckties, all sitting elbow to elbow together. The air of the place was very anti-government. The younger people wanted something more than Soviet-style oppression. Hana and Sonya, both of whom worked in the British zone, had already had enough time in the Western zones to grasp the huge differences between East and West Berlin and the philosophies of those who governed them. They had been filling Lotte's ear since she arrived. They had turned into anti-left dissidents. Their message was sinking in.

Lotte, meanwhile, was starting to develop an enhanced vision of her surroundings, something she had picked up from

## REVOLT IN BERLIN – Part One          NOEL HYND

Bill Cochrane. She often watched what was going on in the background when something important played out in the foreground. And she watched for small details, "little things that told a big story" her control had said.

Oskar, who looked as if he were in his mid-twenties, had the nerves of a professional troublemaker and hadn't yet learned to keep it under wraps in a country that was less than free and democratic. He had shaggy blond hair, a nose that looked as if it had been punched a few times, and round wire-rimmed glasses – the same type that Trotsky had worn, which sent a message and not a good one, as Trotsky was still viewed as the "anti-Stalin" by Stalinists.

Oskar was a student of how the world worked and didn't mind showing off his wisdom to the girls or guys or men with greasy neckties or anyone else who would listen. Most people in this place were talking in low murmurs. Not Oskar. He was a few decibel levels above everyone, though there was another kid across the room who was doing more than okay playing American movie tunes on a harmonica. He had an audience about the size of Oskar's. One half of the room was tuned in to Oskar, the other to the boy with the tin sandwich.

Oskar said he was from Magdeburg in central East Germany. "But I'm on my way to the West," he boasted. "I have an uncle in Amsterdam. I'm going to visit and not going to leave."

Oskar had brought a girl with him. She was a good five to seven years younger than he, and probably the prettiest female in the place. She had her head on his shoulder, love in her dewy eyes, and her arm linked around his, as if she didn't want to let her escape ticket to Holland disappear into the mist.

"You should keep your plans quiet," said another young man. "The snitches are everywhere."

"Screw 'em! I'll be gone by noon tomorrow," Oskar said. "Ugly Ulbricht is a pig's ass. Why should I be governed by a pig's posterior?"

There was nervous laughter around Oskar's part of the room, except from the men in the narrow neckties. One of them got up abruptly and left, his drink unfinished. Lotte watched the way the man purposefully left – the stride, the immediacy – and she smelled trouble coming.

Oskar then unveiled something that was not exactly a state secret, but which was not often discussed in a public place of assembly. Namely, the overall success of the inner German border fortifications had backfired on the Ulbricht government. Although the East Germans had slapped a fortified set of barrier strips between East Germany and West Germany, the Ulbricht government still had not done anything about Berlin. They – with shortsightedness and incompetence once again in play – had made the situation worse for themselves. Nothing could stop young East Germans from traveling to their capital, East Berlin, then strolling casually by foot into West Berlin and proceeding as quickly as possible to Berlin rail or Allied-protected highways to flee to the West. Hundreds of thousands of young educated East Germans were doing this, some settling as far away as Canada and the United States, who were accepting the relatively easy immigration from northern Europe.

Lotte watched carefully now. The brash kid with the harmonica got to his feet and began to wander the room, bringing music, warmth, and mirth with him. The man with the tie who had departed shuffled back in, trying to look casual. Two servers circulated. Someone relit two of the candle-in-wine-bottle lamps and the lighting changed.

*Gemütlichkeit*, all around. Solid cheer. For several minutes, it could have been very pre-1933. Then outside the bar, quiet as a wolf in a Bavarian forest, a gray car pulled up to the curb. Two large men in long coats jumped out while a driver remained. Lotte could see them clearly through the half-window in front of the bar. The men barreled forward through the door, knocked over anyone they wanted to, and came straight for the table where Oskar, the dissident chatterbox, was holding court.

Someone yelled, "Stasi!" and within a second the room exploded.

Some of the girls screamed as one of the Stasi pulled out a truncheon. Some of the young men tried to slow the two intruders by blocking their path, but the men in the long coats threw them aside like dolls. Oskar turned and saw the threat. Lotte could see his face, the expression leaping from bold confidence to fear. Hana and Sonya joined the screams and Lotte tried to move forward to put up a defensive arm in front of Oskar, but it was too late. Berlin of the early thirties had turned into the Berlin of the late thirties.

The first man grabbed Oskar by the neck, crunching a grip on him, and hauling him forward. His girl tried to help him, but with his free hand, the man holding Oskar pushed the girl hard, propelling her backward several feet. The assailant then kneed Oskar in the midsection and then the groin. Oskar howled in fear and pain as the man punched him repeatedly in the face and head.

There were two gashes suddenly on Oskar's face, one on his cheek, the other on his forehead. Blood flowed. One eye was already shut. The man who held him threw him toward the front door. The second man beat back the crowd. The second man drew a pistol and fired a shot in the air. Then another.

The crowd of young people stampeded toward the exits but changed directions as the first Stasi agent dragged Oskar out to the street. Lotte followed the melee as it rolled out of the bar.

The second agent knocked over two girls as he closely followed. The first agent threw Oskar to the pavement. When the boy tried to scramble to his feet, the first man grabbed him and hurled him forward. Oskar crashed his head against the side of the car.

Oskar went into a turtle position and tried to cover his head, but the Stasi kicked him, their shoes landing with loud thumps. His screams and pleas did nothing to stop the beating. From the bar across the street, The Red Boot, several larger men poured out. Then, the crowd from the tough-guy bar coalesced and moved as one. These were men who felt they had already been betrayed by their government and had no love for the new oppressors. They charged.

One of the Stasi picked up Oskar and tried to force him into the car. Seeing a hostile crowd surging from across the street, the Stasi lost interest in arresting Oskar and instead rifled his pockets, coming away with what was obviously his travel money. Oskar pleaded with them not to take the money, but the larger of the two men threw a fist that uppercut into his jaw. He smacked against the car again and slumped down.

By this time, the crowd from across the street had surrounded the car. One man had climbed on top of the hood and another old soldier from The Red Boot was mounting the car's roof. Oskar lay on the sidewalk, clutching his injuries, and rolling in agony. His girl finally reached him.

Lotte's indignation finally bubbled over. She circled behind the car. She slapped the rear trunk of the car as it tried to move forward. Then the auto jerked backward, trying to escape the mob that surrounded it and shake off the combatants that had climbed onto it.

The car hit Lotte hard. She stagged backward.

Someone with strong male hands caught her from behind and steadied her. She kicked at the car and missed. The two men who had been on it fell off. The car began to move. Lotte's hand came out of her pocket with the Browning pistol. She didn't care what the Stasi did to her. She would bloody them just as they had bloodied the young man from Mecklenburg.

From behind her came a powerful arm on her right side. It pushed her arm downward toward the sidewalk before she could pull the trigger. A male head came close to her ear.

"Nein, nein, nein!" the man said. "Don't do it.! They'll come back and kill you! They'll shoot everyone!"

Lotte tried to protest and push him away. But his hand covered her mouth, silencing her. She tried to bite him. It didn't work. His other hand took Bill Cochrane's pistol away, his fingers easily peeling hers away from the weapon as he took possession.

The Stasi car pulled away. Oskar remained on the sidewalk trembling. An array of bottles flew through the air from the crowd toward the unmarked police car.

Most missed, crashing onto the sidewalk and street. Two hit the escaping car.

On the sidewalk, Oskar whimpered. Two of the old soldiers from the bar tended to him. A woman in Der Edelweiss emerged with ice. Oskar's girl was sobbing. Lotte turned, trying to make sense of what she had seen, a flash riot, a Stasi assault, and an angry assemblage of citizens with nowhere good to go.

Lotte looked at the man who had restrained her. He had a strong body and a steady face. No discernible wounds, no mean expression. A former soldier, no doubt. Civilian clothes: state-issued. Then he gave her a slight smile.

Two other men of similar size and build settled in behind him. His friends, she assumed.

"There will be a better time for revenge," Wolfgang said to Lotte. "That time is not now."

Wolfgang handed back her pistol. She quickly pocketed it.

Shaken, her two friends, Hana and Sonya, came to her side. For a long moment, no one said anything. A beautiful night had turned into an ugly nightmare.

"We are drinking across the street," Wolfgang finally said, indicating. "Join us for one vodka?" he asked. "You three ladies."

"*That* place?"

"Even Stasi is afraid to go in," Wolfgang said with a laugh. "We sit in there at night and make plans. We drink and tell dirty jokes about the Stasi, the army, the Russians and the government. It's safe for friends. Come with us, hey?"

Lotte, still shaken, glanced at her two friends. Hana suddenly had a mischievous glint in her eye. She gave Lotte a small quick nod.

*REVOLT IN BERLIN* – Part One          NOEL HYND

Wolfgang smiled. His eyes danced. Lotte eased. Lotte looked back to Wolfgang.

"Sure," she said. "*Danke.* Why not?"

**No caption, just a suggestion that East Germany was a warm and fun place.**

# Chapter 36
## East Berlin – August 1952

They navigated a crumbling, creaking stairway as they walked up to the sixth floor in suffocating, late-summer heat. They were five men, two Russians and three Germans, all armed, sweating like the devil, and all wishing they were somewhere else. They were in a single-file parade that might have been a cortege, but the funeral had not yet happened. Men would die that day and maybe a woman would as well. But no one yet knew where and how.

Vishinski led the way, cocky, brutish, and in civilian gear as he so often was. He wore a long coat. It concealed his sidearm, his Tokarev TT-33 which was on his right hip. A smaller piece of artillery, an eight-round Korovin pistol was on his left ankle.

He reached the top floor, hardly breathing. "Hurry, hurry," he said to his followers in heavily accented German. He wondered why Germans had a reputation for punctuality when he had to kick their defeated backsides so often, particularly these three men: Reymann, Poulgar, and Kregg.

Kregg was the worst of the bunch, Vishinski had decided. The Russian had been in the military long enough to spot the beginnings of a defeatist or a subversive. He had already decided that as soon as Comrade Reymann had hunkered into his first lethal snipe in Berlin, the Kregg bastard could be cut from the program and sent for "reeducation."

It was typical that Kregg was a Berliner, Vishinski thought furiously, with a layer of sweat across his forehead. The Berliners were always stubborn "big-city" types who liked to stick a thumb in authority's eye. Well, Kregg would learn, damn him, probably when being led off to execution. "Good riddance!" he concluded furiously. He'd be happy to shoot the bloody German himself if anyone asked. But that wasn't the way the Soviet army worked these days. If it did, there would be a lot fewer of these stubborn Krautheads. He glared at the younger three men, the Germans, with uncompromising contempt. They had been sluggish the last few days and had big circles under their eyes.

Vishinski stepped carefully around the clutter in the room. He folded his arms and waited impatiently for the men in his charge. Why were these men dragging their feet so badly these days? Were they staying up late drinking or sneaking out? He'd get to the bottom of this!

This afternoon's drill was to last five hours. The surly little chain gang would not be expected back until seven PM. Maybe he should just run them up and down the streets, he thought to himself.

The three snipers finally tossed their small bags of personal equipment into a corner and assembled in the middle of the scorching room. There were open windows on all sides. The windows were actually just big, gaping holes. This had been a factory and a warehouse. Soviet deconstruction teams had taken everything, even the window frames, and shipped the haul back to Poland where it was reassembled. There was a big, gaping hole in the west wall, also, where the metal door of a trash chute had been ripped away.

Nonetheless, targets had been set up on other rooftops anywhere from a hundred to four hundred meters away. Some summer target practice would do these intransigents some good on such a day. No water for them till dinner.

"Hey!" Vishinski finally demanded. "The army should have shipped you imbeciles off to Poland with the rest of the junk they stripped from this place! What's the matter with you today?"

No one answered.

Vishinski was disgusted. He waited for the armorer Mikho to set down the gun bags near the front window. Then he gave Mikho a jerk of the head to get him to depart. He was going to give these men some hell. He watched as Mikho went down the steps. He listened for an extra minute until he heard the sound of the ignition turn over on the army truck that had been used.

The three men shifted uncomfortably.

Vishinski went to the window and watched the army truck leave. It would only attract visitors and the curious if it were left to stand there. Mikho's instructions were to lock the door from the outside and return in several hours.

The truck turned the corner as Vishinski leaned partway out the window and watched. Then the truck was gone. The Russian turned back to the three Germans and was startled. He froze. He suddenly realized he was a dead man. But he didn't have long to reflect on it.

Kregg was pointing a Mauser at him from ten meters away. Kregg's hand was unsteady. He almost fumbled the pistol. But he was in "can't-miss" territory.

"Kregg!" Vishinski barked. There was not much else to say.

Kregg pulled the trigger three times. The pounding of the blasting ammunition filled the hot, suffocating room and could be heard all over the neighborhood. But it aroused no suspicion because everyone knew there were target sessions in these buildings.

The full force of the bullets hit Vishinski in the center of the chest, took a chunk out of his heart, and shattered his sternum. He was still gasping when he hit the floor. Wolfgang might have gone to him and kicked him, but instead, he was repulsed by this whole episode, even as he knew that he might land on death row awaiting a bullet in the brain if he were captured.

Now it was Kregg who said, "Hurry."

Poulgar assisted as they hauled Vishinski's body to an upright position. They dragged him across the room toward the trash chute. His feet kept catching on debris. Reluctantly, Wolfgang assisted and helped the other two snipers get the Russian to the chute. Then they pushed him up and over the top. Vishinski's body made a strange sound as it went over the edge.

Wolfgang assumed that there had still been some life in the Russian. But from the sound of the impact when the body hit the bottom of the chute, that was no longer an issue.

They made a quick effort to clean the blood off the floor. They threw everything that left a trace of Vishinsky down the chute. They knew that the body would be discovered eventually, but it would throw the Stasi off their trail for a few hours at least. It would be dark by the time anyone came looking and put the details of the murder together.

All three men had killed before and knew there was a good chance that they would kill again. For now, they had a plan of escape and, they hoped, a waiting accomplice. If the accomplice had failed them or didn't show up, they were as good as dead.

And they knew it.

*REVOLT IN BERLIN* – Part One  NOEL HYND

# Chapter 37
## West Berlin – September 1952

Bill Cochrane had not been sleeping well of late. Bad dreams had been haunting him, as had a general sleeplessness. Generally speaking, over the course of his professional life, he had presided over successes. There had been short-term setbacks – he refused to term them failures because everything in life could be viewed as an operation in progress – and some that broke evens.

He supposed every man lost an agent in an active career. He had once spent time with a fellow who worked for the OSS in World War II and the man became an alcoholic after he had to personally bury two agents – a French couple in their thirties in Morocco – who had been slaughtered by French fascists.

He lay awake at night reminding himself that the Berlin game was a long one, there would be wins and defeats, gains and losses. But every time he looked at a map, or, for example, the bulbous globe in Bernard Kreitler's office, he saw Berlin as the most eastward bastion of the European non-communist world. Then he would think of the nature of the enemy – the abduction of Walter Linse remained fresh in his mind – and he would remind himself that the free world needed warriors, and some of them would fall.

*Kreitler:* Bill had come to like the man and accept him for who and what he was. But Kreitler was an odd piece of work if the truth were known. Bill had recently spent a half hour in Kreitler's office on the day of his next-to-last class of the summer, ruminating about continuing to teach at the university after the summer session ended.

"Stay in Berlin permanently?" Bill asked. "Is that what you're suggesting?"

"Year to year," said the husky academician with a shrug, trying the soft-sell. "It's the place to be for folks in our line of work, don't you think?"

"Which line is that?" Bill parried. "Whichever one you like best," came the sly riposte. "Books and bullets. The days of wine and warriors. Throat Cutting 101. Call it whatever you want."

"I'll let you know in September," Cochrane answered.

"Good. Thanks. I'll put you down as definite and I'll think of something for you to teach."

All of these thoughts fluttered in a repeating sequence through Bill's teeming mind as he tried to sleep. Thirteen mornings after Lotte had disappeared into East Berlin and more than seven weeks after Walter Linse had vanished in the same direction, Cochrane lay turning in his bed shortly after dawn on a Thursday morning.

Laura shoved him twice to wake him. His eyes shot open.

"Someone's at the door downstairs," she said, alarmed.

"What door?"

A low voice, very cautious. "Our front door," she said.

"There's an iron gate," he said, sitting up sharply. "How did—?"

"Someone got past the gate. It doesn't matter how he did it. Bill, take a gun."

Cochrane swung out of bed and onto his feet. He grabbed a robe, barged down the stairs, and heard an accented voice outside. He darted to the study he had on the first floor where he now kept a Colt pistol, acquired recently after giving the Browning to Lotte. A loud knocking, a furious pounding, continued on the door.

Bill stormed to the entrance. "Who is it?" he yelled.

"Sir!" came Helmut's loud, agitated voice in English from the other side. "Open please!" he shouted. "Urgent, Sir!"

There followed a sharp rapping that only stopped when Bill undid the locks and yanked open the door. He and Helmut stood eye to eye looking at each other. Beyond, on the other side of the iron gate, a large, black vehicle was idling and looming, a beast of a big car, the engine growling, the driver watching them. Bill guessed it was a taxi.

"What's happened?" Cochrane asked, returning his gaze to Helmut.

"Someone important got killed, Sir," the barkeeper said breathlessly.

*"Who?"*

"I'm not to tell you, Sir," Helmut said. "You come and see. And hear."

"Where are we going?"

"My place, Sir. Bar Ritter!"

"Good God! Elfriede's okay, yes?" Cochrane asked with a tremor of horror. "Tell me it's not her!"

"Yes, I tell. My daughter's good. Thank you. Sir?"

"What?"

"They're waiting, Sir," Helmut said, throwing a thumb gesture over his shoulder to the waiting vehicle. "Right here. Now. I think you work with those men, yes?"

Cochrane flicked his eyes up and past Helmut's shoulder again. On second glance the vehicle was obviously not a Berlin taxi. This oil burner was big, boxy, and very American. A Ford station wagon. There was a driver and a man in the back seat. Then as Bill scanned more, he realized there was a second car, also with a driver: another Ford with a driver and a man in the back seat.

Then the rear door of the second car opened. William Harvey squeezed out and stared at Cochrane. "Hey!" he yelled. "Cochrane! Shit's blowing up all over Berlin. You coming or do I have to drag you out of your connubial love nest by the gonads?"

"Five minutes!" Bill yelled back.

"One!" Harvey countered. "Hustle!"

Helmut gave him an imploring look, shrugged, and quickly stepped back to the lead car.

Bill dressed and loaded his Colt at the same time. Laura emerged from upstairs, said little, asked nothing. She had seen it before and knew that if she was lucky, she'd see it again. Caroline emerged and looked frightened.

Cochrane embraced her before going out the door. Previously used words came back, a phrase about "taking care of things" and another hokey one about "some important people."

It was closer to three minutes than one.

Bill jumped into the first car, and they began to move. The second Ford followed at a tight distance. William Harvey rode alone with the driver in the second car. Cochrane didn't know if the driver was a bodyguard, but he assumed he was.

In neither car did anyone speak. Someone was dead and that was obviously all that mattered.

## Chapter 38
### West Berlin – Late August, 1952

It was not yet eight AM, around the time when the Stasi abducted Dr. Linse, that the two American cars drove with an accelerated speed from Bill's residence in to the center of Berlin. They neared Tempelhof then veered away and came to a jarring halt in front of the Bar Ritter, half of each vehicle aggressively up on the sidewalk, half on the street. The bar was dark to the outside, but Bill knew the place well enough to catch a sliver of light through the nearly shut door to the back room.

The two drivers flipped Federal Republic diplomatic identifications down on their sun visors. One, in best bodyguard fashion, stayed with the cars, positioning himself on the sidewalk in a position between the two. The other driver-bodyguard stayed with Helmut who led Cochrane, Kreitler, and Harvey and forged along down an alley to the rear entrance where the garbage cans stood and where disabled war veterans sometimes loitered.

Helmut came to the rear door of his bar, did a quick double knock, and turned a key. The bodyguard remained outside. Helmut led the visitors in, flipping on a light in a back pantry as he proceeded. Cochrane kept pace.

There was a muffled murmur of voices somewhere up ahead, but Cochrane couldn't discern much because Helmut was talking over it. He thought he heard at least two men and a woman. They were speaking in German and occasionally laughing. The laughter, Bill thought, the chatter, sounded nervous.

"Your anti-bugging agents, Jameson and Torres, were here during the night," Helmut said breathlessly. "Discovered I had visitors. They knew that Sgt. Pearson was one of your 'reliables' at Tempelhof."

"Yes. I told them that," Bill said.

"Pearson was working night cargo, keeping an eye on things. So Torres went over and got Pearson then they called me, and I came to see you. Jameson stayed here till Sgt. Pearson came over."

"I follow," said Bill.

Bill followed a lot already. He recognized Pearson's voice. And then he pegged the woman's voice at the same time that Helmut pushed open a squeaky door to his back room. Helmut led Cochrane in, followed by Bill Harvey and Bernard Kreitler.

The woman, Lotte, rose from where she had been sitting. She grinned, but the grin was mixed with relief or apprehension. There were three young German men there, as well, guys in their thirties who looked as if they had beaten the odds and survived the war. They stood also, jittery and looking as if they didn't know whether they were going to be rewarded or shot.

Harvey and Kreitler stood on either side of Cochrane, a half-step behind him. Cochrane took a half-glance at them and caught them staring at the assemblage in complete disbelief. Harvey, a hard man to shock, had his mouth wide open. Jimmy Pearson was sitting on a table, keeping his distance, a massive sidearm on his right hip – it looked like Colt .45 with the new postwar frame.

Jimmy's twitchy hand wasn't far from his weapon, but he looked more amused than frightened. Two of the many things Bill Cochrane liked about Sgt. Pearson: he could roll with the punches and he was always ready for anything.

"Okay," Cochrane said. "What's going on?" He looked at Lotte. They spoke English. "Who are your new friends?"

"German snipers," she said.

*"What?"*

Very politely, Lotte repeated.

"All three?" Bill asked.

"All three. War veterans. Decorated. More than a thousand kills among them."

"How do you know that?"

Lotte switched to German and recounted.

There were several evening meetings in Die Edelweiss and a few in Der Rote Stiefel, she said. A trust developed. Vodka flowed. And flowed some more. Talk loosened. The three young men wanted out – faraway-type out – from East Berlin, not a career as cogs in a peacetime assassination and terror unit. There had been, they explained, a Soviet training officer who was a prime recruiter for snipers into the Stasi. They were going to be used in Berlin against Western targets. Abductions would be out, and the new terror would be the long-range rifle bullet for those who dared to speak out: troublemaker pro-West politicians, nosy journalists. These young men, Lotte continued, owners of three of the most lethal trigger fingers in the postwar world, were being trained. They decided the recruitment was not for them.

"There was a regrettable accident with a weapon," she said with no passion in her voice whatsoever. "The Soviet man perished. The body was disposed of. The recruits feared for their lives and fled."

"So they shot their recruiter and took off?" Bill said.

"It might have happened that way, yes," Lotte says. "Who knows? I wasn't there."

"But you helped them escape."

"Maybe," she said.

"How fast were you out of the Soviet zone?" Cochrane asked.

"Within an hour," Lotte said. "Long before the body could be discovered."

"Did you go through checkpoints?"

"We walked, Sir," Kregg announced, speaking suddenly but respectfully.

"Two by two," Lotte chipped in. "Me with Herr Reymann. The other two boys together. We traveled about fifty meters apart. Four eyes ahead of us, four watching the rear."

"Armed," Poulgar said.

"A couple of pocket Mausers. No big stuff," she said.

"Mostly back streets. Building basements. Sewers," Kregg said.

"No problems?" Bill asked.

Lotte again: "A bed of sweet red roses. Just didn't smell like roses, you know?"

"How did you know how to do that?" Bill asked. "The route?"

"He grew up in north Berlin," Lotte said. "You can tell by his accent, right?"

Kregg grinned like a kid when she said that. Lotte continued. "We went down into a building basement in Pankow, went through a couple of walls, crawled a little where the overhead was hanging low, walked under the border through a sewer tunnel, and came up in Reinickendorf. Magic."

"Holy Jesus," Cochrane muttered.

Pankow was in the East. Reinickendorf was in the West. But the whole thing had an even sharper edge. Pankow, Bill knew, was also where most of the big shots in the East German government had their elite homes.

"You made your getaway right under their noses?" Cochrane asked.

"Her idea," Wolfgang said. "This girl, she thinks."

Lotte shrugged. "I figured the last place the police would look was the in the power corridor," said. "Our Berliner knew a direct path through," she said, indicating Kregg. "So we talk it."

"We walked fast," Reymann added with a chuckle.

"But not *too* fast," Lotte said.

"We burrow away like the famous Old Mole," Poulgar said. "Pop up where no one expects us. In West Berlin."

Everyone laughed.

At that point, Cochrane, remembering that William Harvey's German was nonexistent, took a time out and translated the whole shebang.

Harvey liked what he finally heard. "Keep it going," he said. "This is good. Ask if anyone saw them."

Lotte translated the question.

"*Ratten. Wilde Katzen. Niemand der auf zwei Beinen ging,*" Wolfgang answered, looking at Mr. Harvey. Cochrane translated it back to the boss. "Only rats and cats," he said. "No two-legged creatures."

"That's great if it's true," Harvey said. "Does that mean the concealed pathway is still open? Alleys? Sewers? Basements?"

Again, Kregg knew enough to nod.

"And if not, there are others," Lotte said, translating what Kregg had added to her in German.

"I'm liking this underground stuff more and more," Harvey said. "So this fucker's the expert?" Harvey asked, indicating Kregg.

"He's the one," Lotte said. But she also admitted she had used the routes also in the past. She was becoming adept with them, also.

"Why don't the Reds just block them off?" Harvey asked.

The answer to that came easily also.

Black market dealers used them at night with flashlights and compasses, Lotte explained. There were payoffs to local authorities. And the Russians had put men in charge in that sector who were loyal communists but from the east of Germany near Poland. They weren't Berliners. They didn't know the city or understand what happened on the streets. What happened below the streets was something they couldn't even imagine.

"Where's the Soviet officer now?" Cochrane asked, returning to the Germans. "Where's the body?"

"It's in a deep place in East Berlin," Wolfgang said, continuing the conversation in German.

"The Russians or Stasi will find it," Kregg said. "Eventually."

The three Germans had inside information on Stasi recruitment and Soviet support, Lotte continued. They were willing to talk. They were even willing to serve in a Western army in exchange for asylum, maybe as instructors, maybe in the field.

"They want to go to the West. They hate the Russians," Lotte said in English.

The boys knew enough English to nod. Or maybe they were just inclined to trust their new favorite female.

"Everyone hates the fucking Russians," William Harvey said, lighting a smoke, and tossing his pack on the table, offering smokes to the new recruits. "It's the new growth industry, didn't you hear?" He turned to Kreitler, who had been quiet but attentive. "Any of this stuff been on Radio Berlin yet? Or Red Radio?" he asked.

Kreitler shook his head. "There's activity in the Soviet zone indicating there's some big search going on."

"That would be this," Cochrane guessed. "But you know how secretive the Russians are. They wouldn't admit their underwear was on fire until they sent tanks into the fire department." A pause then. "May I make a suggestion?" Cochrane added.

"Sure," Harvey said. "You're dealing the cards pretty good right now. Keep drawing aces."

"Let's keep a lid on these guys for a couple of weeks and have some of our people talk to them individually. If their story holds, we just struck a little gold. We also delivered a hit to their sniper program."

A moment, then, "We can stash them for a while," Harvey said. "We got a safe house out in Potsdam that's empty right now." He stood. "Might be wiser to get them out of the country sooner rather than later, though. We'll keep them under wraps and move them out there this morning."

The room fell quiet.

"Anything else?" Harvey asked.

No one had anything.

Harvey stood.

"Hey, where do you get an American breakfast around here? Anyone?"

"Tempelhof's across the street," Cochrane said. "Sgt. Pearson will show you the way."

# Chapter 39
## West Berlin – Late August, 1952

The body of Comrade Vishinski was found a day later. The Russians brought in dogs, broke down the walls outside the old rubbish shaft, and made the grisly discovery. William Harvey celebrated by inviting Bill Cochrane back to the Neue Oklahoma Café for more square dance music, German cowgirls, and a lengthy meal that Cochrane could have done without.

But there was some business to discuss, so sensitive that it was one-on-one.

Harvey updated Bill on where things stood, and in East Berlin, most things stood upside down. Ulbricht was furious, and Erich Mielke was beside himself with anger. Mielke was convinced that the Americans had pole-axed his Stasi and their Soviet sniping contact. But there was not yet any admission in public by the East Germans as to what had happened. The people at Radio Berlin had part of the story but were sitting on it. The Stasi didn't know whether the three missing snipers were going to turn up floating in one of the Berlin canals or sitting on a beach in Florida.

Therefore, Mielke's perplexity.

Therefore, Mielke's fury.

Therefore, Mielke's pursuant demand that arrived at the American embassy that morning that he have the privilege of talking to someone of authority working for the United States intelligence community in Berlin. In Stasi-speak, what he really wanted was to talk directly to the CIA bureau chief in Berlin. But he didn't know who that was.

"Needless to say," Harvey said. "I'm not going anywhere near that little slimeball. And I'm not setting foot in East Germany. You been over there, Bill, on the other side of the city?"

"More than a few times," Cochrane answered.

"You're a brave man," Harvey said.

"Or I'm crazy," Bill said with a rueful laugh. "It's gotten worse in recent years. Their economic system doesn't work, personal freedoms are nonexistent, and the younger people want blue jeans, jazz, blues records, and Coca-Cola. It's just a matter of time before the whole place blows up and the Soviets have to send tanks and troops in to restore order. You can feel the eastern part of this city starting to seethe."

"That's your analysis?"

"Informally, yes. And by the way, if you won't travel to the East, any meeting with Mielke's a nonstarter. The warrants for the Bülowplatz murders in 1931 may still be valid. Mielke wouldn't risk it."

"Too bad," said Harvey without meaning it. "We'll just ignore their demand. That's what they do to us."

Harvey was savoring his fourth drink, puffing his seventh cigarette, and enjoying the atmosphere at the fake old western bar. He brought with him that night a carton of Lucky Strike cigarettes and was tossing them around to the staff as gifts. The smokes were well received. After dinner and close to two hours of this, he beckoned to Bill and asked him to lean in closer to listen to something.

Cochrane obliged. He leaned in as Harvey bent forward to speak, stone-sober despite more than eight ounces of booze. "Ulbricht and Mielke are going batshit over this. You know that, right?"

"You mentioned it twice, yes. So I know it."

"Know what I love about it?" Harvey confided.

"What?" Bill asked.

"In order for the Reds to complain that we – or someone – killed their Russian sniper capo, they have to admit that that's exactly what he was. They can't pass him off as a cultural attaché or a tractor specialist. And if they admit what he was, how do they explain why he was in Berlin and what he was doing here?"

"Seems to me they never explain anything," Cochrane said.

"Ha!" Harvey laughed. "Yeah, right. They never do. Against their religion, not that they have any, right?"

After a moment, "You know what else?" Cochrane offered thoughtfully.

"What?"

"They can't even demand that we return their three defectors. The three Germans got away so cleanly that no one saw anything. Or no one saw anything they're going to talk about. So they can't ask for the three German shooters back because they don't even know where they went. Ain't that a kick in the head?"

Harvey leaned back. He started an eighth cigarette and ogled a cowgirl as she trotted by. She winked back, touched Harvey's shoulder in passing, and kept moving. Harvey's attention, diverted momentarily, came back to Cochrane.

"You're a fucking genius, Bill," Harvey said from behind a cloud of cigarette smoke. "Damn! You're good, man!"

Cochrane declined the accolade.

"I didn't do anything," Bill protested, "other than get lucky. Lotte was the agent in place. She took the risks and made the decisions. She worked with what she had, took some big personal risks, came up with something operationally successful, and dropped it in our laps. All credit goes to her."

"Who put her in that place to make those contacts and make those decisions? Right place, right time, and all that bullshit?" Harvey asked.

"I suppose *I* did," Bill said.

"You 'suppose'?" Harvey coughed and laughed. He coughed again, a noisy, wet hacking cough, leaned over, and spat onto the sawdust floor. "Screw yourself, man," he said, laughing gleefully and returning upright, his merry, foxy eyes dancing in his mortar shell of a face.

"Now, you tell me again who put Lotte in that place," Harvey demanded.

"Okay. *I* did."

"As I said," Harvey responded, slapping an open palm on the table. "You're a fucking genius."

Bill leaned back. The waitstaff had congregated on stage and were doing an impressive massacre of "Some Enchanted Evening." When the musical flogging was finished, Cochrane threw a pitch at his big boss.

"If I'm a genius," Bill said, "may I make a suggestion? A course of action?"

"Sure," Harvey said. "Anything. Talk to me."

"Accept the meeting with Mielke. But inform him that since you don't speak German, you'll send a trusted representative who can respond on your behalf to any inquiries he might have."

"You serious?" Harvey asked, his brow scrunched.

"Damned serious."

"Where do we meet? They won't come over here, and I don't want any of our people going over there."

"We meet at one of the border-crossing checkpoints," Cochrane suggested. "They stand on their side. We stand on ours."

Harvey's eyes narrowed. "Maybe. Who do I send? Kreitler? DeWinter?"

"No. Me."

*"You?* Why you?"

"Two reasons. One, Lotte suggested a way we can shut down the Stasi sniper program cold. It's bold and it takes some chances. I'll share it with you if you wish."

"I wish."

"Keep in mind that the Russians don't give a damn about anything you say or threaten. They only understand what you do. You make a statement by acting, by showing what you're capable of doing. Even if it's small, it can loom large," Cochrane said.

"I know that. Said it many times myself to anyone willing to listen. So what's this plan you have?"

Cochrane talked. Harvey listened, laughed, and approved it.

"We can give it a shot?" Bill asked.

"Ha! I like your way with words. Hell, yeah, man! We give it a shot!" Then, "Now, the second reason?" Harvey asked.

"I want to grill Mielke personally about a different subject."

"Which one?"

"Walter Linse," Cochrane said. "People are starting to forget about Walter Linse. But I haven't."

"Genius. A genius," mumbled Harvey, pointing a plump index finger at Cochrane through his veil of tobacco smoke. The music on stage concluded for the evening and applause filled the room.

# Chapter 40
## West Berlin – Late August 1952

The next day the American embassy proposed a meeting to Erich Mielke's office as Bill Cochrane and Lotte Meidner had conceived it. To everyone's astonishment, Erich Mielke accepted, and a time and place was set.

Accordingly, William Harvey contacted Dr. Kreitler at the university. Kreitler caught Bill in the second-floor corridor. Cochrane had just wrapped up his final class of the term. On his walk home, Cochrane stopped at a nondescript brick building that had been requisitioned by the U.S. Army after the war. The building was two blocks from the former General Albertson residence where Bill Cochrane and his family now lived. It had been converted into short-term, bug-proof, studio apartments. Some terms were shorter than others.

Lotte was in residence there. Cochrane conferred with her for several minutes.

Two evenings later, Lotte and Wolfgang used another underground route to pass undetected into East Berlin. They looked like any other needy eastern couple who might have been going to shop at one of the farm markets at the far border of the city. They each carried a shopping bag with an assortment of mechanical parts – clocks, farm equipment, pieces of war weapons, and so on – plus a collection of used clothing that might be used for barter.

Instead of shopping for produce, however, they found their way to the wooded preserve that lay adjacent to Erich Mielke's more countrified residence. From a certain vantage point, they could access a view of the rear of Comrade Mielke's second home, a distance of a hundred fifty meters. As recently as ten days previously, Wolfgang had picked off twenty of twenty-one wine bottles from East Berlin rooftops at two hundred meters. This, of course, had been before Comrade

Vishinski had suffered his lamentable accident and training had sadly been suspended.

There in a knoll with heavy foliage not dissimilar from areas in Poland, Hungary, and Slovakia where Wolfgang had excelled during the war, the couple waited.

They waited until the time would come in the twilight of the next day when Wolfgang would deftly assemble the pieces of his Karabiner from the two bags. Then he would go to work one more time.

Lotte remained with him and served as lookout.

Reymann would fire one shot. Hit or miss, they would then flee and be back in the West within a few hours. She already knew the routes they might take.

Like most battle plans, everything was proceeding perfectly. But then again, the first and only shot had not yet been fired.

# Chapter 41
## East and West Berlin - September 1952

There were many routes passing at surface level from East Berlin to West Berlin in 1952. There were already rumors about someday having to build a wall, but nothing had yet risen.

The busiest crossing points had checkpoints, booths staffed by armed soldiers and police, but most visitors were free to pass. The crossing points survived on the simple, straightforward, unimaginative names that the American military had dropped on them in 1945.

Checkpoint A. Checkpoint B. Checkpoint C. And so on.

All checkpoints had bold white lines drawn across their center points, a finite definition of where the Eastern world ended and the Western world began, and vice versa.

Checkpoint C, which would eventually be better known worldwide as "Checkpoint Charlie," was a crossing point found at the junction of Friedrichstrasse, Mauerstrasse, and Zimmerstrasse. It was also the point where the meeting would take place between Erich Mielke and Bill Cochrane, the emissary "chosen" by the chief of American intelligence in Berlin.

Soldiers from the U.S. Army and East German Army closed the area around Checkpoint C fifty meters in all directions promptly at seven PM on the warm evening of September 3. There had been late afternoon thunderstorms, loud thunder, and lightning with heavy rain. The air was heavy and muggy, the uneven street was wet.

On the eastern side, a Soviet-made Zil limousine emerged from the gray jagged contours of East Berlin at about seven-thirteen. A light rain continued to fall. The GDR flag flew from both front fenders. The Zil proceeded toward the checkpoint.

On the other side of the checkpoint, a tan Chevrolet sedan sat and waited, backed by several armed members of the United States Marine Corps. Bill Cochrane, when he saw the Zil approach, stepped out of the back seat of the Chevrolet, leaving William Harvey and Larry DeWinter behind him in the car.

Cochrane walked toward the white line in the middle of the checkpoint. He wore a dark suit, a regimental tie, and a hat against the rain. He carried nothing in his hands. He stood one step on the western side of the line and waited. His eyes rested on the Zil.

After several minutes, the rear door swung open on the right side of the Russian limousine. Erich Mielke stepped out. He took two or three short steps and adjusted his suit. He walked toward his side of the white line, a cocky pattern of steps. When he came within a foot of the line, he stopped. He glowered.

Cochrane was several inches taller than the stocky little second-in-command of the Stasi. Mielke folded his arms and stared as if to assess, as if to say his adversary was not even good enough to be there. Bill aimed to let Mielke talk first. Bill also planned to speak last.

The rain continued. Mielke started to steam. Cochrane knew the man could be impetuous. He was set on waiting him out. Finally, the rain - or overall impatience – got to the smaller man. Mielke launched into a rant, which built itself into an overall tirade about a dead MGB officer and three vanished military personnel. It reached its crescendo when Mielke took out a handkerchief, wiped the rain from his forehead, removed water from his glasses, and raised his voice to a gruff bark.

Cochrane stood quietly. He said nothing.

"Well? Are you just going to stand there?" Mielke snapped. "We demand to know why Colonel Vishinski was murdered."

Cochrane spoke in nearly flawless German. "We know nothing about any colonel by that name. Perhaps your missing soldiers went out on a hike together, found some Western women, and got lost."

Mielke, enraged, spat on the ground.

"Where is Walter Linse?" Cochrane asked.

"How the hell would I know?" the smaller man snapped back. "And that's not what we're here to talk about."

"What have you done with Linse?" Cochrane asked.

"Ask the Russians," Mielke said.

"We have. They suggested that we ask you. They have a point: we know your people recruited abduction teams in the German prisons. We even know the names of the perpetrators. So where is Linse?"

"Burning in hell, as you religious people would say."

"Moscow?" Cochrane asked. "That's what we now hear. We demand his return."

"You'll have nothing of the sort. Where are the three German soldiers who have gone missing? We demand them back."

"We know nothing about this," Cochrane said. "Which soldiers are you speaking of?"

"You know full well," Mielke insisted.

"I know nothing about three missing soldiers," Bill Cochrane said. "But," he said, shifting his voice and posture to something less formal, "I will tell you what I do know."

"What's that?" Mielke asked.

"You speak of soldiers," Cochrane said. "Snipers perhaps. Well, let me explain something to you then," Bill Cochrane continued. "Suppose I told you that we recently recruited some of the best snipers in the world. A trio of them, maybe. Maybe we did this because we have learned that in addition to your unlawful abductions of West Berlin residents, you imported a Soviet sniping specialist and are exploring using highly trained shooters as killers in this city. Believe me here and now, you should abandon this idea if you value your own life."

Mielke tried to protest and interrupt. Cochrane kept talking.

"And suppose I told you that our people could get anyone in East Germany within their sights. Including you, Comrade. And suppose we instructed one of our men to give you one warning shot. You get the courtesy of one near miss. In the extremely near future. The second sniper bullet will be marked with your name. When it hits you in the head or the back of the neck, your skull, limited brains, and blood will explode so quickly, and your death will be so immediate, that you won't even know what hit you. That's probably a kinder fate than what you've arranged for Walter Linse."

"You're a fascist warmonger!" Mielke said.

"We have nothing further to talk about," Cochrane said. "Unless you tell us where Linse is and set a date for his return."

Mielke's eyes blazed. He spat again at Cochrane's feet.

Bill turned to go, then turned back and spat on Mielke's shoes. "You see. Your own actions will be turned against you." Bill smiled, tipped his hat, and spoke politely. "Have a pleasant evening."

Mielke made a half-motion to cross the white line. Then he thought better of it, stopped himself, stared, glared, and retreated to his car. An East German army officer with an umbrella met him halfway and guided him back to the Zil.

The ignition of the huge Soviet car roared, the vehicle screeched backward, did a U-turn, and disappeared eastward.

"Looks like you pissed him off pretty good," Harvey said to Bill when Cochrane slid into the tan Chevy.

"I think so," Cochrane said.

"Did I see you spit on his shoes?" Harvey said.

"Yes, you did."

"Whoa. You got a brass pair, don't you? That guy has killed people."

"So have I," Cochrane said. When Harvey turned quickly toward him, he added, "In the war. I'm not proud of it, but it happened." Bill drew a breath. "Look, like most bullies, Mielke is a coward. We'll see how the rest of this plays out. Won't we?"

Harvey thought about it. "I have a hunch you did well," Harvey said.

"Sure. And I've turned into exactly what I deplore," Bill said.

Harvey shrugged, grinned, and slapped Bill Cochrane on the knee.

"Congratulations," he said. "It happens eventually to the best of us. Don't let it get to you. You'll start drinking too much." A pause, then, "I got a question for you though."

"Go ahead," Cochrane said.

"When he spit at you, how come you only hacked one back? Why didn't you slap him a good one, right across the chops?"

"Two reasons," Bill said. "First, I didn't want to reach across that white line. And second, to tell you the absolute truth, I didn't want to start an atomic war."

Harvey nodded and let go with a low laugh. "Admirable," he said. "Admirable."

# Chapter 42
## East Berlin - September 1952

Late the same evening, lurking in the wooded game preserve behind Erich Mielke's retreat, Wolfgang Reymann was elated when the lights illuminated Mielke's study, including the fine Fabergé lamp that he kept on his desk.

The Stasi's operational commander was furious over the evening's meeting with the degenerate American. He raged and fumed. How dare these uncivilized upstarts from North America even be in Berlin! Vishinski might be dead, all right, and the crazy Yanks may have even been able to abduct three of his best snipers. But he, Mielke, would go to Russia and talk to Stalin again. He would get ten dozen more of their best marksmen, bring them back to Berlin, train them, and—

Mielke never finished his thought.

He was in mid-rant when a bullet came through the window two feet behind him, exploding the antique panes and then smashing into the stained glass of the Fabergé lamp a fraction of a second later.

The bullet reduced the priceless relic from the tsar to shards of glass and a twisted frame as it spun wildly from his desk, sending burning oil in every direction, igniting prized carpets, a velour sofa, and antiques looted from Jewish merchants during the war. The impact was so close to his head that several fine pieces of glassware cut a swath of deep scratches across his cheek and his eyeglasses flew from his head as he dived for cover.

Mielke's screams awakened his small household staff of Turkish servants. They dutifully extinguished the fires. But they were unable to suppress either the promise or the threat that came through the window with the bullet.

Message sent. Message delivered.

Less than two hundred meters away, Wolfgang Reymann swiftly broke down his Karabiner. Lotte had dug a hole with her hands in the soft earth under some young linden trees. She and Wolfgang buried the weapon so as not to be caught with it and pushed a small boulder onto the earth that had been displaced. It would take Stasi investigators days to find it, if ever. Then they walked from the wooded area and continued westward on foot, cagily staying in the shadow of buildings on the dark streets and avoiding automobiles.

Even plain cars were often Stasi. At one point on Wisbyerstrasse, before they crossed to the West at two in the morning, an inquisitive East German police car slowed down beside them. Its occupants eyed them and shined a heavy beam on them but then couldn't be bothered. The car and the city police in it kept going.

Wolfgang and Lotte crossed again from East Berlin into West Berlin via alleys, cellars, and sewers. They arrived at a prearranged corner of Schiller Park in the American sector the next morning where they saw Bill Cochrane seated on a bench waiting. Kurt was sitting next to him. From there a team of helpful people, including a couple of tough guys from Mr. Harvey's office, took over.

Three days later, after the two visitors from East Berlin had been debriefed, Sgt. Jimmy Pearson drove a civilian truck from a location in the American sector to RAF Gatow in the British zone. He had three passengers: a woman in her twenties, a German national who was a war veteran, and an American man who was currently a lecturer at the Free University.

The drive was uneventful, the conversation subdued. No one took much notice as Sgt. Pearson drove directly onto the tarmac. The two Germans boarded an otherwise unnoteworthy freight Dakota that was nearly empty. It was returning some aircraft parts to an RAF Molesworth maintenance team. The American walked to the airplane with the two Germans, waved as they boarded, and saw them off, heading safely out of the country to await the next chapter in their lives.

The Dakota would land in Cambridge. The woman would go home and live quietly, at least for the short term. The German would be chauffeured to London where the U.S. Embassy would assist him until things calmed down in Germany. Two other German defectors, former military people who brought with them unique skills, remained temporarily in Potsdam.

There, American intelligence agents listened carefully to all they knew of the sniper program in Berlin.

# Chapter 43
## West Berlin – October 1952

Bill Cochrane's star was on the rise yet again in the American intelligence community in Berlin. Sometimes these unsavory things were in the back of his mind as he continued to teach classes at the Free University. Dr. Kreitler had talked him into continuing on, not that it took much talking. Meanwhile, William Harvey surveyed ongoing underground operations – a tunnel, literally – to subvert Soviet intentions in the divided capital.

Dr. Walter Linse remained painfully on Cochrane's mind.

Rumor had it that Beria's security goons had moved him to Moscow. Bill shuddered when he thought of it and the brutal prisons that existed there. Not by coincidence, though, abductions had suddenly stopped happening in West Berlin. And there had been nothing resembling sniper activity.

"Think we scored a small victory?" Bill asked Dr. Kreitler one day with the door closed in Kreitler's office.

"I'll give you a firm and unequivocal 'maybe' on that one," Kreitler said.

"Sure. Thanks," Cochrane answered.

"Look, that agent girl you sent over scored a big-time win. I don't know what you folks did to shut Mielke down for a few weeks, but it must have been damned good."

"Harvey never told you?" Cochrane asked.

"No," Kreitler said expectantly. "I was not included."

"Then I'm not talking, either. Sorry."

"Bastard," Kreitler said with a wink.

Bill shrugged.

"Look, just enjoy yourself while you're here," Kreitler continued. "When you're needed again, you'll know real fast. So enjoy your downtime from your 'second' job. Okay?"

"Did you mean that I should enjoy myself while I'm here in the sense of while I'm in Berlin or in the sense of while I'm alive?" Bill asked.

A long, simmering pause, then, "Only *you* would ask that question. Both," Kreitler said. "Just live a little, okay? None of us is going to fix the damned world. Now get out of here, you're getting on my usually impervious nerves."

"Sure," Bill said. "I'll scram."

Kreitler winked and gave him a friendly thumbs up. Bill left the office. He already had a self-assigned chore he wanted to tend to at home as soon as possible. He had noticed anew that the window in his and Laura's bedroom afforded a view of distant rooftops. If he and his wife and daughter could see distant rooftops then anyone on one of those rooftops could see them, particularly if looking through binoculars or some sort of scope or sight.

He shivered at the thought.

So Bill changed the glass from clear to something cloudy and opaque. No point in inviting a catastrophe. He also put a new lock on the window, one that no one could tamper with.

And Bill Cochrane *did* take Dr. Kreitler's advice.

For a while in the early autumn of 1952, he tried to enjoy himself. He took solitary walks in the afternoon and evening, trying to calm down from the tensions and anxieties of the summer operation with Lotte, Wolfgang, and the vicious Erich Mielke. Cochrane knew that there was another shoe that could always drop; the communists were like that – always plotting another stunt. He only had to wait. The stunt would happen soon enough. He would be ready for it when needed. And so would his network, his German team in exile, as he thought of it.

In the meantime, however, he needed to decompress.

To do so, he turned inward and turned to his family. The decompression worked best when in his off-hours from the university he now included his wife and daughter with him on his walks so that they, too, could bear witness to Berlin's miraculous mid-century reawakening.

The zoo had reopened and so had the Berlin Opera, though the old opera house was in ruins and new productions were at Theater des Westens. The Tiergarten, the gorgeous, vast park in the center of the city, was starting to show a rebirth and so were the great museums. The Soviets always kept the pot bubbling, but the United States refused to retreat from Berlin. So the city would remain the focal point of world tensions, even though the air of renewal was everywhere.

As a father, Bill Cochrane wanted his daughter to be able to remember when Berlin was climbing up off its feet after the war. Great cities always rebounded, he felt. Berlin would be great again.

Caroline was just beginning to understand what had happened in this place and why there needed to be a rebirth. As gently as possible, Bill and Laura tried to explain who and what Adolf Hitler had been, what the evil was that he had represented, and what a staggering price the nation continued to pay. Discussions were free-wheeling, and Bill tried to answer all Caroline's questions. Sometimes the conversations drifted into talk of Dwight Eisenhower who, it appeared by October of 1952, was going to emerge from the role of a victorious wartime general and become the president of their country.

Bill wished he could also have explained more about what he was doing in Berlin, his personal stake, how it had evolved, and what his second job was in addition to teaching.

But all that was still a family secret. The full revelation would have to wait for another day, just like the multitude of secrets, good and bad, that Berlin still tenaciously held.

# THE END

*REVOLT IN BERLIN* – **Part One**　　　　　　**NOEL HYND**

**Third Reich War Poster.
But Some Things Never Change.**

# Coming in winter 2024/5

## Acknowledgments and a note on sources.

    My primary source of research for this series has been a lifetime of travel and reading, poking around in war and espionage museums, trying to learn languages other than English, talking and listening to people more knowledgeable than I am, and a challenging education in the United States, France, and Switzerland.

    Beyond that, credit – or blame - my own runaway imagination for these realistic stories based on fact, premised on fact, loaded with real people, but which in the end are works of fiction – much the way the late William Harvey respectfully appears here but in a fictional context. I'm often asked if an event in one of my books really happened. My response usually begins with. "Yes, as a matter of fact, it did. But. . ."

    I would, however, like to acknowledge acquiring details and background about postwar Berlin from the *New York Times,* the *Washington Post,* History.com, *Le Monde, Die Zeit, Frankfurter Allgemeine Zeitung, Die Welt,* Wikipedia, www.history.net.com, *The Encyclopedia Britannica,* The Office of the Historian at the U.S. Department of State, and www.PBS.org.

    Thank you again for reading. And don't forget my e-mail address below. I'm happy to hear from you.

NH, December 24, 2023

Nh1212f@yahoo.com

*REVOLT IN BERLIN* – Part One    NOEL HYND